MW01386034

Kelsey folded her arms acro
table strewn with the remnants of a blind double date gone horribly, horribly wrong.

She couldn't fault the jazz playing at just the perfect volume in the background or the way the candles and warm lighting glinted off the expensive crystal. Nor did the burden lie with the sumptuous feast they had consumed or the unobtrusive yet well-timed service.

No, the force behind the disaster sat directly across from her at a table set for four, but seating only two.

She held her tongue while the waiter cleared the plates but shot Ryan a look he would immediately understand.

You are gonna pay for this in chocolate.

He was often on the receiving end of that one.

Ryan held up his hands in mock surrender. "Don't look at me. This was all your idea."

She rolled her eyes. It had seemed like a good one at the time. Ryan was her best friend; it should have been plausible that they could manage to set each other up with compatible and interesting dates.

Their dates were compatible all right—with each other. After lame excuses and hasty goodbyes, she and Ryan were left alone—with the tab. Elise and Brandon, their respective dates, were going to "share a cab home".

Right. Share a cab. Probably share a bed too.

And Kelsey had worn her lucky Little Black Dress and everything.

"Ryan, that was the worst date ever...." She halted her erupting tirade as the waiter positioned a decadent piece of Chocolate Cherry Torte between them and handed them each a fork. It was their second dessert, but desperate times called for desperate measures of chocolate.

"Second worst." He dug in greedily. "The worst date ever was when you set me up with your cousin from Hoboken."

She winced. To be fair, that was more her mother's idea than hers.

If you don't want to marry the handsome, eligible doctor, the least you could do is pass him on to someone else in the family, Mom had told her.

Her cousin Marissa was a poor match for anyone who didn't like monster truck rallies. Poor Ryan. He'd been the perfect gentleman, something Marissa wasn't used to, so she'd decided he was gay. It made for interesting family gatherings whenever Kelsey brought him along. Uncle Bill, thinking he was open-minded, always asked Ryan for decorating tips.

One Touch, One Glance

A Sweet Romance Anthology

by

Gwen Hayes, M.E. Ellis, Maryann Miller, Adelle Laudan, K. Starling, Trinity Blacio, Debbie Gould, Ava James, Faith Bicknell-Brown, Savannah Chase, Lisa Alexander Griffin, Kensana Darnell, Nicolette Zamora, Kathleen MacIver, Missy Lyons, and Jambrea Jo Jones

Freya's Bower.com ©2011
Culver City, CA

One Touch, One Glance
A Sweet Romance Anthology
Copyright © 2011
by multiple authors

For information on the cover illustration and design, contact Posh Gosh.
Cover art Freya's Bower © 20011

Editor: Faith Bicknell-Brown

ISBN: 978-1-935013-50-1—ebook
978-1-936222-74-2—print

All rights reserved. No part of this book may be reproduced or transmitted in any form without written permission from the publisher, except by a reviewer who may quote brief passages for review purposes.

This book is a work of fiction and any resemblance to any person, living or dead, any place, events or occurrences, is purely coincidental. The characters and story lines are created from the author's imagination or are used fictitiously.

Warning:

This book may contain graphic sexual material and/or profanity and is not meant to be read by any person under the age of 18.

If you are interested in purchasing more works of this nature, please stop by
www.freyasbower.com.

Freya's Bower.com
P.O. Box 4897
Culver City, CA 90231-4897

Printed in The United States of America

Editor's Note:

This anthology has a mixture of brand new authors to well-established ones in it. They have typed until their fingers and their heads ached; they have all endured my grilling them that they can do better, that they need to fix this, rewrite that, tweak this phrase, develop this character.... They have all gone to great lengths to create stories that make the reader fall in love all over again. And...they have all made me very proud of them.

Ladies, take a bow. You deserve it.

With much respect,
Faith Bicknell-Brown

Table of Contents

5 A.M. on a Sunday Morning
by
Gwen Hayes

Best friends since college, Ryan is ready to tell Kelsey how he really feels.
But is Kelsey ready to hear it?

She Said

Kelsey folded her arms across her chest and glared at Ryan over the table strewn with the remnants of a blind double date gone horribly, horribly wrong.

She couldn't fault the jazz playing at just the perfect volume in the background or the way the candles and warm lighting glinted off the expensive crystal. Nor did the burden lie with the sumptuous feast they had consumed or the unobtrusive yet well-timed service.

No, the force behind the disaster sat directly across from her at a table set for four, but seating only two.

She held her tongue while the waiter cleared the plates but shot Ryan a look he would immediately understand.

You are gonna pay for this in chocolate.

He was often on the receiving end of that one.

Ryan held up his hands in mock surrender. "Don't look at me. This was all your idea."

She rolled her eyes. It had seemed like a good one at the time. Ryan was her best friend; it should have been plausible that they could manage to set each other up with compatible and interesting dates.

Their dates were compatible all right—with each other. After lame excuses and hasty goodbyes, she and Ryan were left alone—with the tab. Elise and Brandon, their respective dates, were going to "share a cab home".

Right. Share a cab. Probably share a bed too.

And Kelsey had worn her lucky Little Black Dress and everything.

"Ryan, that was the worst date ever...." She halted her erupting tirade as the waiter positioned a decadent piece of Chocolate Cherry Torte between them and handed them each a fork. It was their second dessert, but desperate times called for desperate measures of chocolate.

"Second worst." He dug in greedily. "The worst date ever was when you set me up with your cousin from Hoboken."

She winced. To be fair, that was more her mother's idea than hers.

If you don't want to marry the handsome, eligible doctor, the least you

9

could do is pass him on to someone else in the family, Mom had told her.

Her cousin Marissa was a poor match for anyone who didn't like monster truck rallies. Poor Ryan. He'd been the perfect gentleman, something Marissa wasn't used to, so she'd decided he was gay. It made for interesting family gatherings whenever Kelsey brought him along. Uncle Bill, thinking he was open-minded, always asked Ryan for decorating tips.

Kelsey sighed. "I believe I apologized for that and suffered through an entire season of the Yankees to make up for it." Baseball bored her to near suicide. Give her football all year round and she'd be happy. But she went to every home game with Ryan that year.

Every single one.

He balked at her. Not attractive with a full mouth of chocolate, Ry. "You didn't exactly suffer. You caught the home-run ball."

He couldn't be serious. Kelsey gaped and then snaked the cherry off the torte and chucked it at him. "Ryan, you caught the ball! After I stopped it with my forehead." She absently rubbed the still present, but smaller knot. "I had a headache for a month."

"It was a great stop." He grinned goofily at her, raising his eyebrows. God, she loved his smile.

When Ryan grinned, it was impossible to stay mad. Kelsey knew he was doing it to distract her, but it didn't stop her from grinning back. He knew her too well.

"Plus, I let you keep the ball."

True enough. It now sat in a place of honor on her mantle next to all their other treasures—playbills, photo booth strips, squashed pennies—all the hokey, touristy stuff they both loved.

He'd stayed with her all night for the concussion too. One of the perks of having a doctor for your best friend was house calls.

Despite the headache, that night remained one of her best memories. They had stayed awake watching their favorite movies from their high school days. Nobody believed they hadn't met each other until college. Even though they grew up four states away from each other, they managed to have all the same favorite movies and songs from their teen years. Nobody but Ryan understood her fascination with Wayne's World.

"Kelse?"

She looked up to find him studying her. He wore the tie she'd given him for his birthday. The gray matched his eyes perfectly.

"How could you think I would like Elise?" He looked honestly perplexed.

"I'm sorry. What was the problem? Was she too blonde? Too tan? Too drop-dead gorgeous for you? What was wrong with her?"

He grimaced. "She was vapid and one dimensional. You surprise me." He stabbed at the chocolate.

"Me?" Kelsey speared another forkful as forcefully as he did. "I am the most conservative person you know." She realized people were staring, so she toned it down. "What would possess you to set me up with a vegan who owns a metaphysical bookstore?"

The guy wouldn't even sit next to her because she'd ordered a steak. Which was how they ended up playing musical chairs so that Barbie and Birkenstock could get snuggly.

He shrugged. "I thought opposites attract...and my sister always told me she thought Brandon was cute. What do I know?" He sat back in his chair, leaving the last bite of cake for her.

"We're pathetic, aren't we?" She stared at the remaining cake. He always did that. Even if it was clear she'd shoveled in more than him, he was always considerate and left her the final bite.

She took the morsel he offered and let the chocolate do its magic with her eyes closed. She reopened them to find him staring at her. "What?"

He shook his head. "I just like watching you enjoy your food."

Her cheeks heated. "Why?" She hoped it wasn't because she was wearing it on her face. She self-consciously wiped her mouth with a napkin.

He smiled. "Because you are cute." He leaned over and tapped her nose with his finger.

She wasn't sure what to think of that. She felt the flush from her cheeks radiate towards her scalp too.

After a couple of false starts, he said, "This is going to sound strange...."

"Stranger than our double date turning into a scene from When Harry Met Sally?" she asked.

"Why do you always do that?"

"Do what?"

"Whenever I try to tell you how I feel, you make a joke." Resolutely, he reached over and covered her hand with his before he began again. "This is going to sound strange...." He sent her a warning look to quell another interruption. "But I am starting to think that the reason I hate dating so much is because I keep expecting the women to be more like you."

She stared at their hands. It wasn't the first time he had held her hand, but it felt different tonight. His magical hands that saved lives every day, fixed her leaky faucet at two a.m., and brought her gingerbread lattes at a moment's notice were holding onto her like a man holds onto something that is precious to him. Suddenly, it became very hard to swallow.

"Kelsey, look at me." She reluctantly met his silver-gray gaze, so he continued, "I know it's scary, and maybe I shouldn't have waited so long to tell you how I feel. You don't make it easy." He sighed, and she ached for him, knowing how hard this was for him to say it and knowing how scared she was to hear it. "A part of me was hoping you'd be the brave one." His grip tightened, yet his tone softened, making her aware of her own thudding heart. "We both know that nobody else is ever going to be able to put up with either of us."

Tentatively, she placed her free hand over the one holding hers. "I confess." Deep breath. "I knew you would hate your date tonight."

His gaze beseeched her for more of an explanation, and she knew he was waiting for her to make the next move. "The thought of you liking someone more than you like me makes me crazy."

He Said

Was she serious?

Ryan didn't let go of her hand and hoped his eyes were saying all the things he couldn't find words for. Kelsey was the first thing he thought of when he woke up in the morning and the last thing he thought of when he...well...guys are guys after all. But he did think of her right before he fell asleep too. He wouldn't tell her about the other times he fanta—thought of her just yet.

"Kelse, I can promise you that I could never like another person more than I like you."

She bit her lip, and an answering tug on his insides responded. That drove him crazy. Someday he was going to nibble on that lip. Whenever she licked her lips lately, he had to cover his lap.

If he were honest with himself, he'd admit that he'd loved her since the day he met her. Sophomores in college, they shared a house with four other students—well, technically the other four were students. He couldn't remember ever seeing them go to class. Kelsey was different, though, so serious. He probably wouldn't have gotten into med school if she hadn't encouraged him to keep studying.

That first day in the house, her baby blues had struck him blind with lust, but she had a long-distance boyfriend then. By the time they'd broken up, Ryan was dating someone else. Their timing never synched, but their friendship only grew stronger. When he'd finally finished school, he'd thought it was too late to change their relationship.

But he never stopped wondering.

Ryan tried, every now and then, to coax her into thinking about him differently, to see him in a new light. For some reason, the conversation always caused his fearless take-charge friend to become skittish and fidgety.

The waiter set the check next to him, breaking the spell. He knew what came next. She'd retreat. Maybe crack a joke or cajole him with a story about one of the eccentric artists she'd had to deal with at the gallery today. The moment would be lost, and he'd have to start again.

Maybe it was for the best. If she didn't return his feelings, he could lose her. The thought sucker-punched him in the gut.

Resigned, he said, "Come on. I'll take you home."

She Said

What just happened?

Kelsey wrinkled her brow. Weren't they just about to embark on a more-than-friends topic? The temperature in the room dropped ten degrees as Ryan shuttered all emotion from his face and pulled out his wallet.

Fine. It was better this way. It would be stupid to ruin a perfectly good friendship with a doomed romance. Because both of them sucked at romantic relationships. What they shared now far surpassed an entanglement that would lead them down the road of goodbye.

Really, this was better.

Once the stinging sensation in her heart stopped, she'd be glad he'd dropped the topic.

"I want to pay for half," she said, not knowing why. It always pissed him off when she made a stink about going Dutch. Oddly, she suspected that was why she offered. She'd rather deal with a perturbed Ryan than a frosty one.

Except he didn't even acknowledge her taunt.

The rollercoaster of emotion needed to stop. She left her stomach on the last drop. Life would be easier if they stuck to the plan. She swigged the last of her wine back and reached for his.

"Did you want to order a glass to-go?" He punctuated the question with a perfect eyebrow parenthesis over one eye.

"I know you practice doing that in the mirror."

"Women like it." He stood up and walked around the table to her chair.

"I don't."

He offered a hand. "Yes, you do. It usually makes you—" He stopped short as she put her hand in his and rose so that they were face to face.

Kelsey's breath hitched in her throat, and her heart hammered, the sound pounding in her ears. His steely eyes darkened like storm clouds, and he lowered his gaze to her mouth. Before she could stop it, her tongue instinctively slipped out to wet her lips. Ryan inhaled sharply.

What would it be like to, just once, lose myself in his kiss?

"Kelse...," he whispered.

It wouldn't really be getting lost, would it? It seemed more like it would be going home.

"Ry...," she said, her voice raspy and huskier than normal.

She reached for his cheek, touching him for the first time even though it must have been the thousandth. Her fingertips glided over smooth skin, but she knew tomorrow it would be rough with stubble because he never shaved on Sunday if he didn't have to.

She knew everything about him, didn't she?

Except what his kiss tasted like.

She stretched to close the distance between them.

His beeper went off.

He Said

You've got to be kidding me.

Ten years. Ten years he'd waited for this moment.

Ryan grabbed her elbows. "Wait right here."

Kelsey nodded, her eyes glazed with that shine only a woman on the edge of passion possesses. God, finally.

Ryan called his service from the lobby. He turned around to find Kelsey behind him.

"They're trying to reset the table," she explained. "I didn't want to be in their way. Do you have to go to the hospital?"

He nodded. "I'll put you in a cab."

"Sure." She smiled. Weakly.

"Kelse—"

"We'll talk later, Ry. You need to go."

Regret left a bitter aftertaste in his mouth. He loved his career, really, he did. But at that very moment, he wished he sold life insurance in an office from nine to five. Closing the cab door and sending her away made him shake with emptiness.

Damn it.

Six hours later, he showered and changed back into his suit. He considered the jeans and t-shirt he kept in his locker, but superstition won out. Kelsey had looked at him with new eyes in that suit—he needed all the luck he could get on his side.

The ride across town at four in the morning gave him too much time to think. He talked himself out of talking himself out of going to her. It couldn't wait. They had waited too long already. His stomach clenched, churning the metallic, stale break-room coffee he'd known better than to drink. He loosened his tie and tried to breathe.

What was his problem? He shouldn't be so worried. But God. If he screwed this up....

He let himself in the lobby door with the key she'd given him long ago, but thought better of entering her apartment with it. He knocked on her door while he called her cell.

"Hmmm?" she answered groggily.

"I'm at your door. Come let me in."

"Ry?" She groaned, and the shuffle of sheets followed. "What time is it?"

"Kelse, just come to the door." He rested his head on the wood. "Please?"

"Just a sec."

5 A.M. on a Sunday Morning

He didn't hang up. Neither did she. He heard the thwap of her slippers on the carpet as she crossed her apartment mumbling into the phone. One...two...three locks, and the door opened revealing everything he ever wanted...wearing pajamas with cows on them.

"Hi," he said into the mouthpiece of his phone.

"Hi," she answered into hers.

Silence stretched between them.

"May I come in?"

She Said

"I have to go now," she said into her phone. "Somebody's at the door."

Kelsey snapped her phone shut and stepped aside so he could come in. She brushed her hands down her wrinkled jammies, wishing suddenly she was the kind of woman who slept in a negligee.

And full make up.

She carefully locked the door—not because she was worried about someone breaking in, but because it gave her something to do with her trembling hands.

She inhaled deeply and pivoted around to find him standing in the middle of the room staring at her. He looked awful. She never understood how he could function on as little sleep as he ever got. He should have gone straight home and to bed.

"Are you hungry?" she asked.

"No."

His stomach growled.

"Well, maybe a little. But I don't want to eat."

"What do you want, Ry?"

He loosened his tie some more. "I want you, Kelsey. I've always wanted you." Ryan hadn't moved closer, but his words spilled over her as if he were touching her. They soothed her, but they also excited her. "The question is...do you want me?"

More than anything, she wanted to yell out. "I'm scared."

That propelled him towards her. He grasped her shoulders. "What are you so afraid of?"

"What if we can't make it work? What if I take a chance and lose you?"

"I've been here for ten years. If you had a prayer of scaring me off, it's long gone by now."

"Ryan—"

He pressed his fingers to her mouth. "The question is still do you want me?"

Snippets of their life together played across her mind like the home movies in her parents' attic. The post-date rehashes, studying for finals, road trips, the flu—his and hers. Through the good times and her lowest days, he'd been there. It had always been Ryan.

He still had his fingers over her mouth, so she nodded. He lifted his hand, and they collided together, raining hard kisses wherever their lips could reach. Finally, their mouths found each other, and the world stopped as she melted into his arms.

Ryan, Mr. Calm in a Crisis, kissed her madly with a kind of abandon she never knew he had. And she answered with a heat that threatened to sear her from the inside out. All she could do was respond to her body's demand to get closer to him.

He wrenched himself away, holding her shoulders in a firm grip. "Wait."

Wait? The look in his eyes did not say "wait".

"Why?" Kelsey stepped back into his embrace, but he held her firmly.

"I knew you wouldn't like your date either."

Huh? She shook her head. "I think we've moved past dissecting all the reasons the date didn't work, Ryan."

"I just wanted you to know. I fouled it up on purpose."

"I get it." She attempted another step, but he wouldn't let her budge. "Ry—"

"I love you, Kelsey. I've never said that to another woman. It's always been you."

He brushed the tear from her cheek, and she realized that the best moment of her life was happening at five a.m. on a Sunday morning while she wore the dumbest pajamas on the planet.

She was going to have to bench the lucky Little Black Dress. Apparently, the only luck she needed didn't care what she wore. Or how she looked— he'd definitely seen her at her worst—yet here he was.

"Oh, Ryan. I love you too. I always have."

He pulled her back into his arms, and she wondered how it was she hadn't been there all along. This time, he gentled his kisses, but they warmed her just as much as before.

Ryan's stomach growled again. Loudly. They both laughed and held hands on their way to the kitchen. He would make the omelet; she was in charge of toast. They knew this routine by heart, but suddenly it seemed fresh and new.

And a really good way to start.

Author Bio:

Gwen Hayes writes Romance and Young Adult fiction. She likes to think she is saving the world...one love story at a time. Please visit her at: www. gwenhayes.com or www.fictionistas.com.

I Heard You, You Know
by
M.E. Ellis

After a rocky divorce, how hard is it to say "I love you" again?

I've just been caught shoplifting. Well, I didn't intend to pinch the mascara, but my mind had drifted off into Romance Land, and before I knew it, I stood outside the department store with the incriminating evidence in my hand. Bad Lashes would have apparently made my eyes look stunning. Instead, they probably resemble one of those sodding zoo animals now. You know the kind—the ones with eyes too big for their heads. Lemurs, is it?

Anyway, I'm not complaining...at the moment. The security guard is a bit of all right. His hand on my shoulder—and don't I wish it would gravitate south to clutch my arse?—sends shivers of delight right down to my lady garden. Speaking of lady gardens, mine hasn't been touched in a long while. Not since my divorce. Shame that. That's why I wanted Bad Lashes to spruce myself up a bit and capture a fine looking specimen.

Ironic that he captured me.

Shit.

"Come this way, madam," he says.

Madam? Do I look *that* old?

I toddle beside him in my black heels down a corridor above the department store. Seems I'm going to get reprimanded in this office here because he unlocks the door and ushers me inside.7

"Please take a seat." He gestures to a grey desk chair complete with ripped fabric and escaping foam.

"Nice place you have here." I smirk, can't help myself. Situations like this always bring out the immature side of me. Besides, I've been reduced to experiencing my childhood again by his sneer. Feeling ten years old at my age isn't funny. I mean, I'm forty, for God's sake, wearing a decent suit, no less.

Act your age, you silly cow.

I clear my throat and battle away another smile. "I'm terribly sorry, sir, but this is a mistake."

He plops down on the other chair behind the desk and grips the arm rests, swings the seat on its castors. A fellow who harbours childish tendencies too? No. That can't be true. Security guards don't have a sense

20

of humour, do they? His black hair flops over his forehead, and I wonder if he's been on holiday recently or has a penchant for tanning beds.

"You can say that again," he says.

"But it is! I didn't mean—"

"That's what they all say."

His loud sniff of derision gets right on my tits, and I whiz from one end of the emotion scale to the other. Indignant, I state, "But I'm telling the truth!"

"They all say that as well." He laughs—nice straight teeth—and I fight the desire to claw at his face with my nails. That'd teach him. That'd ruin his gorgeous face.

Why did I have to be detained by a good-looking bloke?

I stare at the grotty beige carpet—don't they employ cleaners? Its decoration of crumbs, chocolate wrappers, and balled-up plastic wrap disturbs me. Any manner of germs could lurk down there. I lift my feet and rest them on a tall box of printer paper. Whoops, my skirt dangles down and reveals the underside of my thighs. How naughty am I? Who would believe that at my age I've been apprehended and now show off my cellulite-splattered legs to a hunky bloke?

Cellulite-splattered!

Sod the germs! With the haste of a fly zooming onto shit, my feet touch the floor again. I straighten my skirt, and the blush of the momentarily insane burns my cheeks. What the bloody hell was I thinking?

"So, please explain why you walked out of this store without paying for this mascara." He holds it up, examines it, his eyes so narrow I imagine that's what he'd look like when he's.... *Stop it, you filthy woman, you!*

"Well, I, uh, I...."

It's no good. He isn't going to believe me, is he? Who would?

His attention, now on my face, heats my cheeks another degree. The urge to cry is so vast that the lump forming in my throat is bound to cut off my air supply and render me a gasping wreck on that scabby carpet. And I don't want to get filth in my hair or on my clothes. No. Not in front of him, anyway.

"Well?" He leans back in his chair; seems to be settling in for a cosy chat, what with his legs now resting on the desktop, his trouser hems rising, thick, dark calf hair exposed to my eager view.

Lady garden alert! Oh, the tingles!

I squeeze my legs together and clench my bits in an attempt to quell the rage going on in my nethers. My face is so hot.

And so is he....

Inhale! Exhale! Think good thoughts.

I must make a visit to the supermarket and buy some sausages.

Sausages! Oooh, shit!

Try again. Quickly, he's staring at me!

I must remember to put the rubbish out tonight. Stinky, mouldy refuse, spores, gunge, filth!

Filth...imagine being filthy with him.

"Arghhh!" I yell and jump up from my seat. I didn't mean to say that out loud. I didn't!

He's up on his feet now, mascara brandished in front of him, a weapon of miniscule destruction if ever I saw one. "Sit down, madam! You'll accomplish nothing by being aggressive!"

I flop down onto the chair, my breaths heavy pants—pants...I wonder if he wears briefs or boxers? Shut. Up! I try to calm myself.

"I'm sorry. Sorry, I don't know what came over me."

He smiles, that roguish smile some men get when their mind switches to innuendo mode. Oh, crap.

"I didn't mean that as it sounded. I mean, I-I...oh, fuck it!" I release such a whoosh of air that it dislodges a sheet of paper from the desk. It floats to the floor and lands by his feet.

He bends to retrieve it, gaze fixed on me, mascara still held out as a warning. "Sit still, madam. No funny moves now. I'm watching you."

Shame he isn't watching me in any other way except to gauge whether I'm going to leap at him, a madwoman gone madder. Shame he's going to telephone the police and tell them I stole Bad Lashes and tried to attack him in his office, even though I haven't done either of those ghastly things.

I would attack him, only not in the aggressive sense.

Back in his seat, upright position displaying his authority, he points the mascara at me to emphasize each word. "What were you doing stealing this mascara?"

"I didn't steal it. I forgot I had it in my hand." What a lame excuse.

"You forgot?" His eyebrows quirk, and my stomach flips.

"Yes. You see, I was daydreaming—"

"What about?"

Is that a smile tugging his lips there?

No sense in fibbing. "About finding a man, if you must know."

"Were you now? How...interesting."

"Yes, well, that's the truth of it. Now either ring the rozzers and get me arrested, or slap my wrist and ban me from this shop. One or the other."

His brown eyes match the shade of mine. They soften and stare at me with such intensity that I'm forced to look down...at the infernal carpet.

"You really do need to clean up in here." Why did I just say that?

His laugh startles me, and I glance up, meet his gaze once more.

"My house needs a woman's touch as well."

Is he flirting with me? Hinting that he's single? No ring adorns his left hand—no telltale band mark from one either—but that doesn't mean anything these days, does it?

"Hire a bloody cleaner, then," I say, much harsher than I'd intended.

Let's face it. I'm crap at flirting. May as well just get this over and done with, hope I don't get taken to court, and move on to the rest of my life, alone.

Boo-bloody-hoo. Those violins pain my ears, tug at my heart, and bring tears to my eyes.

Tears to my eyes? What the hell's that all about? Angry, I swipe them off my cheeks. I bet all the thieves he's brought up here cried too. Great, I'm a typical woman, nothing he hasn't seen before, and I so wanted to be... different.

"Why are you crying?"

"Because I am. Hurry up and do what you have to do, will you?" The sight of the carpet is getting on my nellies, so I lift my head, stare into his eyes again, and wish we'd met under different circumstances.

"Name?" He picks up a pen, roots through a desk drawer, and brings out a sheet of official-looking paper. Head bent low, hand poised to fill in the form, he waits.

Despite my previous mood shifts, immaturity reigns once more.

"Polly Pocket." I tamp down a giggle.

His head snaps up. "Very funny. Name, please."

"Dora the Explorer."

"Look," he says, nostrils flaring, lips quirking—*quirking*? "Be serious, otherwise, I'll be forced to telephone the police. Name—the *proper* one this time."

My sigh of relief kisses his hair, and his fringe sways a little.

Oh no. I had a cheese baguette for lunch. With garlic mayonnaise. He winces. *Winces*, for frick's sake! *Way to go! Put the bloke off with your disgusting halitosis!*

"Sorry. Sorry for the breath." I fiddle with my hair. It needs a trim; bloody split ends—they remind me of dried-out tobacco. I really need to buy some intensive conditioner, maybe invest in a set of those straighteners. I bet even those wouldn't tame my mad, frizzy locks.

"What?" He frowns, smiles a little.

"My breath. Sorry about it. I had garlic mayo in my lunch, you see, and I just sighed, and my breath went in your face, and you winced, and—"

"Please, madam. *Please*, just give me your bloody *name*!"

He swore. He just swore! Oh my goodness.

"Pamela Anderson."

"Right! That's it. Enough is enough!" Irate now, cheeks aflame, lips pursed, he snatches the phone from its cradle.

"No! Sorry! No, please! I'll be serious now. Honest!"

He glares at me, and those eyes, jeepers....

My. Lady. Garden. Is. On. Fire.

"My name's Goldie."

He snorts and grits his teeth so hard his jaw muscles spasm. "Hawn, I suppose."

"No. Porn."

"Oh, for fu—"

"I'm serious!" I dive into my handbag, bring out my purse, and lay a credit card on the desk.

He stares at it, then at me. "Oh, right, well...Miss *Porn*, what's your address?"

* * * *

This is nice, isn't it? A tasteful restaurant, this, what with the posh décor—all pine-paneled lower walls and blush-pink wallpaper above. The tablecloths match the drapes and napkins—even the candles. It costs an arm and a leg to eat in here. I should know. I've been here before, you see, on my first date with that security guy.

"I could have throttled you that day," he says. His eyes reflect the lights from the overhead chandelier. "I had no intention of shopping you to the police, you know."

"Really? And all these years I thought I'd got away with it by using my insane wiles." The memories coax a smile to my lips, and I look at him looking at me, and well, I could cry right now, I really could.

I love him so much it hurts my tummy.

"I almost willed you to steal something."

"What?"

"I'd been trying to get up the courage to approach you and ask you out on a date." His smile does things to my bits, as always.

"Honestly!" After a sip of wine, I ask, "So why are you revealing this now? We've been married for ten years!" I cut into my steak and pop a piece

24

into my mouth.

"I'm not sure. Maybe I just wanted you to know before...well, we're not youngsters anymore, are we? I want you to know everything about me so that there's nothing left to tell. Then we can sit down and enjoy each other's company with no secrets, nothing."

That's very sweet, isn't it? He says things like that all the time. A lump forms in my throat, and I find it difficult to swallow my steak. It goes down, a hard stone, and I gulp some wine to help the meat along its way. A thought strikes me then, grips my chest with scared fists and shakes me, doesn't let go.

"Is everything all right? You're not ill or anything, are you?" A thundering, adrenaline-fuelled heart isn't good for someone of my age. Fifty now, see. I breathe long and deep to steady the painful thumps.

"Who me?" he says, eyes wide, hand on chest. "Of course not. Don't be daft. Whatever gave you that idea?"

After clearing my throat and sipping more wine, I say, "Well, uhm, I think I'm just being a bit silly. You know, old age creeping up and all that. Made me think...." Oddly, a wave of self-consciousness claims me, and I fiddle with my hair. My straight hair (I bought the straighteners!).

"Don't you want to tell *me* everything?" he asks.

His smile, so genuine, stills my thoughts, my tongue. I know what he's waiting for, what he wants to hear, but I've never been able to say it. My last marriage wrecked my ability to express my feelings in any other way except joking. Besides, who wants a mushy, serious wife?

"I do tell you everything!" I bluster. "You know I do. Only the other day we discussed how Melanie annoyed me by cropping her side of the dividing hedge in our back garden so low that I saw her sunbathing in the buff. I wouldn't mind, but since seeing her, I keep envisaging her tits hiding under her armpits, which led me to get on our bed without any clothes on and check if mine do the same. And I told you they do, told you how it made me feel to have saggy boobs. Not every wife would confess that to her husband, would they? You know, they got undressed in the middle of the day and... and...."

Goldie, stop waffling.

His rich laugh ensures other diners look our way and smile. He has that way about him, this husband of mine, that draws people to him. I often joke that he's a magnet where I'm concerned. He's a magnet, and I'm a pin. As soon as he passes by me, I'm stuck to his side, where I always want to be. Tears prick my eyes. I never thought it possible to love someone so deeply that the waves of emotional love attack me with such fervour that it produces a physical pain. God bless the day I saw that Bad Lashes advert and walked into the department store to steal—to *buy* some.

"Goldie, you're funny. You've made me so happy, d'you know that?"

Something in his tone frightens me. My stomach clenches, my heart rate accelerates, and my knees—if I stood now my legs wouldn't hold me up.

"Martin? Martin, what's wrong? Something's wrong, isn't it?"

He reaches over and pats my hand, stops the fork clanging against the plate where I'd shook, shook it to the point of terror. "No, nothing's wrong. Nothing at all. I love you, daft Mrs. Forbes."

I swallow, smile, blink. "I know, Mr. Forbes."

* * * *

It smells in here, smells of disinfectant and lemon polish. And the sounds: squeaking shoes, the jangle of curtain rings as they swish along poles, medicine trolley contents clacking against one another, nurses riffling for their blood sample test tubes, their rubber gloves, their....

"Mrs. Forbes?"

A nurse stands beside me, body bent forwards, her face saying a thousand words. Sympathy resides in her expression, along with sorrow, pity...and I don't want her goddamn pity. I just want Martin, my rock, my life, to be well again. Will she tell me what I dread to hear? Will she? Will she break my heart with her next sentence—delivering my sentence?

A life without him.

Stop it, Goldie, just stop it. Think positive.

"Yes?" My voice doesn't sound like mine. Sounds like some old lady I used to know when I was a kid. She used to smell of urine—must have wet her knickers on many an occasion—and we'd rip the piss out of her. Or we would have, if she hadn't have done it herself.

The nurse sits beside me in this stark, primrose-painted corridor. The air huffs out of her seat as she settles on it, her hand on my arm, tears in her eyes. "I'm afraid it's bad news. Your husband's going to need an operation, or...."

Pure, unadulterated fear throttles me, tries to murder me with its intensity. "Or what? What? *What?*"

"Or things could go from bad to worse. I'm so sorry." She squeezes my arm, and though I realise, even with my current state of mind, that she means well, that she seems sincere, I want to shirk her off, rail at her, tell her she knows nothing, *nothing* of what I'm feeling inside.

I Heard You, You Know

What will I do without him? He's going to be taken away, isn't he? Taken away, up there with the angels, and what good is he up there? I need him down here, with me. *Oh, God...God, if there's any justice in this world, let my Martin get through this. Please don't take him. Not yet. Not without me too.*

"I've got to see him. Now." I stare at her and try to convey how urgent it is that I have my request granted.

"You can have five minutes, then he has to go down to the operating theatre. He's sleeping now, though."

Disappointment crashes through me on feet of spite, feet that crush and destroy and obliterate and.... Oh, God, I've got to speak to him, tell him. Tell him....

Almost blind with tears, I follow the nurse into Martin's room. She pulls back the curtain. Oh, Jesus. Where did his weight go? He's only been here five hours, and the weight has dropped off him, just disappeared. This is it, isn't it? This is all the time I've been allowed with him. Twenty years. And it wasn't enough, *wasn't enough*! We'd planned so much: so many places to go, people to see, sights to soak up, joys to experience. We couldn't have any children, so I won't even have them to fill my days. No. *No!* I won't have it. I won't have his life cut short like this. Not without saying....

"I'll leave you to it, Mrs. Forbes."

I nod, listen to the swish of her skirts as she leaves the room, and sit down in the visitor's chair beside his bed. The crêpe-like skin on his hand—when did that happen?—forces tears to spill and my lip to wobble just like it did that time when Dad caught me carving my name into their new dining room table and he shouted at me, shouted so loudly.... And I hold Martin's hand now, hold it, will it to squeeze mine like it always has when I'm scared.

And I am scared. Falling apart.

"Martin?"

His eyelids flicker, but my voice elicits no other reaction. None at all.

Oh, *God.*

"Martin?" More urgent this time.

No flicker. Nothing.

The clock ticks, the sound so loud in this room containing my whole world.

"Martin," I whisper. "I'm here, okay? Here. With you. Where I'll always be—where you know I'll always be. And when you wake up, I'll be here then as well. Right next to you, okay? And you'll get better. You will. I'll help you fight this. Did you have it all this time? Did you know and not tell me? Right back then? I had a feeling something was wrong, didn't I? Didn't I say that?

27

Knowing you like I do, you didn't want to worry me, kept it all to yourself, even though you said you wanted to tell me everything. Oh, Martin. Typical you."

No reaction.

Come on, hand. Squeeze mine. Eyes. Open. Please open so I can look into them again, if only for one more time.

Please. *Please*?

Nothing.

"Time's up, Mrs. Forbes."

No. It can't be. That wasn't five minutes. That was seconds. Seconds!

"Please, just a little longer. Please, I'm begging you. I need to...I have to...please."

The nurse backs out of the room, and I can't stand the look on her face. Can't *stand* it!

"Martin?"

His dear face, how I love it. Every line, wrinkle, and crevice.

"I love you, Mr. Forbes."

A tidal wave of emotion engulfs me, and I topple off my chair and onto the floor, a soggy, sobbing mess.

* * * *

This is nice, isn't it? A tasteful restaurant, this, what with the posh décor—though it isn't the same as it used to be. Still, I suppose I have to accept that things change, times change. It's all re-vamped in here now. Made trendy for the youngsters, I imagine. Oh my, I'm seventy years old and still dining out. Who'd have thought it? Mind you, I'm not eating steak tonight. My bloody dentures won't allow it. Not in public, anyway. It's okay when they pop out and land in my gravy at home, but here? No. Wouldn't want to make the other diners ill.

Those brown pools opposite me, I love them. Have since the first time I looked into them, even though they held a hint of anger back then. Not since, though. They hold love, sincerity, desire—yes, even that. Years ago, I always thought old people didn't do it, but I don't feel old, you know. My world there, he keeps me young and can still reduce my lady garden to a mass of mulch instead of a cultivated landscape. I'd like to say my privet hedge is still nicely trimmed, but I confess, I let that kind of thing fall by the wayside ten years ago when nursing Martin.

Tough times, those, and I never want to go through them again, though I would. For him. Anything for him.

I Heard You, You Know

"Back here again then, love," he says, his hair no longer dark but white, eyebrows to match.

"I love coming back here every year. Never tire of it, do you?" I sip my wine.

Martin leans across and strokes my cheek, a soft smile on his lips.

"Damn this getting old business," I say and grit my teeth.

"Well, at least you haven't got a beard."

"Yet. I'm cultivating a moustache, so the beard won't be long behind it."

He laughs, and oh, how I love the sound. I won't ever tire of that, either. I drink in the sight of him, and memories from our past saunter through my mind. Days at the beach, quiet Sunday morning breakfasts, watching TV holding hands.

I wish we were immortal.

Martin clears his throat. "Goldie?"

"Hmmm?"

His face holds mischief—it reddens, his eyebrows rise—and he fiddles with his napkin, just like a naughty little boy. "Did you ever throw that fake credit card away? You know, the one you showed me when you said your name was Goldie Porn?"

"As a matter of fact, no. I kept it. Why?"

His grin widens, and his lovely eyes sparkle. "Shall we give it to the waiter when he brings the bill? You know, for a laugh?"

I giggle and sound young again, *feel* young again. "We could do. His face'll be a picture."

"Always up for a laugh, is my Goldie." He grasps my hand, squeezes it tight, and I'm safe, always safe with him.

He clears his throat. "You know when I got ill?"

"Oh, God...." *Please don't tell me it's back. Tell me anything but that.*

"No, no, don't worry. Nothing like that."

Relief visits my extremities, leaving me weak and thankful. He wouldn't keep it from me—not again. He promised.

He gazes at me, his eyes conveying everything I'm sure mine tell him. Our connection is like that—intense, strong, so right.

"Well, do you also remember that conversation we had in here twenty years ago? The one where I said—"

"Yes, yes, I remember." Embarrassment jiggles in my tummy, releasing the caterpillars from their cocoons. Oh, hell. He's going to ask me to say it.

"I just want you know that you don't have to worry anymore. I mean, I know you try and say it, but you don't have to. Your actions tell me fine enough. I know everything about you."

"You do?" My heart thuds, and love surges through me, so intense it steals my breath.

"The day of my operation?"

"Yes?"

"I heard you, you know."

Author Bio:

M.E. Ellis is a novelist and also an editor with Wild Child Publishing, Freya's Bower, and Dred Tales Magazine.

New Love
by
Maryann Miller

Love can be just as sweet the second time around. And there are no age limits.

"What am I doing? Acting like a love-sick teenager, that's what."

He made the personal indictment aloud while driving slowly down the tree-lined street checking addresses. Ten hours of driving had left him with burning eyes, and the shadows of near dusk were hard to penetrate. It didn't help that he hadn't been here in ten years. What if she'd moved since they had last seen each other? What if she didn't want an eighty-year-old man showing up on her doorstep with courting in mind?

"You're a fool, Patrick David Williams. A silly old fool."

Then he saw it. Her house. A little yellow frame structure nestled between two sprawling brick ranches. It was so unique, he should have remembered the distinction and not bothered with trying to read addresses. He started to stop in front of her home, but panic struck and jangled his nerves. *What if she's married again?* Accelerating, he drove past to the end of the street. There, he pulled to the curb and took a couple of deep breaths. Leaves of gold and red scuttled down the sidewalk driven by the evening breeze. *God, Patrick, why didn't you think of this sooner? A simple phone call would have answered that question.*

He pulled out his cell phone and looked at it. It was a present from his kids. They had all agreed they would feel better if he had one while he was traveling. His son had programmed all the important numbers into the phone to make it easier for Patrick to call them. But he didn't need numbers programmed for him. He might forget a lot of things. But not numbers. Even after all these years he still remembered Jean's number. He could call now, and if a man answered, he'd hang up.

That thought elicited a chuckle. Was his life now a cliché?

The choice was clear. He could sit here until someone became alarmed about him loitering and called the cops. Or he could drive off and forget this crazy idea. Or, the third choice: He could go to the door and see what happens.

He eased the car back onto the street and looked toward the intersection leading to the highway that would take him toward Detroit and his daughter. If he started now, he could be there in about three hours. He sighed and glanced back at Jean's house. Might as well chance it, he reasoned. If there was a new man in her life, she would still be hospitable to a traveler. That was her way.

He used a nearby driveway to turn around and head back. He doused the lights, stilled the engine, and sat looking at the house. It needed a new coat of paint, but the grass was neatly mowed, and marigolds bloomed along the walkway. Orange fingers of sunset stretched across the expanse of sky beyond the house roof, and a light shone in one window. He considered the light a sign: *Welcome. Come on in.*

He opened the car door, slid out, took a moment to get the circulation working in his legs, and walked up to the door. His finger trembled as he reached for the doorbell, and he drew his hand back. He took a moment, pulled himself as straight as the catch in his back would allow, and punched the black button. The chime buzzed in the interior, and a few seconds later, a flash of brilliancy blinded him as the porch light flickered to life.

"Who is it?"

Jean's voice was the same. Soft, melodic, and oh, so sweet.

"It's me, uh...Patrick."

The door flew open, and wide brown eyes regarded him. "Oh, my gosh."

Hoping for some sign of excitement or welcome, he watched a myriad of emotions play across her face. Surprise. Confusion. Concern. Then he saw it—delight.

"Come on in." She opened the door wider. "But I must say you're the last person I expected to see on my front stoop."

The nervous flutter of her hands, along with the quick look around the room, as if assessing how it looked for company, amused him. He smiled. "I was in the neighborhood."

"Oh." She reached to clear some newspapers from the sofa, but something stopped her. "I thought you lived in Texas?"

"I did. I mean, I do. But I get up here every now and then."

She looked at him for a long moment, and he knew what was coming next. "Is Regina with you?"

Now it was his turn to look everywhere but at her. "No. She, uh...she died last year."

"Oh."

For a moment there was nothing but the single word. Then he felt a light touch on his arm, as if a butterfly had landed there. He turned to the touch and saw her eyes swimming with compassion. "I'm so sorry," she said.

"Thank you."

He turned away again, glancing around to see if there was any sign of a male presence in the room. Nothing. No telltale pipe or slippers or beer bottle by the lounge chair. Just a knitting bag on the floor and a book on the small table beside the chair. The book lay face down, as if hastily put there. She must have been reading when he rang the bell.

"Are you taking an inventory?" she asked, a smile touching the corners of her mouth.

He glanced back at her. "Uh, no."

Oh, that was brilliant, Patrick.

They stood in this silent tableau for a moment, his nerves creating pools of sweat at the small of his back. Where could the conversation go from here? Did he just blurt out the reason he'd come? He covered the confusion by angling toward an armchair that seemed to beckon his weary body. "Could I have a seat?"

"Of course." She dropped the papers on a low table. "What can I get you? Coffee? Something stronger?"

"A glass of ice water would be nice. Didn't stop much on the way up."

She headed toward the kitchen, but paused with one hand on the doorjamb and looked at him. "You drove all the way today?"

"From Lexington."

"That must be...what? Six, seven hundred miles?" She walked toward him, the water apparently forgotten.

He considered for a moment. "About."

"What on earth caused you...?"

He wasn't conscious of sending any signals, but something stopped her question. She sat down slowly and looked at him. "Why are you here, Patrick?"

Whew. Here's the moment. He put a hand on the knee that had started to tremble and cleared his throat. "There was a time we were right fond of each other."

He let that statement stand alone a moment, giving her time to adjust. When he thought she was ready, he continued, "I was hoping we could maybe...see each other."

"You're asking me for a date?"

"I know it sounds a little silly at our age." He shrugged. "But, yes. I'm asking if you'd like to have dinner with me."

"When? Tonight?"

"I am a bit hungry."

He offered a smile and watched carefully as she appeared to process everything with a thoughtful expression on a face that had weathered the years well. Laugh lines had made deep grooves on her cheeks, and crow's-feet accentuated her dark eyes, but in his eyes, those things only added to her appeal. Little flutters of movements as her fingers played with the crease in her tan slacks betrayed a nervousness that matched the thumping of his heart.

He would die if she said no.

"I suppose it wouldn't hurt," she finally said, straightening her back and stilling her hands. "I could just freshen up a bit first."

"Sure." He let the relief out with a large whoosh of air. "I'll, uh...I'll just wait here."

"There's another bathroom downstairs." She gestured to the stairway just off the living room. "If you need it."

Jean disappeared down a short hallway, and Patrick sat a moment, before deciding that a trip downstairs was a good idea. He relieved himself and washed his hands, checking his face in the mirror. The stubble of beard could use some attention, but he hadn't brought his toiletry bag inside. Should he go out and get it? Did it matter that he was a little rumpled and unkempt? Surely she would understand since he'd just driven all that way.

But what if she saw it as an indication that he didn't care enough to clean up for her? He never thought stuff like that mattered, until marrying Regina. She had a fine sense of what proper gentlemen and ladies should do before presenting themselves in public. In fact, he remembered the first time they had to call the ambulance when her heart trouble started. She made him get her pearls from her dresser so she could put them on. She said a lady never went out without her pearls.

The memory brought a sting of tears behind the chuckle. "Oh, girl, you were something else. And this has nothing to do with how much I loved you."

Patrick waited a moment in the stillness, almost as if waiting for her to respond. He sighed and again considered a trip to the car. The twinge in his knee was the deciding factor. One trip up the stairs was probably all he was going to manage.

As a concession to propriety, he ran his fingers through his hair, still thick after all these years and still mostly black with just a sprinkling of gray. He splashed his face with cool water and swished his mouth with some mouthwash he found in the cabinet beside the mirror. This would have to do.

He started up the stairs, glad there was a turn with a stopping point halfway up. *Damned arthritis.* When he reached the top of the staircase, Jean stood there, watching him.

"Your knee giving you fits?" she asked.

"A bit." He noted with some relief that she had not gone to great pains in "freshening up." She'd done something to make her auburn hair fluff nicely around her face in soft curls, and her lipstick looked darker. But she still wore the tan slacks and lavender blouse. A black shawl lay across one arm, and a purse hung over her shoulder.

"Why don't I drive?" She dug in her bag and pulled out some keys. "I've got a brand-new car."

She led the way to the garage that housed a light blue Lincoln Town Car. Patrick settled back into the soft leather and decided this beat the hell out of his little Pontiac Vibe. Great gas mileage wasn't always worth the sacrifice of luxury.

"There's a little diner just up the road a bit," Jean said as she backed the car out of the garage. "Sound okay to you?"

"That would be fine."

They drove a few blocks in silence. Patrick wondered what she was thinking, but he didn't dare ask, afraid that she was thinking him a fool.

"I can't believe we're doing this."

The pronouncement stopped his breathing for a second. "Uh, do you want to go home?"

"No, silly." She glanced at him with a quick smile. "It's just... I don't know. I haven't done something this impulsive in years."

Relief washed over him. "Me either."

She turned her attention back to the road, and a more comfortable silence settled on them until she pulled into the parking lot of Foster's Diner. "Where Home Cooking Reigns" a sign proclaimed. "I remembered you are a meat-and-potatoes kind of guy," Jean said as they made their way to the entrance.

The business of getting settled and placing their order occupied them for a while, but once the waitress left, they exchanged nervous smiles and seemed to have difficulty speaking again.

* * * *

Jean took a sip of water, set the glass down, and looked over at Patrick. "How long do you plan to stay?"

"I don't know."

"Are you on your way to Detroit?"

"Eventually." He rearranged his silverware for what had to be the third time since they had sat down.

"I don't mean to pry, Patrick, but do your children know where you are?"

"Do you mean in Central Michigan, or sitting here with you?"

The jest was so classic Patrick, she had to swallow a rush of emotion before she accepted the invitation to banter. "Don't be smart."

His smile took ten years off his face. "I told them I'd be stopping along the way. Not to worry."

So, okay. Did he tell them specifically that he would be stopping to see me? Jean almost voiced the question, but she wasn't sure if she wanted to hear the answer. She stifled her curiosity with another sip of water, relieved when the waitress brought their salads and they both had something to do for a few minutes.

Then her maternal instincts kicked in. If she was traveling, her kids would want to know exactly where she was. That concern brought a mixed bag of appreciation and irritation. It was nice to be so cared about, but she hated being reminded that they were now watching over her like she had watched over them when they were toddlers.

She pointed at him with her fork. "You should call."

"I will," he stirred the lettuce on his plate, "when I know what I'm going to say to them."

There were layers of meaning under his words. At least, Jean thought there were. A flush started to warm her neck as she thought about what he might be implying. Was it just another tease?

Jean couldn't remember the last time she felt so rattled. She prided herself in maintaining a steady emotional balance through almost anything. But from the time she had opened her door and saw Patrick standing there, she had felt like a gymnast slipping off the balance beam in slow motion.

As if sensing her discomfort, Patrick gave her another smile. He was about to say something, but was interrupted when the waitress arrived with their dinner plates. Meatloaf smothered in mushroom gravy for him, and baked halibut for her.

After the young woman determined that they had everything they needed, she left, and Jean watched Patrick cut his meat into neat little pieces. That was more like the Patrick she knew. Precise. Consistent. Predictable. Totally unlike the man who had appeared on her doorstep this evening. What was she to make of this other man? Was she ready for what she thought he had on his mind? Or did she even dare consider it?

Ten years ago she had been ready. Barry had been gone two years, and she was almost desperate for someone to share the lonely nights and that very large bed. She was also ready to admit that there had always been a bit of something special between her and Patrick. She had felt it all those years the men had worked together and the families had played together.

Jean had never been sure what to call that feeling. It wasn't exactly a sexual attraction. At least not the kind she had shared with Barry. It had been more like some of the bonds she shared with close girlfriends; an easy comfortableness that was deep, solid, and seldom needed words. She enjoyed Helen, Patrick's first wife, but when the foursome was together, she was drawn to him a little bit more than to Helen.

When she realized that and acknowledged that it was a form of intimacy, Jean had been careful to keep the friendship within the proper boundaries. That was especially true at those times when it was clear that emotional intimacy could easily lead to something more. There was no way she was going to be "the other woman" and ruin two families. At a point when that precaution didn't seem necessary, at least from her standpoint, Patrick had been too fresh with grief over Helen's death to notice another person beyond the pain.

Jean had never been one to waste time with wishes and what ifs, so she had merely accepted that their lives would probably go in different directions when they no longer had work and spouses to tie them together. They had kept in touch through sporadic holiday greetings and an occasional letter. That's how she found out he'd married Regina a couple of years later.

Now, everything was changing again. Regina was gone, and here he was, back in her life with something obviously on his mind.

Jean pushed her plate to one side and watched Patrick mop the puddle of gravy with a roll. Was he ever going to broach the subject, or should she just take the initiative?

As if perhaps sensing the question on her mind, he looked up and gave her a brief smile.

She took a deep breath and asked, "When you said could we 'see each other' what exactly did you have in mind?"

Patrick carefully wiped his mouth with his napkin before setting it beside his plate. "I thought maybe I'd stay here in Ann Arbor for a while. We could go out some and see where that takes us."

"Well, I don't want to sound pushy. But how long is a 'while?'"

He shrugged. "A few months?"

"Are you asking?"

"I thought it would be presumptuous to assume."

Jean refolded her napkin, using the slight delay to find enough courage to be direct. That had been part of the problem ten years ago. Neither one of them had the courage to say what needed to be said.

"You can stop me if I'm wrong, but something stronger than casual interest prompted you to make a long, arduous trip to see an old friend. And if I'm right about that, I'm guessing that you'd like this to lead to something more than a few dates."

She paused to give him time to respond, but he sat silent, an odd expression on his face. It was so unreadable she almost panicked, but she swallowed the fear and continued. "So my question to you is, what are we waiting for? It's not like we're young with all the time in the world."

* * * *

Patrick hoped the tightness in his chest was from excitement and not a sign of a pending heart attack. "You're saying you might be interested in making this something permanent?"

"If that's what you're wanting."

Suddenly, the years melted away. He was eighteen again, and Maggie Crenshaw had just smiled at him. If he passed a mirror and saw himself, he'd swear he'd even be standing straight and tall again.

"I know what I've been wanting," he said. "But I need to know about you. And I don't want to rush you."

She reached across and touched him. His hand tingled where she made contact.

"How old are you?" she asked.

"Eighty."

"I'm seventy-six. I think rushing might be necessary in this case."

He laughed so hard, people at nearby tables gave him startled looks. He grinned at them. "I think she likes me."

"Patrick, hush." Jean touched a hand to the flush on her cheek. "This is embarrassing."

"No. This is right." He leaned toward her. "Just right."

Author Bio:

Maryann Miller is an author, scriptwriter, and editor. Her recent novels are One Small Victory, and Play it Again, Sam. Visit her Web site: www.maryannwrites.com.

A Ride to Remember
by
Adelle Laudan

*Dinner with her student's grandfather has fifty-year-old Desiree
wondering...is there really such a thing as fate?*

Desiree would never have guessed at age fifty that she'd feel freer to be herself than ever before—no pretenses, no facades. No longer did she live to find the ultimate party, having just celebrated ten years of sobriety. How liberating to be yourself without watching others for clues about what to think or say. If she learned nothing else in her recovery, she'd learned you must be the change you wish to see in the world.

She settled back on her porch swing, setting it in motion. The morning sun danced off a blanket of dew that created a prism effect. Inhaling deeply, she stood and followed the scent of fresh-brewed coffee—one of her favourite aromas—toward the last gurgles of her coffee machine. She hummed to herself while filling a mug.

Incessant barking caught her attention and drew her back to the front porch. A small dog, maybe a poodle mix, ran in circles on her front lawn as a man played tag with the pooch's leash.

"Sadie, you stop this instant," he grumbled, missing the leash again. He stood with his hands on his hips and shook his head at the rambunctious animal.

Desiree giggled behind her coffee mug. "I think she wants to play rather than listen."

The man turned to face her. Friendly blue eyes sparkled with laughter. "She's too saucy for her own good."

Desiree's breath hitched. His gaze enveloped her like a warm embrace. Her hand fluttered to her cheeks. "Coffee is hot if you'd care to join me." She offered her hand. "My name's Desiree Janson."

"Nice to meet you. Albert Tanner, but my friends call me Tanner." He wiped a hand on his faded jeans before shaking her hand. "If I can catch Sadie, we'd love to sit for a spell."

"Why don't you just close the gate and let her tucker herself out?"

"Now that sounds like a plan." He closed the gate and stepped up onto the porch.

"Please have a seat," she said, "while I get you a cup of coffee. Cream and sugar?"

"Just milk. I'm already sweet enough." He winked and sat down on the swing.

Desiree chuckled and hurried inside. She braced herself against the counter, closed her eyes, and took a deep, steadying breath. "Get hold of yourself, Desiree. You'd think you never saw a man before."

She poured Tanner's coffee and took it out to him. As she leaned across to him, she noted he smelled of soap and fruity chewing-gum. Sadie scampered back and forth, barking at anything and everything.

"I swear I don't know what has got into her. You'd never guess she's eight years old by the way she's acting." He drank from his mug.

"Spring is in the air."

He held her gaze. "Ah, that must be it. A time for new birth and new love."

Desiree cursed the heat rushing to her cheeks and quickly averted her gaze. "Are you from around here? I don't remember seeing you, I mean, Sadie, before."

"I'm here visiting my daughter who just made me a grandfather again last week." He reached into the inside pocket of his windbreaker and pulled out a cigar wrapped with a pink band. "I don't suppose you smoke, do you?"

Desiree took the cigar. She rolled it between her thumb and forefinger before passing it under her nose. Amusement danced in his eyes as he watched her. Laughter bubbled up from within her and burst out. She pointed at him. "You should see your face." She wiped the moisture from her eyes. "Did you really think I'd smoke it?"

Tanner shrugged. "You never know nowadays; anything goes."

She handed him the cigar. "Congratulations, by the way. Your daughter wouldn't happen to have an older daughter named Emily Simms, would she?"

His brow arched. "Why yes she does. A proud big sister, I might add. Do you know my Carol?" He took his wallet from the back pocket of his jeans and flipped it open. "Here's Emily. I don't have a picture of the new arrival yet, but she's the spittin' image of her."

Desiree smiled. "I thought so; I'm Emily's second grade teacher."

"Miss Janson?" Tanner laughed. "I've heard your name mentioned quite a few times. Well isn't this a small world?" He put the cigar back in his pocket and whistled. "Come here, Sadie old girl."

Sadie bounded up the steps and danced around their feet. She stopped in front of Desiree, her tail thumping against the porch.

"Hello, Miss Sadie." Desiree rubbed behind the dog's floppy ears. "I think she likes me."

"What can I say? She has good taste." He held her gaze. "I hope you don't think me too forward, but do you have any plans for dinner this evening?"

Desiree's pulse raced. "No, I don't." She hadn't been on a real date in over ten years.

"Good. Can I take you out for a meal? Let's say six?"

"That sounds like fun. I look forward to it."

Tanner stood and grabbed Sadie's leash. "I'll let you get on with your day, then, and pick you up around six." He leaned close and brushed her cheek with his lips. He scratched the top of Sadie's head as they descended the porch. "I guess I owe you a great big soup bone."

Desiree smiled, watching him walk away. He certainly was handsome, maybe three or four inches taller than her. She'd been a big fan of salt-and-pepper hair ever since Kenny Rogers started going gray. He stopped outside her gate and turned to face her.

"Oh, you might want to wear pants tonight, okay?"

Her brow creased. "Sure," she agreed, thoroughly confused.

He smiled mischievously and continued along the sidewalk. She couldn't help but remember the last man in her life. She'd woken after her final drunk in the emergency room. Her husband of five years had brutally beaten and raped her before emptying their bank account and fleeing the country. Needless to say, it left a bad taste in her mouth when it came to men.

Her sponsor had insisted that a recovering alcoholic woman shouldn't have relationships during her first year of sobriety. Desiree had more than welcomed the condition. Since then it became easier to abstain than deal with the painful memory. A shudder ran the length of her body, and she glanced at her watch. She had exactly eight hours to find something to wear. Hopefully Marci would fit her in for a wash and curl this afternoon. She gathered the empty mugs and hurried inside to use the phone.

* * * *

"Honestly, Marci, I feel like a teenager getting ready for a big date."

Marci massaged her scalp under a steady stream of warm water. "I'm sure you'll have a wonderful time." She helped her sit up and wrapped a towel around Desiree's wet hair. "Now let's make you beautiful."

Desiree sat in front of the mirror assessing her face. The words of her sponsor replayed in her mind.

"There are days when we need to make the conscious decision to love ourselves moment by moment. You will never be able to feel the love someone has to offer until you can love yourself."

She feathered the tiny lines at the corner of her eyes. They wouldn't be there if she hadn't had laughter in her life. A slight chip showed on her bottom tooth—a constant reminder of what happened when she drank.

Marci appeared behind her reflection. "So what is it going to be? Do you want it up, or down?"

"I'm not sure. He told me that I should wear pants tonight. What's up with that?"

Marci combed through Desiree's shoulder-length hair. "I don't know." She shrugged.

"How about we leave it down for a change? I wear it up for work five days a week."

"Good. I'll use the flat-iron and make it really shine. Did I ever tell you how jealous I am of your hair? You can't buy this shade of blonde in a bottle."

Desiree smiled. "I think you might have mentioned it a time or two."

"I hope this guy knows how lucky he is that you're giving him a chance after what that jerk of a husband did to you."

Desiree waved a hand. "That was a very long time ago, Marci. It's high time I stopped being a victim, don't you think?"

Marci nodded. "So are you going to wear jeans?"

Desiree laughed. "The only jeans I own are over ten years old."

"If you like, I can take a break when I'm done with your hair. Why not treat yourself to some nice jeans and a top to show off your curves?" Marci expertly trimmed the ends of Desiree's hair as she chatted.

"I don't know about all that, but I'd love your help."

"It's settled then. I'll finish drying your hair and iron it. Then we can head over to the mall."

"You're a good friend, Marci."

"No big deal. It'll be fun."

* * * *

Desiree stood in front of her full-length mirror. Panic rose up in her and played havoc with her nerves. She liked the looks of the woman she saw. The dark wash trouser jeans made her legs appear a mile long. A short-sleeved, white cashmere v-neck under a black embroidered, short jacket completed the outfit. She ran her hand down the length of her shiny blonde hair, smooth as silk. Not one for wearing make-up, she'd opted for mascara and liner to cover her blonde lashes and pale rose gloss on her lips.

A Ride to Remember

About an hour ago she started worrying about the date. *What if he drinks? Can I enjoy a meal with someone who does?* She realized that over the past ten years she'd isolated herself from the drinking world. When she really sat and analyzed the situation, she'd agreed to go off with a stranger. For all she knew, he could be a serial killer.

Her laughter reverberated through her small bedroom. *Now you're being ridiculous.* She was going out to dinner with the grandfather of one of her students. What harm could there be in that? Despite her pep talk, she pressed her hand to her tummy in an effort to still the butterflies doing aerobatics in her stomach.

A thunderous roar reverberated outside her window, and she dashed over to look out the glass. The biggest, blackest motorcycle she'd ever seen pulled up to the curb. Her heart raced so fast her chest hurt. The rider hiked a long leg over the iron beast and took off his helmet.

Oh...my...god.... Her jaw dropped. The rider was Tanner, her date. She stood staring in disbelief until a knock on the front door startled her. Flustered, she left her bedroom and hurried to answer the door.

Tanner stood on her porch dressed in a black leather jacket. He wore a smirk on his face that was highly contagious, and she found herself smiling in return.

"Well, aren't you full of surprises?" She glanced past him at the motorcycle.

"I hope you're okay with it. I didn't want to scare you off, so I thought I'd surprise you."

"Mission accomplished. I am indeed surprised to say the least."

She smoothed her recently ironed hair. *So much for my hair.* "I'm guessing you want me to get on that thing with you?"

Tanner laughed. "That would be the plan."

"I've never been on a motorcycle before. Do you think I can do it?" The closest she'd come to bikes or bikers was her favourite movie, *Mask*, with Cher and Sammy Elliot. In fact, Tanner did have a slight resemblance to the sexy biker from the movie.

"If it was my low-rider, we might have a problem. This baby is like sitting on your sofa."

Desiree glanced at the comfortable-looking seat. It even had armrests for the passenger. "Am I dressed okay for a bike?"

He eyed the length of her. "I'll be the envy of every biker for miles. Do you have any boots?"

"Actually I do. I'll just be a second. What about my hair? Do I need to put it back?"

"Here. Loosen your jacket."

Desiree did as asked. He pulled the jacket back from her neck and allowed her hair to fall down the inside. "It would be a shame to mess it up. Do up your jacket, and your hair should be fine until we get to the restaurant. You might want to bring an elastic band for the ride home, though."

Excitement and fear coursed through her veins. Who would ever imagine her taking her first ride on a motorcycle at age fifty? She snatched a hair tie off of her dressing-table and looped it around the end of her brush before tucking it in her purse. Her black boots sat on the floor in her closet; she hadn't worn them since her drinking days. She wished she had thought to give them a quick polish.

Tanner waited by his bike with an extra helmet in his hand. She took a deep breath and locked her front door. *You can do this.* She smiled broadly and walked toward him.

"You look great tonight, Desiree."

She accepted the helmet from him. "Thanks. I'm not sure how great I'll look after wearing one of these, though."

"No worries. The restaurant isn't far. I hope you like seafood."

"You can't grow up in Port Dover and not like seafood." She chuckled.

He showed her how to tighten the strap under her chin and how to get on the bike. Instead of foot pegs, this bike had floorboards. The seat was as comfortable as sitting in an armchair. A small microphone extended from the side of her helmet to a point in front of her mouth. She heard a slight crackling, and then his voice filled her helmet.

"Can you hear me okay?"

Desiree laughed out loud. "This is not at all what I expected."

"Hold on!" His motorcycle started with a flick of a switch. The rumble between her legs wasn't so terrible. In fact, he rode to the first stop sign, and she fully understood how people 'lived to ride.'

Tanner weaved his bike effortlessly through the traffic. In less than fifteen minutes, they pulled into the restaurant parking lot. Desiree wished for a longer ride.

He got off the bike and turned to face her, searching her face expectantly. "Well, was it so bad?"

Desiree shook her head. "It was great! You have to promise to take me for a spin after we eat."

He held her hand as she got off the bike and helped her undo her helmet.

She smoothed her hair out and laughed. "That was fun!"

Tanner tilted his head back and laughed too. "You look like a little girl right now." He stared intently into her eyes and smoothed down her hair.

"See? Perfect."

At the intimate gesture, a tingling sensation traveled the length of Desiree's body. She shifted her gaze and set her helmet on the passenger seat, her attention caught by the sticker on its side. Happiness and relief flooded her. "Friend of Bill W?" Bill W was one of the founders of Alcoholics Anonymous. Bumper stickers were often put on members' cars to identify themselves to other members.

Tanner looked nervous for the first time. "Yah, is that a problem? I totally don't mind if you want a glass of wine with dinner or something."

Desiree shook her head and riffled through her purse, taking out a medallion and putting it in his hand. His brow creased, and he flipped the medallion over on his palm. "Ten years? Well, how about that!"

"What about you?"

He lifted the lapel of his jacket to reveal a string of bars, eight in total.

"What are the odds?" She matched his gaze as he took her hand and lifted it to his mouth.

"I'd say there's something magical in the air tonight." He lightly kissed the top of her hand before tucking it in the crook of his arm and ushering her into the Fisherman's Wharf.

The restaurant was on the upper-class scale for Port Dover. Desiree had only been inside one other time for a Christmas party. Tiny pot lights twinkled above them, and a small fire crackled in the stone fireplace. Very romantic.

"It's beautiful," she whispered at his side.

"I'm glad you like it. Have you been here before?"

"Only once, but it wasn't quite so roman...." She hadn't meant to say it out loud, grateful for the darkness that hid the warmth of her cheeks.

His eyes sparkled as he lifted her chin and forced her to look at him.

"Yes, it *is* romantic, and I couldn't be happier to be here with you tonight."

"Table for two?" A waitress dressed in the customary white shirt and black skirt showed them to a table for two by the window with a perfect view of the lake.

"Can I get you something from the bar?" the woman asked.

"No thanks. I'll have coffee, and what would you like, Desiree?"

"How about iced tea?"

The waitress nodded and left them with menus.

"Do you want to order a platter of seafood and we can share?" Tanner suggested.

"That sounds like a good idea. Then we can taste everything. I so love a good feed of fresh fish."

"I usually drop by the Dairy Bar whenever I'm in visiting my daughter, or for the Friday 13th Biker Rally."

"I must confess, I usually leave town for those. I find the whole streets-filled-with-bikes-and-leather thing rather intimidating."

"I can understand that. I bought my first bike when I celebrated five years of sobriety."

"You never had a bike before then?"

"That's a good thing. I probably would have killed myself on one during my drinking days."

Desiree laughed along with him. "If you met me in my drinking days, you never would have let me on the back of your bike."

The waitress returned with their drinks and took their order. Desiree looked out at the lake; the setting sun cast a pink glow on the calm water.

"Red sky at night, sailor's delight," Tanner recited the old fisherman's expression.

"Red sky in morning, sailor's warning," Desiree finished the verse.

Tanner shook his head and reached for her hand. "So where have you been all my life?"

Desiree didn't bother to hide the fact her cheeks were inevitably stained pink. She smiled warmly. "I was on a very long journey of self-discovery."

"You and me both." He rubbed his thumb across her palm, sending tiny electrical shocks up her arm.

"Where do you live?" she asked.

"Niagara Falls. About an hour and a half away on a good day." He squeezed her hand. "But after today I have a feeling I'll be spending a lot more time in Port Dover."

"This is crazy." Desiree giggled behind her other hand. "Do you know I haven't dated once during my sobriety?"

"I guess you were waiting for the right man to come along. At least I hope that's how you feel."

Desiree sighed. "Do you believe in fate?"

He brought her hand to his lips and kissed her fingertips. "I do now."

Author Bio:

Adelle Laudan, best-selling author of the Iron Horse Rider Series, lives in Southern Ontario with her two teen daughters. It is her dream to change the image of bikers, one book at a time.

Sweet Tea Maggie
by
K. Starling

Maggie lives and works at a Savannah B&B. Escorting a new guest back to the house is unusual but fun...and leads to romance.

Chapter One

Maggie added a twig of fresh-picked mint to her sweet tea. The 2x3 patch of land out back produced enough herbs for the Mydnyte Garden Bed-and-Breakfast. She even dried some from the rafters of the old shed to use during the winter.

"Fill me up, Sweet Tea Maggie." The prominent local architect kept an office two rows down.

"Sure, Mr. Cole. Didn't you already drop by this morning?"

"You make tea so well that I need at least one refill per day. Don't tell me you haven't noticed me making a nuisance of myself, girl." He winked, but Maggie didn't give him a second thought.

"Have a great day, Mr. Cole. See you tomorrow."

"If not sooner," he called right before the door shut behind him.

"Why do you let people call you Sweet Tea Maggie? It's ridiculous." Mrs. Kohn peered over her shoulder. "Did you brew the thirty gallons of tea for tomorrow yet?"

"Yes, ma'am. And I did it just the same as always with three cups of sugar, six bags of tea and five sprigs of mint. The jugs are sitting on the stoop."

"Some northern transplant had the audacity to order *unsweetened* tea yesterday. I told her she wouldn't find any of that on West Jones Street."

"Of course not, ma'am. Just the usual."

"Perfect. Now, next time you tell that man your name is Maggie. Last week five different locals used that silly nickname, and I don't like it."

Maggie nodded and walked into the kitchen to start on the morning dishes.

"Maggie, dear," called Mrs. Kohn from the parlor.

"Yes, Mrs. Kohn."

"I'd like for you to pick up fresh crabs at the market today. Mr. Joansen assured me that he would keep some back for me. I plan to serve them this evening for dinner. Sara can work on those dishes. She takes too long to come back when I send her anywhere. I trust you more."

After all these years? You think so? "Of course, ma'am."

A gnarled, arthritic hand dismissed Maggie with a wave.

Maggie enjoyed doing the errands and it got her out of the house.

* * * *

Maggie breathed in a lungful of fresh air, crisp and clean. Before long, the wretched, foul odor from the paper plant would invade every nostril from Garden City to the coast. Residents hoped for a constant ocean breeze to keep the smell away.

A basket hung on the crook of Maggie's arm. "Humm, mmm," she hummed while she walked, glad to be out of the ornate dwelling where she spent her days and nights. *I'm luckier than most. At least I have a place to lay my head when the sun drops below the Savannah River.*

Not one piece of trash littered the sidewalk or the street that she passed on her cockcrow journey. The last street sweeper made its way to the warehouse to park for the night. Storekeepers washed windows, swept dust and turned the air-conditioning units on high. They had another scorcher in store for them. Tourists would occupy parking spots, seats and benches within the hour. Businesses with air-conditioning always attracted hot, weary travelers.

Savannah is my city. It owns me, and I doubt I'll ever leave, even if that means working for ol' lady Kohn the rest of my days. If only...

Daydreams constantly filled her mind. Images of a man, a business, and life-long friends passed before her eyes. All of her dreams took place in this city. How she hoped for at least one of those dreams to turn into reality.

"Miss Maggie, so nice to see ya. I reckon ya came for Mrs. Kohn's crabs. I got 'em right here. Let me pack 'em up tight so as you can tote 'em real careful. Do ya need to see 'em first, dear?"

"Thank you so much, Mr. Joansen. I'm sure she'll be quite pleased with your selection. I'll be back soon to gather them up."

I need a few moments to myself.

A band set up their instruments by the new parking deck and practiced a few old Irish tunes.

I wish I could see this town through the eyes of a stranger. I'd love to be able to lounge here at the City Market. I'd drink Mojitos and listen to the live music, but hopefully not alone.

She looked through the window of *Vintage Lace* and peeked at the hand-stitched collars, dresses and tablecloths. The purple, velvet-brocade bonnet was her favorite. It would accent her brown hair. The sign read: *You'll be the belle of the ball in one of these hats!* Too bad her wages didn't allow frivolities. How elegant she would look in church on Sunday with one of those hair covers. Mildred made the hats herself and sold them at an extravagant price. Maggie dared not enter since the shop owner frowned upon window shoppers, especially those she knew by name.

Children milled through the Praline Kitchen next door. Free samples drew people in. Maggie grabbed a dark-chocolate praline sample as she passed. Mmm, the bittersweet chocolate mixed with the nuts was Heaven. The toy train that traveled around the room on an oval track caught her attention. *What a fun store this is.* She waved to Sara Jo, who was overcome with customers vying for freshly made fudge. The local owner had lost her husband the year before and counted on the tourist season to keep her five children fed and clothed.

Her stroll down Congress Street turned up many items of interest. Families lined up to eat breakfast at the famous Myrna's Kitchen. They featured homemade biscuits with eggs, grits, bacon and red-eyed gravy. All-you-could-eat buffets were a favorite with city residents and out-of-towners alike. One man from Tennessee told his waitress the food was 'Good enough to slap his momma and bring his daddy back home!' She overheard that story in the market one day and laughed every time she remembered it.

One of the trolley tours dropped visitors off here every morning at seven. Myrna had an agreement with the trolley owner, Charlie Parker. She promised to feed his customers, and he assured her that he would pick them up in thirty minutes. Dawdlers were discouraged. Myrna and Charlie were in concurrence most of the time. Nearly everyone credited that to the fact that they were kin.

Up ahead, her favorite Belgian mare swished her tail up and down. "Hey, Hedi. I've got something for you." The apple from breakfast that morning came out of her pocket and went into the white draft horse's mouth. The sixteen-hands-high animal snorted in appreciation, and Maggie patted her head before moving on. The horse's repeated attempts to follow and one drawn-out neigh worked. Maggie stopped for another few minutes to pet the soft hair between Hedi's eyes. "No more snacks, sorry."

Maggie turned the corner to make her way back to the seafood stand and ran smack-dab into a tourist.

"I'm so sorry, sir. I should've paid better attention. Are you alright?"

"No harm done." He looked at his map and turned it completely around—twice.

"Let me help you. I know every street in Savannah. Where are you headed?"

"How far am I from...Ranburne, Alabama?" He laughed.

"Alabama, sir? Surely you know you're in Savannah, Georgia."

She couldn't help looking up to scrutinize his tall frame. His wavy brown hair was cut short and barely peeked beneath his hat, but she could just bet those waves turned into curls when, and if, he ever grew it out. This man had a firm jaw at the end of his oval-shaped face with a day's worth of stubble.

"Why your teeth are as bright as a fence on whitewash day."

The man laughed, the sound deep and robust.

Her face grew hot. *I can't believe I said that out loud.* "I'm so sorry. You must think ill of me. How can I help you?"

"Don't worry none about that, ma'am." His blue eyes twinkled, and the corners of his mouth drew up. Laugh lines engraved the outer edges of his lips. He boasted a full head of brown hair combed to the side. A few wisps of gray touched the edges.

"Just a little dry humor that didn't work so well. People call me Stanley Howard. You can call me Stanley or Stan, but you won't ever call me late for dinner."

The overfriendly man patted his stomach as he said this.

"My name is Maggie...Ms. Maggie Ruthledge."

"It's nice to meet you, ma'am. My daughter brought me down here to this fool place to visit a college. We have schools in Alabama. Don't know why she can't go there. Wants to be a restorer or something like that. Heck, I don't know. If I had my way, she'd stay home and run the pig farm. It's not like I don't need the help."

"I'm sure you're talking about our local art school. The main office is over on Bull Street. Let me show you where that is on the map."

The fact that he was a pig farmer was too much information for Maggie. She looked at his fingernails for dirt but found not a speck. *How rude of me. I must remember my manners.*

Her breast brushed against his arm as she leaned in.

Stanley jumped back a little and looked into her eyes.

"Sorry about that. My mistake." Neither of them voiced what the mistake was.

"Here it is, only three streets over," she said. "I've heard wonderful things about the school. I do hope your daughter decides to make Savannah her home, at least for the next few years, that is. It was very nice to meet you."

He smelled of clean earth and freshly mown grass. It brought back memories of her childhood. Her daddy used to hold her on his legs during his laps around the yard. That accident had changed her life. She simply had to focus!

Maggie moved to return to the seafood stand, but the man took hold of her elbow and wouldn't let go.

"Excuse me, sir. Do unhand me before I create a scene like you've never been party to in your whole miserable life."

He abruptly let go.

"Please, ma'am. I meant no harm. I only wanted to thank ya and give you my card." The card read: Stanley Howard, Swine Trader, Ranburn, Alabama.

A tingle emanated from his fingertip to hers. Maggie ignored it.

"My daughter and I will be staying for several days, and I wondered if you could recommend a place? We want to be within walking distance of the college."

Her first instinct was to hurry away, but something told her to stop avoiding life and live it.

"Oh, fine. I work at a very nice bed-and-breakfast not far from here. It's two blocks from the main office of the college. We have a few rooms open. You do understand that the art school is spread out all over the city, don't you? You won't be able to walk to all of it. I can show you where it is, but I have to stop and pick up dinner first."

"I'd be much obliged, ma'am. I don't mind walking and I have a car parked down by Bay Street. My daughter's buying souvenirs. I don't know who she's loading up for. Pigs don't need knickknacks." It was a corny joke, and she did her best to hide the grin that covered her face.

Stanley Howard didn't say another word until they reached the seafood stand. "I'll carry that for you. A pretty woman like you shouldn't have to carry nay a thing. What in tarnation is that awful smell?"

Maggie laughed. "That would be our paper plant. Some days are worse than others. We've kind of gotten used to it."

"My pig farm smells sweeter than that! Sit with me for a moment before we leave this magnificent market place."

Once again, Maggie let her common sense roll into the wind. "I'd be happy to join you for a spot of Coke, Mr. Howard, but only if you can find me a bag of peanuts." Maggie cleared a chair of leaves and set her parcels down on one of the wrought-iron tables. *So nice to take a short break.*

"Can I bring you something to drink, ma'am?" The young girl smiled as she wiped the dust from the tabletop.

"Two large Cokes in to-go cups, please. My friend will be right back." *Ruth and I usually only order one and share. Guess saving money shouldn't be a factor here.* Maggie wasn't used to social encounters. *Get yourself together, girl. He's just a man, albeit the first one you've spoken to on a social level in about three years, but a man nonetheless.*

Her hands moved over one another repeatedly. Maggie stood and pushed in her chair about to go.

"Where ya off to, darlin'? I bought your precious peanuts at the candy store. Should I go inside and order the drinks?"

There was no insistence in his voice, his clothing was clean and ironed, and he'd been a gentleman hence far. A typical *nice guy.* "No, I've already ordered them. Let's sit."

Stanley pulled her chair away from the table and held out his arm. It was a sweet gesture, one that many men forsook for lint years ago.

"Thank you." Maggie appreciated it, she wasn't a women's libber or anything. In fact, she expected to be made a fuss over. Ruth always joked about how feminism didn't make it past the Mason-Dixie line, and that was just fine with this Southern belle.

"Tell me about this place where you work, The Mydnyte Garden, you called it. Do you own it?"

"No, I've worked there with my friend Ruth for many years. It's the only home I know. My parents died in a horrible accident back in eighty-seven."

She paused. Stanley laid his hand over hers. She resisted the urge to pull it away.

"Ruth took me in and has watched over me ever since." Why in the world did she feel the need to share intimate details with this stranger?

"I'm sorry about your parents. I lost mine at the ripe age of twenty. Losing people close to you is something you don't get over." Stanley's gaze shifted to the cobblestone at their feet.

"You're right, Stanley, it is hard. I know they're in a better place, though. I have to believe that. I'll see them again someday."

"You keep on believing that if it brings ya comfort, missy. We'd better be going."

Chapter Two

Maggie was gone way too long. She'd have to hurry through her duties to get caught up. Mrs. Kohn was sure to yell. At least she'd brought back a boarder with money. That might placate the old bat. It was past time to prepare lunch. The Mydnyte Garden had lost seven out of ten employees the past year. Not many people could get along with the rough owner, who possessed no people skills, but Maggie knew she had a good side to her, even if she did keep it well hidden.

They entered through the massive oak double doors only because Mr. Howard accompanied her. Usually, the back entrance was the only way she was allowed to come and go.

Mrs. Kohn appeared in the foyer to greet the new guest. "Maggie?"

"Yes, Mrs. Kohn. This man and his daughter are visiting from Alabama. They need a place to stay, and I told them that your establishment was the cream of the crop."

The elderly woman beamed at the compliment. "I'll check you right in, Mr.?"

"Mr. Howard, ma'am." Stanley held his hand out, took her hand in his, and kissed it right below the wrist. He followed the baffled owner to her registration table and signed his name in the guest book, but turned to stare at Mrs. Kohn, who looked over his shoulder. She didn't appear the least bit embarrassed.

"Is there a Mrs. Howard?" Her eyelashes batted so fast that one of them came askew. She turned her body to readjust it. A smirk passed over Stanley's mouth, but he made sure she didn't notice.

"There is no Mrs. Howard, ma'am. Taylor-Anne's momma passed away the day she was born. It's just been the two of us for the past seventeen years, and now she's going away to college. I miss my wife more than a gaggle of geese in the wintertime. I'd better go tell her where we'll be staying. What time's dinner?"

"Seven o'clock, Mr. Howard. Casual attire encouraged. We'll see you when you return and we can't wait to meet your daughter. I can have someone bring in your things."

"I wish you could, but my things are packed up in a truck down on Bay Street. I reckon I'd better get down there and pick it up, along with Taylor-Anne before she spends all my money on souvenirs. We'll be back shortly."

He stepped out onto the brick stairway, and Mrs. Kohn ran after him. "Here's your key, Mr. Howard. You will be in room two-eleven, and your daughter will be right next door in two-twelve."

"Thank you kindly, Mrs. Kohn." The man tipped his cowboy hat and walked out the door.

The two women waited until the devoted father left before they looked at one another.

"Don't be getting any ideas, Maggie-Mae. He's too old for you, and I don't think he's looking anyway."

"Why, Mrs. Kohn, of course I have no such notions. I have never given you the idea that I was interested in finding a man. I have plans and dreams, none of which include being tied down to a, well a...country bumpkin pig farmer from Alabama!"

"He didn't look so country to me, dear. He comes from good stock. Hard to find a man such as that these days. If I were younger, I'd snag him myself."

Maggie couldn't believe that Mrs. Kohn would say such a thing to her. Marriage was in her long-term plans, children too. For now, her work and small garden were enough to sustain her. Trolling for men was not on her agenda.

She had money saved up to start a garden center. Her paper plan called for around thirty-thousand. Maggie loved to garden and wanted to share it with others. Customers around these parts were known to spend huge amounts every season to spruce up their yards. Some even hired designers to plan the landscaping. If she enrolled in a few classes, she'd be able to design those yards and earn that money. It was her dream, and determination had set in a long time ago. No man would deter her from a lifelong desire.

* * * *

Back in her own room, Maggie laid on the bed. She took her break every day at noon. It usually lasted an hour and a half and it began with a nap. This day was no different. The before-lunch rush had been busier than usual. Greedy Mrs. Kohn invited the locals to dine at the Mydnyte Garden for lunch. It seemed like more of them showed up every day. Seconds after her head hit the pillow, she fell asleep.

She was back in the market district. It was time to open Sweet Tea Gardens. Maggie opened every window and door letting in the rays of sunshine that both she and her plants needed. This was her favorite part of the day: watering time. The rich, brown dirt siphoned the water down to the roots. The sun brought life to the plants' leaves and invaded every pore of her being. It brought her great delight and always lifted her mood. She was nothing more than a tall plant that needed tender care.

The truck crunched the gravel that made up her parking lot out back. It must be Jimmie delivering the herb seedlings that were so popular this time of year.

She pulled on her thick cotton gloves to go help him unload. Her smile lit up as her head lifted from the plants to the familiar man who she had known for years from Garden City. She'd even dated him once back when she worked for Mrs. Kohn. The blue eyes she stared into were not Jimmie's.

Her eyes popped open and scanned the room. She still lay on her bed at the Mydnyte Garden. Her hands felt for the common flannel sheets that she always slept on. Yes, still there. Maggie often dreamed of the garden center she hoped to open one day. Sometimes Jimmie was in her dream. He'd promised to provide her with everything she needed for her establishment. He owned one of those new builder supply companies and got huge discounts on plants. The man in her dream wasn't Jimmie, though; he was Stanley. Why in the world would she dream about an old coot like that? It wasn't like they had an instant attraction.

Enough time spent on silliness. Time to get back to work. The dinner guests would be hungry and thirsty, and it was her job to furnish the tea and desserts. Maggie tugged her uniform back on and rolled her hair into a bun. A few brushes over her apron and she was ready for the afternoon shift.

Mindless thoughts raced through her head. She offered the guests their choice of pecan pie, banana pudding or peach cobbler. The cobbler was picked most often. She made it fresh like her grandmother had taught her.

"Such good desserts, Maggie. I guess you made them?"

Erma was one of the regular locals who dropped by at least once a week.

"Yes, ma'am. Glad you like them."

She should have spent more time with Mrs. Erma, but her mind dwelled on other things.

Stanley and his daughter didn't show up for dinner. She assumed they ate in town somewhere.

"I'm going to retire, Maggie. You don't mind finishing up, do you?"

The end of the day cleanup wasn't fun, but at least she got time alone.

"No, I don't mind, Mrs. Kohn. Sleep well."

"I'll see you in the morning, dear."

The woman never ceased to amaze her. She was never so friendly around the other staff. It was best to get started while the last of the customers finished their desserts. Maggie carried dishes to the kitchen and returned to the dining room to retrieve the remaining cobbler.

The front door opened, and there Stanley stood beside a girl who had to be Taylor-Anne. The teenager's complexion was smooth and fair, her hair a light brown, and those eyes of hers were azure-blue like her father's. There was a light in her eyes that brightened every time she gazed up at him.

The girl turned and smiled. "This place is great, Dad."

"Did we miss dessert?" asked Stanley. "Sugar is a necessity before dinner. Please tell me I don't have to take this young'un out to the ice cream parlor this late."

"Of course not, Mr. Howard. We have plenty of cobbler left, and I may even be able to find some vanilla bean ice cream to scoop on top. Dinner, however, is done and gone. Hello, Taylor-Anne, my name's Maggie." She wiped her hands on the hem of her apron and then extended her hand out towards the young girl. "I've already heard so much about you from your father."

She shook Maggie's hand firmly. This girl had manners. "Nice to meet you, ma'am. I heard about how my dad accosted you in the market this morning. He isn't much on propriety and stuff like that. I hope he wasn't too dreadful."

"Oh no, dear. I think we understand one another just fine. Why don't you sit right here, and I'll bring you a big dish of peach cobbler with ice cream. I'll be right back." The local ladies talked in whispers in the dining room. Their exchanges ended abruptly when she returned with the carton of vanilla bean.

The natives knew an outsider when they saw one. Lord knew they spent enough time complaining about them. It was like they didn't realize this was a tourist town, their bread and butter. They wondered about this tall, dark, and handsome out-of-towner. Even Erma batted her eyelashes at him.

"I understand you're applying to the art college here in Savannah. Several of the teens that attend my church go there. Some of them are even in the choir. If you do come here, I'll be glad to introduce you around."

"Not likely, Maggie. We don't sit well with all that preaching. We live our lives like we ought to and that's good enough for us. I won't have ya putting notions into my Taylor-Anne's head. Fool notions at that. Eat your dessert, Taylor-Anne, I'll meet you upstairs." Stanley left the dining area and climbed the stairs.

Dumbfounded, Maggie stood before Taylor-Anne. She didn't know what to say to the girl.

"Sorry about that, ma'am. My dad still blames God for taking away my momma all those years ago. He still loves her or misses her, I'm not sure which. I used to wish he would find a woman and fall in love; I've never had a momma. Now I just want him to be happy. I guess he is in his own way. Thanks for the cobbler."

"It's quite all right, Taylor-Anne. You're welcome to finish your dessert upstairs. Here, take some for your daddy too. I'll gather the dirties up in the morning."

"Thank you so much, Maggie. I'm glad to have met you. Don't judge my daddy on his comments. He doesn't always think before he speaks, but he really is a great person."

"Oh, I'm sure he is. Don't you worry your pretty little head over that none. Let me know if you need anything else."

"G'night then. And thanks again for the cobbler; peach is my favorite." Maggie watched the teenager take the stairs two at a time to her room. *If only I had that kind of energy. I'd give ol' Stanley a run for his money.* He had a vendetta against God? The only man who had somewhat piqued her interest in the last two years was the closest thing she'd ever met to an atheist. Maggie sat on the plush velvet chair and cursed herself for the glimmer of hope she'd let enter her heart and mind.

"The kitchen's done, Maggie. Should I stay and help you with the dining area?"

Ruth was a godsend. She helped a lot around the old house and cooked better than any mammy Maggie ever had growing up. The two shared the two-bedroom guesthouse out back. She was the closest thing Maggie had to family. Her mother and father died in a plane crash over the Pacific Ocean when she was ten. Many family members took custody of her for seven years after that but only on paper. Ruth dried her tears and fed her. Every time a birthday cake needed to be baked or a doll dress mended, Ruth was there. She made sure that Maggie had a coming-out party at sixteen and that she had a new dress for every prom she attended, albeit most were homemade.

"No, Ruth. You go on to bed. I'll finish up here. Give me twenty minutes, and we'll watch some of that soap opera together that you always tape. I'll bring the dessert."

"Don't stay here too long. This monstrosity of a house might suck ya in. I'll wait up for ya and have our show ready."

She finished the chores in record time and rushed to begin her nightly routine with her closest friend.

Maggie bowed out of the second episode of Gushing Secrets.

"I'll see you in the morning, Ruth. Thanks for waiting up for me."

She was almost out of the room when Ruth spoke.

"You like him. I see it in your eyes. What's holding you back?"

"Who? I don't know what you're talking about."

"Come on now, Maggie. I'm the closest thing ya got to a momma. I know you better than just about anybody. You saw something that drew you to Stanley Howard, but you don't want to act on it, and I want to know why. He seems like the decent sort."

"He blames God for his wife's death."

"And?"

"And? Ruth, The faith I gained since mom and dad died is the only thing that's gotten me through. Before I met you, I gave up on everything. If you hadn't kept at me about attending services I might have wallowed in self pity for years before I got it together."

"Did you ever think that maybe he's your Ruth, darlin'? Sometimes people enter our lives at just the right moment for a reason. That man has every right to be hurtin'. His whole world got turned upside down, just as yours did all those years ago. Who did you blame?"

"For a long while, I blamed myself. After that, I blamed my family. I don't ever remember blaming God, but then again, I didn't have much faith before I met you, anyways. My folks weren't the church- going types."

"There, you see? Everybody blames somebody. He chose to blame God and he's having a hard time getting over it. Some take longer than others. That's just the way of the world."

"Thank you, Ruth."

"For what, child?"

"For coming into my life and for just being you. I love you."

"I love you too. Go on to bed now. I want to sit up a bit longer and watch Roger seduce Jessica again."

"Who would know by looking at you that you're a smut watcher?"

"Hee, hee. Girl, I'm a smut reader too. God don't judge us, and we shouldn't judge or compare others either. What else is bothering you?"

"I've been thinking about Rob a lot today. How things didn't work out for us. I thought *he* was the one."

"I know you did. That boy was a charmer. He even brought *me* flowers once when he was courtin' ya. Told me not to do anything for yer birthday 'cause he was handlin' it. I believe he even drew me up like a pot of butter. Hate that I let him bedazzle ya."

"No, Ruth. It wasn't your fault at all. I'd still be with him if it wasn't for the fact that I caught him in our bed with another woman."

She never told Ruth that he'd invited her to join the two of them. It was too humiliating.

"Sometimes you just have to take a chance. All men aren't Rob

Whitakers. Some are just plain ol' nice guys. Your Mr. Howard might be one of those and he might not. I don't plan to get in the middle of this one. I'm just warning ya that you shouldn't avoid falling in love. I did that one too many times myself. Now skedaddle and get some rest. You work too hard."

Maggie bent down to kiss Ruth on the cheek. "G'night."

Chapter Three

A fitful sleep overcame Maggie that evening. Her subconscious filled with dreams of Stanley, being a mother to his grown daughter, and Lordy-be, she even fed pigs at one point.

It was lucky for her that neither Stanley nor Taylor-Anne came down for breakfast. She wasn't up to chattering with them, and avoidance was a great way to deny her wanton lust. It was illogical to want a brown-headed stranger who she'd only just met. All of those lonely nights had gone to her head.

"Maggie? Maggie, would you please answer me?"

"I'm sorry, Mrs. Kohn. Did you ask me something?"

"I asked you if we were out of apple pectin. There's no more on the sideboard. I asked you three times, Maggie. What's on your mind, dear?"

"I don't want to marry a pig farmer."

"What?" A look of confusion passed over her employer's face.

"Oh nothing, ma'am. I'm so sorry. I didn't sleep well last night. I'll go get the pectin for the biscuits." Maggie hurried away before Mrs. Kohn could question her further.

The cool cellar walls felt good against her back. Her wits would return any minute now. *Only thirty minutes until my break. Get it together, Mags.* Her mother had called her Mags up until her untimely death. Funny that she would think of that now. *I can't afford to break down in the middle of the meal rush.* She smoothed the front of her uniform, tucked her hair behind one ear, and made her way up the old, rickety stairs. With one last deep breath, she pulled the chain that led to the light bulb above, and her emotional order was restored...at least temporarily.

"Maggie dear, where's the apple pectin?"

All that time down there and I forgot to bring it back!

Ruth rescued her. "I forgot to tell you that we're out, Mrs. Kohn. I'll pick some up at the market this afternoon. Maggie, why don't you leave a few minutes early. You look a bit pale, dear."

They both knew their boss lady wouldn't go down in the cellar, so it was a fairly safe lie. Maggie hated it just the same. "Thank you, Ruth," she mouthed and fled out the back door to her room.

This is ridiculous. I'm in love with a pig farmer. It took great effort to admit it, even to herself. *How did this happen? I have my whole life planned out. He isn't part of my plans, and he has some kind of grudge against God.* Her normal coping mechanism was avoidance or sleep. *I'll think about this after my break.* She lay sideways across the bed and fell into a deep sleep.

* * * *

A loud, booming knock startled Maggie awake.

"I need to speak to Sweet Tea Maggie and I need to speak to her now."

She pulled her robe around her gown and walked to the front door of the cottage. She didn't open the door immediately but stood against it. Was it Stanley?

"Come on, Magdelena, we need to discuss a few things before I go back to Alabama."

So it is him. Of course it's him. How many deranged men have knocked on my door in the last five years? None, that's how many.

"I'm on my way, you darn fool. Leave my door alone." She used a gruff voice that showed more confidence than she possessed at the moment.

The knob turned just as she reached to open the front door. "What do you mean barging in—?"

The rest of her sentiment escaped straight into the mouth of Stanley Howard. His tongue first encompassed her words and then lingered over her top lip, planting small, sweet kisses along her chin. He drew back a few inches and held her head in his hands. She sighed and leaned against him.

"Taylor-Anne told me what a jerk I was leaving the room like that last night. I came to apologize. You shouldn't open the door with that sleepy look in your eyes. I imagined you naked and waiting for me." A devilish grin let her know that he wasn't kidding.

"How did you know that folks around here call me Sweet Tea Maggie and that my first name is really Magdelena?"

"I had a long talk with Ruth before I traveled back here to speak with you. She was about to read me the riot act until I told her I owed you an apology. I do declare, that woman scared me more than my drill instructor from the Marine Corps. For a few minutes, I wasn't sure she'd let me out the back door."

"She watches out for me. We're family."

Stanley stepped forward and closed the door with the heel of his right foot. "Mind if I come in? Or should I kiss you on the threshold again for everyone to see?"

Maggie debated for about three seconds before she led him to her bedroom. Once there, she was uncertain how to proceed. *Should I kiss him? Undress? How frustrating. I finally get a man to my room and I don't have a clue what to do next.* Her fingers touched her forehead, heart and both shoulders. Another one of her coping mechanisms. *The sign of the Father, the Son, and the Holy Ghost? Really, how awkward.*

"I forgot something. I should probably be going, Maggie. I promised to take Taylor-Anne over to Bull Street to some new wave gift shop where hairpins cost hundreds of dollars. They say they're made with real gold, but I sure don't get it. They looked like bobby-pins to me."

"I'm sure I'll see you at dinner." Her gaze shifted to the floor. Stanley left without a word. Maggie ran to her bedroom and threw herself across the bed.

Chapter Four

Once she quit crying and fell asleep again, it was all she could do to wrestle away from the warm, safe bed and go inside the house to prepare for dinner. Ruth met her at the kitchen door.

"Are you okay, dear? I spoke to that man friend of yours. He really likes ya. I gave him the what-fer about the way he treated ya, but that didn't seem to faze him. He's a keeper."

"I know. He's wonderful, he's handsome, his daughter is a great teenager, and he left me standing by the bed. I took him there and didn't have a clue what to do, so I stood there. I don't blame him, really."

"Now stop that, child. I doubt he knew what to do anymore than you did. His wife's been gone near seventeen years, and I bet ya a white-haired lizard he's been with nobody since."

"Maybe you're right. I won't have a thing more to do with the man. I have plans for my life and for you and for me. I'm going to buy a house, a real house that ain't behind no mausoleum. We deserve more than we're getting out of life, and I'm going to make sure we get it."

"Calm down, chickadee. I didn't pay all that money to send you to charm school just so ya would use words such as *ain't*. I want more for you, Maggie-Mae, that's for sure. I'm not so worried about myself. I think you're getting rid of a good thing in ol' Mr. Howard myself, but that's between you and him. Let's get through the dinner rush, and then you take the rest of the evening off. You work harder than any young woman should."

"I'll take you up on that, Ruth. What would I do without you?"

They embraced for a few seconds and then hurried off to work.

* * * *

It was Wednesday, and the church was open late. Maggie lit a candle, pushed her dollar donation through the slot and knelt in the first pew. *I need direction in my life, Lord. Give me clarification. And if you see fit, I'd like a man who loves lots of sex, please.*

"Maggie?"

Stanley stood right behind her.

I know you work in mysterious ways, but this is crazy! Good thing I wasn't praying aloud.

"What do you want, Stanley? As you can see, I'm busy right now."

"Of course you are. I'm sorry to interrupt, Maggie. Ruth told me where to find you. I can wait outside 'til you're done. Take your time."

True to his word, Stanley Howard exited through the back doors and sat on the steps, right after he stopped at the holy water and whispered to the Father, Son and the Holy Ghost. She saw him settle down on the cement step just as the door closed.

He's Catholic? Now what am I supposed to do? He didn't get hit by lightning when he entered the worship hall, so he must be okay. Crazy thinking, Mags. Get it together. He wants to talk to me. I'll just lay it on the line. Tell him what I want and where I want to go with my life. He'll take that as it is—or he won't.

Several deep breaths on the way down the aisle gave her the courage to open the large, heavy door that led outside. Stanley rose as soon as she came out.

"Let me tell you something, Mr. Howard. I have plans for my life and I don't need you messing them up. I want to start a gardening business. I want to buy a house big enough for Ruth and me. I—"

"Whoa, slow down. You're like a wild filly during breaking season. I don't want to interfere with any of that. I like Ruth, and any person should be able to start a new way of living if they're willing. I want you, darlin'. More than anything, I want you—forever."

The look of shock must have registered on Maggie's face because Stanley stepped back.

"Look, I don't mean I want you to commit to me for the rest of your blame life right this instant. We'll take things slow. I'll get a small place here with Taylor-Anne, and you and I can get to know one another. I had an offer on the farm last week. A good offer too. Just so you know, I don't hate God. I've just been really mad at him for the last seventeen years."

Smiling, Maggie stood face-to-face with Stanley. "I don't really need that much time, Mr. Howard."

"Let's go back to my room and discuss this further."

"I can't be seen going into your room, Stanley. Why don't we go to a private place I know down by the river? Tourists don't go there because they don't know about it, and the locals are all so busy during the day. Follow me."

The two of them all but ran down MLK Boulevard and around the shops towards the docks.

"Here." She pulled him into a tiny crook of a place. They wouldn't be seen unless someone walked right up on them. The last time a girl got spotted kissing a tourist she was fired from her cleaning job.

She leaned in and pressed her lips to his. They were cool at first, but then she sensed something spark inside the man. Maggie felt a bomb go off, and it ignited the both of them.

Her tongue dipped into his mouth for a small taste, and the resulting zing traveled all the way down to her belly button. Tiny sparks of sensation heightened her senses. Never before had she warmed up so quickly.

One small part of her mind said slow down, but she squished that thought. Her arms wrapped around his strong shoulders. *Oh, God. Don't let it end. Please don't let it end.*

The two of them inched towards the floor of the abandoned building still holding onto one another. Stanley tore off his jacket and threw it to the floor.

"Why don't you join me and lay down?" Maggie smiled up at him.

"I've wanted to do this since the first time I saw you downtown, darlin'."

"Next time, don't take so long acting on your impulses, Stanley."

Words were in the way and almost troublesome now. Maggie's ankles wrapped around his, allowing her to pull even closer to him.

"Hang on. You're an awful good kisser, Maggie. I wish I had you all to myself right now but I don't. Meet me in my room this evening. We can get to know one another there."

"You're right, of course. It's been a long time since I made-out like a teenager!" Images of how he may have looked as a young man flitted through her mind.

"Where are you going, little lady? I'm not through with you yet. The two kissed again, rose and walked down River Street hand-in-hand. They spent hours beside the Savannah River. Huge barges sailed past them.

"That one's from Greece. I've always wanted to go there." Maggie sighed.

"Well that one's from Romania, darlin'. How 'bout we go there too?"

"Oh, my. I'd better get back home."

"Let me escort you, mi'lady."

Stanley was such the gentleman. *And such a hot kisser.* Maggie imagined spending the rest of her life with this man and his daughter. *Wait until I tell Ruth!*

Visions of garden parties, family gatherings and holidays entered her mind. *We'll be a real family.*

The two returned to the bed-and-breakfast right before dinner.

"Let me see if Ruth needs any help."

"Sure thing, missy. Don't forget about our date. I want you all to myself. Maybe we can sit by the window and look at the stars all night."

"And maybe we can spend that time kissing." Maggie giggled and hurried to the kitchen. It was all so perfect. Things would work out after all.

"What are you grinning about, child? You look like the Cheshire cat."

"I'm going to take a chance on romance, Ruth. And I'm going to take it with Stanley. Wish me luck."

Ruth slung her arm over Maggie's shoulder. "You don't need luck, child. Looks to me like you already have love."

Author Bio:

K. Starling still believes in romance, soul mates and true love. She spends time each day with her muse, family and pets in a small-southern town in Georgia. You can find out more about K. Starling at her MySpace: www.myspace.com/kissasssweetside or email her at: sweetromanceauthor@yahoo.com.

Tuesday's Affair
by
Trinity Blacio

Over one year ago, Tuesday's heart was shattered when her husband left. Now, Ike's back. Does she take a chance and let him back into her life?

Chapter One

Tuesday glanced in her rearview mirror into the backseat. Her son, Jared, played with his toy car in his safety seat. Doubts lingered in her mind about staying the weekend with her ex-husband's sister, Pam. The thought of being in the same room with Ike sent shivers up her spine. One year, four months, and six days ago he'd left her pregnant with his child. He'd denied the baby and had abandoned her. Not even the paternity tests and pictures of their son seemed to help change Ike's mind.

"I can't have kids! I told you that from the beginning! The doctors aren't wrong!" Ike pulled at his hair, his fists clenched. "How could you?" he asked as he leveled a look of disgust at her.

Those were the last words he'd said to her. He'd walked out of her life and shattered her dreams. When the news of his reenlistment and the divorce papers arrived, her world crumbled around her. Broken and battered, her heart went on, warmed by the new life she carried. Jared was the only piece of Ike she had left.

She pulled the car into Pam's driveway. She wiped at her misty eyes before she neared the house. With a fake smile, she looked at the home she knew so well. Nothing had changed about this place.

In the circular driveway, Pam stood with a warm smile on her lips. Turning off the car, Tuesday observed Pam approach the car. She peeked inside at Jared. Pam's life resembled that of a fairy tale that Tuesday could only dream of; the woman had a handsome, wealthy and loving man. The small fortune Tuesday's aunt willed Pam gave her freedom.

"Oh, my god! He looks exactly like Ike did as a baby!" Pam declared as she opened the back door to get Jared. "I can't believe that Ike doesn't believe you!"

"Let's not talk about that, okay? It's over. He's moved on, and so have I." Tuesday pulled out her purse and the diaper bag. "We're just here for you to meet your nephew and to have a good time at the masquerade ball. Ike's not going to be here, right?"

"I already told you, Ike called and said he wouldn't be able to make it. He's going to some group thing with his squad, and you know what that means: a whole weekend of drinking. Now quit worrying," Pam called over her shoulder as she carried Jared into the house.

Pam's husband, Bo, walked up to Pam and looked from Tuesday to her son.

"You know I hate to say this, but...well, let's just say I didn't want to believe it. After one glance, anyone with common sense can tell he is an exact replica of Ike." Bo's gaze traveled up and down her body. "I have to say Ike's a fool to have left you! God, what did you do to yourself? Did you change your hair?"

Heat burned her cheeks at his inspection. "I didn't do anything, and let's not mention this again, okay?"

"Will you quit? You've embarrassed her, for Pete's sake! She's here to have some fun." Pam walked up the stairs. "Come on, Tuesday. I'll show you where you and Jared will sleep. I even set up a crib for him in your room."

"What time does the party start?" Tuesday looked around the room. A king-size bed provided the focal point with a crib on the right and a desk on the left side. "This room is big enough to fit my living room and kitchen in it."

"People will start arriving around seven," said Pam. "So what's your costume? You never told me over the phone."

"Good, that will give me time to get him down for bed," said Tuesday. "The nanny should be here around five; it will give me plenty of time to get ready. Oh, and my costume is a surprise. Let's just say I even took lessons for it." Tuesday smiled at Pam, teasing her.

"That's so unfair!" Pam laughed, slapping her arm. "You always do this to me, and it takes me forever to figure out what or who you are."

"Go on so I can put Jared down for an early nap. I still have to get my stuff out of the trunk."

"Okay, I'm going. I'll throw some lunch together for us. We can talk while Jared takes his nap. Say...in about half an hour?" Pam walked to the bedroom door.

"Sounds great. I'll be down in a few."

* * * *

Ike held the phone in one hand and balanced it with his shoulder. Okay, florist out of the way. Now to reaffirm my plans. He dialed his sister's number.

"Hello." Bo, his brother-in-law, answered the phone.

"Hey, bro. Did Tuesday make it? The florist will be there in an hour. Could you let Pam know I'll be there about seven-thirty?"

Ike held his breath and waited for Bo's answer to confirm she was there. Did she agree to come to the party? His fingers tapped on his truck's dashboard.

"She's here, and I'll let Pam know. Do you have a costume?"

Ike heard the laugh in Bo's voice and it grated on his last nerve. He stopped his truck at a light and glanced at the jewelry box next to him.

"Yes, I picked it up yesterday. I'll be the pirate dressed in black," he snapped.

"Great, did you get the ring we looked at last week?"

"I just picked it up from the jewelry store."

"Pam put Tuesday in the same room you stayed in while you were here. I'll see you in a few." Bo chuckled as he hung up the phone.

Ike stared at the disposable phone and wanted to ring his bother-in-law's neck. His whole life depended on this night, and Bo had laughed at him.

* * * *

Bo hung up with a mischievous grin on his face.

"What's with the grin?" Pam asked, opening the fridge.

"Your brother just called. Our plan is in full swing. He'll be here at seven-thirty, and he said the florist will be here in an hour." Bo's gaze wandered down his wife's body and rested on her plump lips.

"Tuesday is going to think I set this all up."

Her comment snapped him out of his thoughts. "It's a masquerade ball. We'll just act surprised when he shows up." Bo shrugged, turned and grabbed a piece of cheese from the party platter. "I mean, it's about time Ike sees his son, and when he gets a load of Tuesday, he's going to drool everywhere." He popped another piece of cheese into his mouth.

"It could work. She does look great, and I saw the expression on her face when we mentioned him. I've always believed they belonged together. He was a fool to let her go." Pam piled sandwiches onto a platter. "Okay, we're on. And you'll never guess who responded to the invitation. Drew is coming too. Can you believe it? This is going to be like the old days. Oh, I can't wait!"

Chapter Two

Tuesday studied the costume in the floor-length mirror. It had cost her plenty. She'd searched the Internet and Googled for belly-dancer costumes, but none except this one had appealed to her. The silk scarves covered her form perfectly. Glancing at her breasts, Tuesday smiled. Some women lost some of their size up top, but not her. Her body blossomed with the birth of her son, and she couldn't be more thrilled with her new shape. She admitted she had trouble finding decent bras, but it was worth it from the looks men gave her when she wore this costume. Her lessons in belly dancing firmed her body in all the right spots which only enhanced her larger breasts. She brushed her long red hair, placed the beads throughout it, and slipped on her mask. A smile formed on her lips. Perfect. No one would recognize her. Tuesday had purposely worn baggy clothes earlier.

The clock read seven-thirty. Taking a deep breath, she made her way to the door. Before she left, she glanced back at her son...sound asleep. The baby looked just like his father.

Stop this! He's moved on, and now it's your time to do the same.

"Mrs. Booth?" The nanny tapped on the door and peeked inside.

"Come on in, Doris, I was just about ready to leave. He should sleep the night for you, but if you have any trouble, please don't hesitate to bring him to me," Tuesday said and closed the door behind her.

Walking down the long hallway, she glanced at the family portraits that lined the walls to the ballroom.

Tuesday looked around. Spotting Pam, she made her way into the grand ballroom. At least one hundred people were in attendance in all sorts of different costumes. Tuesday grabbed a drink as the waiter walked by and made her way to Pam. She watched the people dance and observed Bo and two other men talking to her sister-in-law, one dressed in an all black pirate get-up. The other wore a Viking warrior costume. The men's biceps could stop a tank, and both were well over six feet tall. The pirate's long black hair lay flat against his back, and his mask covered his face. The Viking's helmet held down his shoulder-length blond hair.

She moved closer and stopped in front of Bo, who looked around the room.

"Are you looking for someone?" She smiled up at him.

Everyone turned to stare at her.

"Is that you, Tuesday? My God! If I wasn't married, you would be in trouble right now. I mean, I thought you looked great earlier, but wow! Pam, do you believe this?" Bo turned and kissed his wife's cheek.

"Oh, sweetie, you look great. Are these the lessons that you told me about earlier, the belly dancing ones?" Pam asked.

"Yeah, those are the lessons I was telling you about. It's been a long time since I've been home, so I wanted to make sure I made a great impression with the men. I'm free now. Plus, I love the attention. I have this great instructor in Cleveland. You should try it. We have a ball in class." Tuesday glanced at the two men next to Pam, their gazes never leaving her.

"Honey, you won't be alone too long. Hell, all the men in this room can't keep their eyes off you. Great costume! Oh, I'm being rude." Pam pointed to the Viking. "Tuesday, you remember Drew from high school."

He stepped forward and hugged her.

"God! I haven't seen you in what? Two years? You look great, Drew." Tuesday pulled away and smiled.

"What are you talking about? Look at you. You've got to be the most beautiful woman in the room. Come on, dance with me just like the old days." Drew pulled her out on to the dance floor. Stairway to Heaven streamed through the room.

Tuesday threw her head back and laughed. "You told them to play this, didn't you?"

Drew shook his head. His hand circled around her waist and brought her close. "You know Pam. She loves to play all the old stuff. Now, tell me how the little boy's doing? What is he? A year old now?" He smiled and dipped her.

Each bell on her costume chimed together as they hit the floor. "He just turned one today and he looks...just like his dad. He's an angel, and he even slept the whole night the first week from the hospital," Tuesday said, watching the crowd of dancers.

"I'm sorry, Tuesday. I didn't mean to bring up bad memories. You know Ike's a jerk." Drew shook his head, frowning down at her.

"Hey, it's okay. I have to get over it. I guess he never really trusted me. Maybe I wasn't good enough for him? Who knows? But I won't dwell on it any more. It's been a year, and not a word from him since. I got the separation papers, but that's all. I don't know what he's doing and I don't care. As soon as I get back, I'll have a lawyer find out what's going on, and if he hasn't finished the process, I will. It's time I moved on, especially with all these handsome men around me," Tuesday said, smiling at him.

A cry erupted behind her, and she recognized it as her son's. She glanced towards the door; her nanny carried Jared into the room.

"I'm so sorry to interrupt," the nanny explained. "He wouldn't stop crying. I think he wants his mommy." She handed her Jared.

"That's okay, Betty. He's in a new place, but he'll go back to sleep."

Pam and Bo approached with the pirate between them.

"Is Jared okay?" Pam asked and brushed his hair away from his eyes.

The pirate gasped.

Tuesday looked up into his eyes and recognized them. Ike.

"You told me he wouldn't be here!" Tuesday shifted Jared in her arms, leveling a glare at Pam.

"We didn't know until this afternoon, I swear!" Pam pleaded.

"She's telling the truth. I called this afternoon," Ike said.

"And how would you know the truth?" Tuesday shrieked. She turned to leave, to escape. Tears welled, but she wouldn't let them fall. He'd left her, and she wasn't about to let him affect her again. Even though her body hummed at his nearness, she had to ignore it. Her heart couldn't take any more hurt.

Chapter Three

Ike watched his wife leave the dance hall with his son. God, he had grown since the pictures she had sent him! He looked just like him with the same eyes, hair and facial features.

What the hell did I do?

Slowly, he made his way out of the dance hall and followed his wife. Her body teased him. He'd never seen her look so exotic. Her long red hair hung down her back, the beads in it swaying as she walked, the costume's bells chiming. Her hips...God, her hips moved to a silent rhythm that beckoned him to touch her body.

Grumbling to himself, he felt his shaft growing larger. It had been a year and six months since he'd last tasted her nectar. She slipped into one of the guest rooms, talking to the baby in an attempt to comfort him. He'd always known she would be a great mother.

He listened at the door, and tears welled up; he never cried.

"Your daddy's here, Jared. You look just like him, so handsome, but young man, you're supposed to be sleeping. How about I sing your song to you?"

He couldn't believe she sang the same song his mother had sung to him as a baby. Her voice soft, sad, and filled with love, wrapped around his aching heart. Ike pushed away from the door, his mind plotting out every aspect of his plan.

* * * *

Tuesday wasn't about to let her ex ruin her night. After she put the baby back to bed, she returned to the party. She grabbed another glass of champagne and gulped it down. Drew leaned against the wall across from her. Slowly, she walked up to him. She swung her hips, a faux smile pasted on her lips.

"Hey, baby," she teased, "want to finish our dance?" Tuesday sidled up to his body.

"You know you're crazy, right? Ike's pissed." Drew laughed and let her pull him onto the dance floor.

"That's not my problem. He's the one that wanted to move on. It's time I moved on, too, and what better way than to dance with one of the most handsome men here." Tuesday wrapped her arms around Drew and laid her head on his wide chest, bare for costume effect.

"Honey, you still love him. You two belong together. I know he's a fool to leave you. Hell, everyone in this room knows it, and the way he's staring at us right now...but, I do think maybe making him a little jealous would be great payback." Drew lowered his head, and his lips made contact with hers, giving her a soft, passion-filled kiss for Ike's viewing.

Tuesday looked askance at Ike to see if his famous temper would erupt.

"Hey, Tuesday. Everyone was wondering if you would belly dance for us?" Pam interrupted and pulled Tuesday aside.

"Okay, what is it with everyone interrupting us when we dance?" Drew groaned, but he perked up at Pam's question.

"Please, Tuesday? We'd love to see you dance," Pam begged.

Tuesday laughed. "Sure. I've done shows before. Let me grab my music."

She handed her CD to a band member and took a deep breath. She never danced in front of family and friends, just strangers. Tuesday turned towards the audience. Ike watched her every move.

She closed her eyes and let the music swirl around her body, caressing her soul. Her hips and body started to move with the music; her bells chimed in tune with the song, and her hair swayed with the lyrics. When she opened her eyes, lust filled Ike's eyes and beckoned to her. Heat surrounded her, and the music beat increased, her body moving faster. Ike drew closer. The music ended. Everyone in the room clapped. Tuesday raised her head and stared into the deepest blue eyes—Ike's eyes. Her heartbeat accelerated.

Ike grabbed the microphone from one of the band members. He turned to his friends and family. "I would like to make an announcement, if you good people don't mind. I have an apology to make to a special person who has captured my heart and my soul. I've been a fool for the past year." He turned and gazed at Tuesday. "Years ago, doctors told me I couldn't have children, but they were wrong. I was wrong. I accused my wife of something horrible and wouldn't accept our son."

Tuesday couldn't move. Her mouth fell open.

A single tear slipped down his cheek. His eyes shimmered with more unshed tears.

"My son celebrated his first birthday today, and it's the first time I've ever seen him." Ike kneeled down in front of her, taking hold of her hands. "Please give me a second chance to make this up to the both of you. I've never stopped loving you, Tuesday. I threw the separation papers away a week after I got them. I couldn't do it. My heart has screamed for you since I left."

Tuesday looked around the room, tears filling her eyes. "I can't promise anything Ike. You hurt me, but I never stopped loving you. We can start slow and see where it goes from there. That's all I have to give right now," she whispered and cupped his cheek.

Chapter Four

His gaze held hers. "I received the paternity test you sent me and the pictures of Jared." He held onto her hand, and the band started to play their song, For Your Eyes Only. "I've tried to think of ways to contact you, but I've been so afraid you wouldn't listen, that I had lost you forever."

His arms tightened around her. She felt a slight tremor run through his body. "Why didn't you write, Ike? I waited for any word, but I got nothing."

"After you sent the test and the pictures, I wrote a letter. I had every intention to send it out that day, but...." Terror surfaced in his eyes. "We were captured by a group of hostiles, and all the pictures, everything, was destroyed. Three months later, the other half of our team found us and rescued us." His voice rippled with pain and fright.

"I can see the pain in your eyes, but I needed to know why you didn't come back. I waited. Hearing nothing, I gave up, Ike. The important thing is that you came back to us. Were you hurt?" Tuesday inched closer to his body and laid her head on his chest. Tears slipped silently down her cheeks to land on his skin.

"When they found us, I was in a coma with both legs broken. I was in a coma for two weeks."

"Why wasn't I contacted? I'm your wife!"

"When I reenlisted, I put Pam as my emergency contact. I wasn't thinking, plus I'm glad you weren't there."

"Why didn't Pam call me? She's supposed to be my best friend."

"She did, but you wouldn't listen to her. You hung up the phone on her. Plus..."

"Oh my god, I did hang up on her. I'm so sorry."

"You don't need to apologize, I needed to go through physical therapy and I didn't want you to see me that way, baby." He pulled her face upward with his long, tapered fingers and stared into her eyes. "Don't cry for me. I couldn't stand for that. All I thought of was you and Jared; that's what kept me going." His tongue teased her lips. Tuesday opened her mouth to his silent command. He tasted of wine, his masterful tongue tangling with hers. Ike pulled back as the song ended.

Her fingers touched her swollen lips. "Would you like to see your son?" she whispered. His hand still held hers. They made their way to her bedroom without a word. When he squeezed her hand, Tuesday glanced over at him and noticed his slight limp.

Tears slipped down his face as he watched his son sleep. He brushed a lock of black hair out of his son's face. "He's so perfect! He has your pretty mouth," he whispered into her ear and nibbled the sensitive skin of her neck.

"He is, isn't he? Jared looks just like you; his eyes even mirror yours. I can always tell when he's sad or happy."

"Will you take a walk out in the gardens with me? It's a beautiful fall evening." Ike pulled her out the bedroom door and down the hallway.

"Okay, what are you up to? You have that look in your eyes that tells me you're up to something." Tuesday laughed.

"Just wait. You'll see." Ike drew her around the corner and into the garden pathway. Tiki torches danced with light.

Tuesday stopped, her gaze drawn to the garden's heart. Candles and torches lit up the area. Rose petals scattered the ground, and orchids lay at her feet. Ike tugged her closer and knelt down before her.

"I can't undo what I've done, but I'm going to try and make your dreams come true, even if it takes me the rest of my life. I want to spend it with you and our children. Will you marry me—again?" Ike pulled a gold ring out of his pocket. In the middle of it, a heart-shape Mystic Fire stone sat with diamonds surrounding it. The candlelight reflected its beauty as she stared at it on her hand.

Her eyes blurred with tears. "How did you know? Oh, Ike, it's beautiful," she sighed.

He put the ring on her finger. "I have my ways. Does this mean you'll re-affirm our vows with me? I want us to exchange our vows in this castle I found in Canada. The whole time I stayed there, it reminded me of you. I know you always wanted a big wedding, and we didn't get that last time. I want to give this to you, baby. You'll love it. All our family and friends can come for a week of celebration." He stood, hugging her.

"Yes! God, I love you!" The words had barely left her mouth when he picked her up and swung her around.

"It's about time you two got back together!" Pam laughed. She and Bo stepped out of the bushes hand-in-hand.

"You helped him with all of this, didn't you?" Tuesday smiled, embracing her sister-in-law once Ike put her down.

"Of course, but it was his idea. I didn't have a clue about the ring. I think Bo and Ike have kept me in the dark on that part." Pam stepped back. "Oh, and I've seen pictures of that castle Ike's talking about. It's beautiful. So, when's the big day?" she asked, stepping into Bo's arms.

"I've always wanted a Christmas wedding. Do you think we could have it around Christmas?" Tuesday asked.

Ike drew her back into his arms. "Baby, I'll make sure of it. Now, if you two would excuse us, I have plans for my bride," Ike said and drew her towards the house.

Tuesdays' heart pounded hard against her breasts. Her legs wobbled as she followed Ike. He glanced back at her, his eyes filled with love and promise.

Author Bio:

Trinity Blacio is a devoted writer and bookworm to all genres of romance. To learn more visit: www.trinityblaciosfantasy.com.

Lavender Heart
by
Debbie Gould

What happens when you meet a man with the most beautiful lavender eyes you've ever seen? However, there's one problem: every inch of his face is covered in scars. Do you walk away or do you look deeper into his soul?

Lisa pawed through the classic rock section trying to find the Poison album a co-worker had told her about. She knew they were an old band but come on. The store must have at least one copy. She looked up from the collection and glanced around the store in frustration. Where the hell were all the employees? Not one person was around to ask except the kid at the register, and the checkout line snaked to the door. The heck with it; the stupid CD wasn't worth it. Emily could burn it for her.

Lisa scanned the store one more time and started to leave, but a man with the most stunning lavender eyes caught her attention. Good Lord, she'd never seen eyes that color before. Entranced, she locked her gaze with his and could almost see into his soul. Despair and sadness emanated from him. He seemed a tired lost soul searching for peace.

He was the first to break the connection. Blinking, she tried to shake the impressions. For some reason, this stranger drew her. It was a disconcerting feeling. Stranger or not, she found herself propelled to the end of the store where he stood.

Getting closer, she noticed his face. Not one inch was smooth. Hideous scars covered his skin from forehead to chin and ear-to-ear. Dear Lord in Heaven, what had happened to him? Funny, from the distance, she'd only seen his eyes, and his face had appeared smooth.

Looking at him now, the scars were very prominent, and the lavender eye color had gone, leaving his eyes almost coal black. Immobilized with apprehension, she shivered. The sounds from the store faded away, and once again, her gaze locked with his.

This time it wasn't sadness she felt from him, but instead, heartfelt anger and injustice. This man had given up on humanity, and condemnation rolled off his person. Sucked into a cold black hole, she shook with the fear of never returning from it.

"Have you gotten your fill yet?"

His voice shook her back to reality. "Excuse me?"

"Have you seen enough yet, or should I strip my clothes off so you can see the rest of me?"

Mortified that he thought she'd been staring at his scars, she took a step forward, and he immediately took two steps back. "I...I'm sorry. It wasn't your scars," she said. "Back there, when I caught your gaze, your eyes...they were the most beautiful color I've ever seen. I didn't mean to offend you. I'm usually not this bold, believe me, but I felt drawn to you."

Oh my God, Lisa, what is wrong with you? You don't even know what you're talking about. Turn around and leave the store now before you stick both feet in your mouth and make this extremely intimidating man really angry with you. But her feet seemed fused to the floor.

"Listen, lady, there is nothing beautiful about me, hasn't been for years. If you're feeling sorry for me, don't. I don't need anyone's pity. If you think I'm your next charity case, get over it. Go to the pound and adopt a puppy if you feel the need, but there is nothing about me to be drawn to. Believe me. It could be bad for your health."

He pushed her aside and headed for the door. He'd just warned her off, basically threatened her, but could she do the smart thing and back off? Oh, no, not her. Apparently she didn't have a smart bone in her body.

"Wait, please."

The man didn't stop, though. He kept his stride without a hitch in his step and shoved the door open.

Lisa followed.

* * * *

Grant Monroe shoved the door open, sprinted out of the store and into the fresh air. His lungs burned, and his stomach clenched. He forced the air out of his lungs out in a whoosh so fast it made him light headed.

With the back of his hand, he swiped away the sweat beading on his forehead. The skin on the back of his neck still prickled. He'd known not to go in that store. Observing Lisa from a distance was one thing. Even from a distance his body reacted to her.

Following her into the store had been a stupid and dangerous move, an impulse. One he should've controlled. He'd needed a closer look at the woman who held his future. A future he wasn't certain he wanted.

Too late to take it back now. She'd seen him. She'd seen the scars, looked deep into his soul and didn't turn and run. Damn, he wasn't ready for this. Years of being alone suited him. The scars kept people from coming close. Viktor warned him the day would come when a woman would see past his repulsive side. He said she would save him from a life of loneliness and bring beauty back to his world. But there was nothing left inside him to save. He didn't want it. So why follow her, why go in the same store where she was bound to see him?

Because he hadn't believed Viktor knew what he'd been talking about, but he did now. She'd seen the color of his eyes, and for years, they'd shown black, but she saw the real color.

Grant yanked open his car door, braced his hands on the door casing, and leaned his forehead on the roof. *What the hell am I going to do?*

His heart thudded crazily in his chest. He wasn't ready to feel anything. Too much had happened in the years since the curse. He'd seen and done things no man should ever have to live through. It was too late for him.

Leave. I need to leave now.

A hand on his shoulder stopped him from sliding into his car. Without turning around, he knew it was Lisa. The healing warmth emitting from her spread over his shoulder, seeping into his heart.

No!

Spinning to face her, the movement knocked her hand away, and his heart stuttered in protest at the loss. "What is it with you? Are you so lonely you have to chase after repulsive men? Do you have some morbid fascination with scars, or what?"

"Wow, do you have some morbid fascination with browbeating innocent people? You accused me of some shitty things in the store. That wasn't fair."

"You're not seriously going to stand there, with your gorgeous little body, flawless skin, beautiful blue eyes, and stunning red hair and talk to me about what's fair, are you?"

"Ya know, if anyone else said those words to me, it would be a compliment, but you may as well have sworn at me. You're a mean, coldhearted man." She backed up.

"You don't know the half of it."

"Fine, I'll leave you to crawl back into your cave. Forgive me for trying to strike up a conversation and make a friend. *Jerk.*" Tears formed in her eyes. She turned from him and ran to her car.

Yeah, I'm a jerk and much more. No one needed a friend like him. Yet fury boiled his blood with the knowledge he'd turned away the one person he was meant to be with.

He slid into the driver's seat and shut the door with a jaw-rattling bang. He kept an eye on her little red sports car leaving the parking lot and watched it head down the highway. It was for the best. Slamming his fist into the dash, he shook off the pain and started the car.

Five miles down the road, traffic came to a halt. Four cars ahead of him, a tractor-trailer lay sideways on the road. Frustrated by the hold up, Grant stepped out of the car to see if there was any way around the wreck. The end of a small red sports car lay underneath the rig's big cab. A chill took over his body, and the ground shifted beneath him.

Lisa!

Grant pushed through the small crowd of gawkers, the need to reach Lisa the only thing keeping him on his feet. His heart stuttered, and the contents of his stomach lodged in his throat. His knees threatened to buckle. She couldn't be dead.

Until the moment he'd seen her little red car flattened under the cab of the semi, he hadn't realized how much he'd wanted to live. He'd thought himself ready and willing to go through the rest of his life alone with only his scars to carry his burden.

In the one month of observing Lisa, she'd turned it all around for him. She was warm, beautiful, caring...all the things he'd forgotten how to be. As a natural healer, it was no surprise to see her in the nursing profession.

Lisa had no knowledge of her hidden gifts; no one had ever divulged the secrets of her legacy. He'd told himself this morning that he could let her go and he didn't need his life fixed. Hell, it was his *duty* to remember the fate he'd been given.

Why'd I let her see into my soul, see my colors? I was weak. I fell for Lisa without even speaking a word to her. I gave in to the weaker side of me that wants to be whole again.

He'd also hurt her, sent her away from him in tears. Now, she lay inside that mangled wreck of a car because his pride refused his heart's desire.

Grant made it to the car. Police or rescue were nowhere in sight. *Where are they?* He faltered at the sight of her pale arm dangling from the crumpled metal. Waiting for help wasn't an option. The glow from her aura was fading fast.

"Help me get this door open." He turned to the people behind him, but no one ventured any closer to the wreck. "What is wrong with you people?" A young boy of thirteen or fourteen stepped forward, but his mother quickly pulled him back.

"Dude," said the boy, "the truck's leaking gas."

Grant wrenched on the door, moving it only a few inches. The driver of the truck limped around the corner, blood pouring down his face. He latched onto the door, and together, they drew it back far enough for Grant to squeeze his body into what was left of the front seat.

The driver fell to the ground, and one of the bystanders hauled him away from the wreckage. Grant grabbed Lisa's wrist and felt for a pulse. What he found was almost too faint to palpate, but it was there.

The back of her seat had collapsed, and her body lay flat, the roof only inches from her head. The upper half of her body was free from obstruction, but both legs were crushed under the dash.

"Lisa. Lisa, baby, I'm here. There's nothing to worry about now. I'll get you out."

Lisa groaned and tried to move, crying out in pain. "Hurts. So much."

Grant brushed the back of his hand across her cheek, and she turned her head toward him. Their gazes locked, and she burst into tears. "He came straight at me. I tried to get out of the way...I couldn't. It hurts so much."

Grant wiped the tears from her face and placed his left hand on her right shoulder. The color in her face drained before his eyes. "Tell me where you hurt, Lisa."

"Oh, God, my legs. My legs are crushed." Her chest started to rise and fall too fast.

"Shhh, baby. We'll fix it. You need to concentrate and tell me where else you're hurt. Do it now, Lisa. Close your eyes, take my hand, and show me where you're hurt. Use your training."

She latched onto his hand, and her breathing immediately slowed. Her entire body shook. "I'm bleeding internally. My stomach...oh, the pain." Her voice sounded weaker than before.

Grant still couldn't hear any sirens. He needed to act now or she would bleed to death. He moved her shirt up, closed his eyes, laid his hand on her bare belly, and braced himself for the burning pain he knew would come. He cradled her face into his neck and awaited the inevitable.

Beads of sweat broke out on his forehead, and scorching heat traveled up his arm, scalding his shoulder. He clenched his jaw through the pain and concentrated only on healing Lisa's ruptured spleen and internal damage.

Minutes passed with repairing the damage the only focal point of Grant's attention. All his energy converged and sent out healing waves. A man's voice broke his focus, and he all but collapsed to the ground, his body's energy spent. Lisa held onto his hand even as the paramedic attempted to move him out of the way. She stared into his eyes, her own wide and full of questions, but she remained silent, clinging to his hand with a strength that amazed him.

"Sir, you need to back out of the car so we can get her out. We need to hurry." The paramedic's voice dissolved the connection between them, and he reluctantly let go of her hand and stepped away from the car. Fifteen minutes later, the rescue team had Lisa loaded into the back of the squad; it took off screaming toward the hospital.

Hunched over, Grant trudged back to his car, one arm wrapped around his middle until he was able to sit gingerly in the driver's seat. He knew he'd find fresh blisters and scars adorning his stomach when he pulled his shirt up.

* * * *

Two weeks later, Lisa lay in the hospital bed, staring out the window. Dr. Miller knocked lightly on the open door and entered the room. "You look a heck of a lot better than you did when they brought you in here, Lisa. I must say, I do good work."

"Okay, Trent, there's not enough room in here for you, me, and your ego." She laughed. She'd known Dr. Trent Miller for five years. Working in the ER together, they ran into each other nightly. In his mid-forties and a wonderful doctor, he'd just started to gray along the edges of his hair. "So when do I get out of here?" Lisa asked.

"Well, you're two days post-op on that right leg, and I do believe it'll be the last surgery you need. Everything is healing well, so barring any unforeseen obstacles, I'd say you could leave tomorrow afternoon. How's that?"

"That's wonderful. Thank you."

"You'll need to start physical therapy on that leg next week. I still can't guarantee you won't have a limp, but at least you still have a leg and can walk. So behave and do what the therapist tells you to do. By the way, who is going to help you at home?"

"Home?" Well hell. She hadn't thought about that. There wasn't anyone to help. It was just her. "Um... I'm not sure. I'll figure something out, though."

"You need help getting around. I'll need a plan from you before I can release you." He looked worried.

"You'll get one, don't worry about it."

Except she was worried and had no idea what to do. With only one living family member—her father—calling him was out of the question. There was absolutely no one.

She still hadn't heard from the man from the record store. Whatever it was he'd done at the accident site had saved her life. Strange, after the accident, she'd thought for sure he'd stop by to see her. There had been an undeniable connection made between them, unless it was all her imagination. Maybe she'd dreamt the whole thing.

None of it made sense, no matter how many times she replayed it in her mind. She'd known she'd been dying. Burning pain had been present in her gut. A trauma nurse, she knew the signs and symptoms of internal bleeding. That is, until he'd placed his warm hand over her belly.

She could try to tell herself she'd been in shock and unaware of what had been going on around her, which may very well be true, but she'd felt the life draining out of her.

What had he done?

"Lisa?" Trent's words cut through her thoughts.

"What?"

"I was saying you could stay with me and Josh for a couple weeks if you want."

"That won't be necessary. She'll be staying with me."

They both turned to stare at the man standing in the doorway. *Him.* For one moment, she saw a glimpse of lavender eyes and a flawless handsome face. The image blurred, and once again, the hideous dark eyes and scars were prominent.

In the bookstore, she'd questioned herself. Had she really seen the beautiful eyes and face? Had she really looked into his tortured soul and seen something more?

Now, though, after what had happened at the accident, she knew. There was so much more to this man. The lavender eyes were the real thing, not the dark-abyss ones everyone else saw. Any sane person should fear this man, but she didn't. She was more drawn to him now than ever.

He moved into the room, and Trent's face tightened. "Do you know this man, Lisa?"

She patted his hand in reassurance. "Yes, it's okay."

"Fine, I've got some other patients to see, so I'll be back later to check on you. My offer still stands. Josh and I would love to have you." He leaned down and kissed her forehead. "I'll see you later."

Mystery man moved to make room for Trent to leave but stayed in the doorway.

"Please, come in. You can't make that statement without coming in and explaining yourself. I thought I'd never see you again."

He strode across the room and folded his long, muscled body into a chair beside her bed. Looking everywhere except at her, he seemed uncomfortable as hell sitting there.

"Soooo, do I at least get to know the name of the man who saved my life and plans to kidnap me?"

He sat up straight. "Kidnap?"

"Well, you did just waltz in here and announce that I'll be staying with you. Without my consent, I do believe the word for that is kidnapping." She was trying to say all this with a straight face. The man had absolutely no sense of humor.

"I—you need somewhere to go, someone to stay with. I knew you didn't have any family. I was trying to help, Lisa. I would never force anyone to do anything."

"Ah, I see. I am still at a disadvantage here. You apparently know who I am, and I have no idea who you are."

He sat relaxed in the chair again. "Grant Monroe. And of course I know who you are. You're my salvation. My future."

* * * *

Grant watched her eyes widen and her mouth drop open. The chains around his heart and soul released link by link. Done fighting the inevitable, he already felt lighter than he had in years; it was even easier to breathe. All it took was to admit to himself that he wanted a life. He didn't want to live in the shadows anymore.

He'd never regretted the actions that caused his fate; he'd embraced it. The pain that came with that decision shut him down, heart and soul, until he'd seen Lisa. In the two weeks since the accident, he'd gone back and forth arguing with himself. Finally, realization struck. He had no choice. This woman had opened his heart when he wasn't looking. Now, it was time to make her love him in return.

"What do you mean I'm your 'salvation'?"

"Exactly what it means, but we don't need to worry about it here in the hospital. You will come home with me, won't you?"

Lisa tried pushing herself up in bed and struggled to get comfortable. He rose and stood by her side, offering his arm for leverage. Her hand touched his bare skin, and warmth spread up his arm and across his shoulder, the feeling indescribable.

He'd thought Viktor wrong, but the proof was in this woman's touch. Without looking, he knew the scarring on his left shoulder had vanished. The gypsy had told the truth.

He caught her gaze. Could she feel their connection? She moved into a more comfortable position and released his arm only to glide her fingers down and grasp his hand.

"Yes," she said.

Disoriented by her touch, he'd forgotten the question—oh, yeah, he'd asked her to come home with him. Good Lord, she left him off balance. This newfound tenderness in his heart was difficult to get used to. It felt like the thaw after a long, cold winter. *Please God, don't let the season change on me.*

"That's great, Lisa. I'll make sure you have everything you'll need. You won't want for anything."

"I'm not high maintenance, Grant. I don't need much at all. I do have a question, though."

"Ask away."

"When we first met in the record store, you were very angry with me. Why the change?"

He didn't really know how to answer, so he shrugged and told her what he thought would make sense. "When I yelled at you, you left the parking lot in tears. That accident wouldn't have happened if it weren't for me. I owe you. I was rude to a woman who tried to be nice to me. I guess it'd been so long since someone looked beyond my scars for no other reason than to get to know me that I had no idea how to react or trust. I didn't believe that a beautiful woman would want to get to know a man who looks like me. I want to fix that. I want to make it up to you and I want you to get to know me." Well, hell, that all poured out without thinking. He hadn't meant to say it all. Not yet, anyway.

Lisa dropped his hand and lifted hers up to the rough, scarred skin on his face, running her fingers over the lines and ridges. One by one, the ridges she touched softened. Gasping, she pulled her hand back, and her gaze snapped to his. She didn't understand, and that was okay. Because he knew now; oh, dear Lord, he knew. Joy burst through his heart and broke the final links of the chain, staggering him.

He took hold of her hand and brought it to his lips, placing a soft kiss on her open palm. "I need to go. There are supplies you'll need, and I want everything ready for you. I have a question for you."

"Um...what's that?"

"Why are you accepting an invitation from a virtual stranger?"

"I'm not sure, really. First of all, the accident wasn't your fault. I was upset, yes, but that truck crossed lanes and came at me. I saw him coming but couldn't get out of the way. You saved my life that day. I still don't know what you did, but I'm beginning to believe we are meant to find each other for some reason, and I'm not willing to walk away. Not yet."

Hopefully never.

"I'll see you in the morning. Sleep well tonight." Grant leaned down, his mouth inches from hers, waiting for a sign whether or not to continue. She looked into his eyes; he swore he felt her touch his soul. That was all he needed.

He placed his mouth over her soft lips and fell into the silkiest, most sensuous experience he'd ever known. He savored the taste of her. Bringing his hand around to the back of her neck, he tangled his fingers in her smooth hair.

His thumb traced the sleek skin over her jaw line, and for a moment, he was lost in time, only knowing the magic that was Lisa. Pulling back, he trailed his fingers along her neck, then dropped his hand to his side.

Grant walked across the room and turned back to look at her. She'd placed two fingers over her lips, but a smile covered her face. For the first time since he was eighteen years old, Grant's smile reached his eyes, and he had reason for hope.

* * * *

The next morning, Grant helped Lisa into his shiny black Lexus. After a sleepless night, she was more than ready to get out of the hospital. What sleep she'd gotten had been fitful. She'd dreamt of her grandmother and the stories she used to tell her. Stories of the man she would meet and grow old with.

Fairytales, or so she'd thought, but now she wasn't so sure. Grant Monroe was no man made from fairytales, but somehow she believed in her heart and soul that they were meant to find each other. She didn't know anything about him, yet she'd known him forever.

After stopping at her house for clothes, they headed out of town. "I just realized I don't even know where you live."

"About half an hour out of town on Carver's Mountain."

She turned her gaze from the window to him. "Carver's Mountain? I'd heard the whole mountain was private property, some kind of preserve or something. How is it you live there?"

"It is private property, but not a preserve. I own it."

"Own it? As in you bought a whole mountain?"

He chuckled. "Yes, as in 'bought a whole mountain.'"

Unbelievable. He thinks it's funny. The man owned a mountain and acted like it was an everyday occurrence. "Why?"

He glanced over at her before returning his gaze to the road, his smile gone. "Look at me, Lisa. I didn't want to live in town. I'm a freak. I didn't want to be around people at all. I guess you could say I was running away from my fate. But it always seems to find me."

Lisa shifted in her seat. "You're not a freak. Do you know the first time

I saw you, your eyes were lavender and your face smooth as a baby's. It wasn't until you met my gaze that I saw the scars. I think I have everything figured out, but you need to tell me. What's your fate, Grant? What caused all these scars, and how am I involved?"

He was silent for a moment, intent on the asphalt ahead of him as he turned off the main road onto a dirt one. Carver's Mountain loomed over them, and they began the ascent up the steep, winding lane. "We're almost there. I'll explain it all then, I promise."

The end of the road opened up to a wide expansive field. Several horses grazed on the long green grass, tails swishing in the wind. At the end of the field, a beautiful, huge A-frame house sat at the edge of the forest. Windows covered the entire front of the home, and on the second story, an enormous wraparound deck had baskets of flowers hung from every corner.

Grant slid the shifter into park and shut the car off. At first, she thought he was going to stay there in the car, but he finally took his hands off the steering wheel and got out. He opened the door, walked to her side and knelt in front of her.

"When I was eighteen years old, I lived next door to an old, crazy woman. At least, I *thought* her crazy. She was Greek and always yelled at us in words we never understood. She was fiercely protective of her property and pitched a fit if anyone even got near her house. The whole neighborhood thought she was loony. No one ever took her seriously. I came home from work one night and saw flames coming from the top floor of her house. I didn't think twice. I ran to her place and tried to bust the door down. It wouldn't budge, so fool that I am, I dove through the glass plate window in her living room, sliced my face all to hell. You'd think I would have grabbed a rock or something to break it first, but not me." He laughed, shaking his head.

"Anyway, I ran up the stairs, calling her name and searching from room to room. I found her lying in bed, staring at the fire in her bedroom, watching it grow. I grabbed her off the bed and threw her over my shoulder. She hit, kicked, and yelled at me the entire time, but I got her out of the house. The place burnt to the ground, but I saved her life."

Lisa swung her legs out of the car so she sat face-to-face with him kneeling between her legs. "I'm sorry you were hurt, but you saved her life, that's a wonderful thing."

"You'd have thought so, wouldn't you? She was angry, really angry. She'd wanted to kill herself, and I'd saved her. In the ambulance, she'd stopped yelling in Greek long enough to tell me she'd cursed me. If I'd wanted to save lives so badly, then that would be what I was destined to do.

But not without a price. With every life I saved, that person's wounds would scar me instead of them."

Grant lifted his shirt. Scars covered his sculpted abdomen. A fresh one stood out, and Lisa covered it with her hand. It was an impulse she couldn't ignore. She wanted to take his pain away, she wanted him.

"This is because of me, from the accident, isn't it?"

"Yes."

"Oh, Grant. How could she have done this to you? You've had so much pain in your life." She removed her hand from the wound, but it was gone. Quickly, before he could stop her, she ripped open his shirt, mindless of the buttons flying everywhere, and peeled it off his arms.

Tears flowed from her eyes. She inspected each and every mark on his upper body. Horrified for him, she pulled him flush against her body and ran her hands up and down his back while she moved her lips along his jaw line to his mouth. When her lips found his, she poured all the love and passion in her being into the kiss in an attempt to take away all the pain he'd lived through.

She framed his face with hers hands and stared deep into his lavender-colored eyes. The black spheres that held so much pain were gone. Some scars remained, but many had vanished too. Twenty years would take some time to heal.

"Grams told me about you. She told me about a man with a hard shell but a lavender heart. She said lavender hearts were ones to be cherished, and I would be the only one to heal his wounded soul."

He seemed serene as he tugged her even closer and buried his face in her neck.

"My grandfather told me about you, also, although I didn't believe him. After all this time, I'd given up finding love. But he told me a healer would come along, that I'd have to open up and be able to love, or you wouldn't be able to help me." He looked into her eyes. "And I do, Lisa. I love you with everything that's in me."

He wiped the tears from her cheeks with his thumbs and rested his forehead against hers. "Can you love me?"

"I can love only you."

His smile lit up his face, and he let out holler that startled the horses from their grazing. With her arms around his neck, Grant lifted her out of the car and faced the house. "Welcome home, my love."

Lisa laughed. "You know, Grams also told me our children would be blessed with our healing powers and destined for greatness. Do you suppose that's true?"

"I'm a believer, honey. Our children, huh? Wow. I can't wait," he said, taking off at a run toward the house. Her laughter echoed throughout the mountain.

Forever Found
by
Debbie Gould

Kelly is a single mom in the Air Force and has learned the hard way men can be irresponsible and only out for themselves when the father of her child signed off all his rights and fled. Can Jason prove to her all men aren't like the ones in her past?

Jason slowed his pace just enough to let Kelly catch up to him. Swiping the sweat from his brow, he fell in line with the newest addition to the squadron. At six a.m., the Florida heat and humidity was already a force to be reckoned with. Even so, doing PT-physical training at six a.m. was a heck of a sight better than three p.m.

For two weeks, he and Kelly ran their three-point-four mile run in companionable silence. A 'hello' at the start and 'have a good day' at the end. In the beginning, that was fine with Jason. He'd just wanted to get a closer look at the cute five-foot-three-inch girl with light brown hair tied back into a bun and the single most amazing pair of blue eyes he'd ever seen.

In excellent shape, she sported trim legs and arms with a hint of definition to the muscle. It was apparent she took her training seriously. The first day, when he pulled up alongside her, they had exchanged names, and he asked if she'd mind if he ran with her. With a million-dollar smile, she told him 'not at all,' and they'd fallen into the pattern ever since.

Now, it was getting to the point where he tossed and turned at night and he'd stare up at the ceiling, thinking about those blue eyes and that bright smile. He wanted to get to know her better.

Something was different about her today, though. The light seemed gone from her eyes, and she struggled to keep her usual grueling pace.

"Hey, Kel. You feeling okay this morning?"

"Huh? Oh, yeah, I'm fine. I was up with my son all night, so I'm a bit out of it today."

Son? Aw, heck. She wore no ring. He'd never thought she might be married. Never dreamed she might belong to someone else. *Stupid, stupid, stupid.* He'd been so drawn to her he'd begun to think of her as his. Which was foolish, since all they did was run together every morning. Well, so much for that. Dim-witted maybe, but stalker no, and he didn't poach on someone else's territory.

"I'm sorry to hear that. Is he feeling better?"

"Yeah, he appears to be." She glanced at her watch. "Six-fifteen and no call from the sitter yet. That's a good sign. I'll be glad when this run is over, though." She chuckled.

"Yeah, I imagine. The good news is we're three-quarters of the way there. We'll be done before you know it."

At the end of the line, they said their goodbyes and headed to their different offices. For some unknown reason, he couldn't let her go without one last flash of her smile. "Senior Airman Fuller," he bellowed at her back. She whipped around, eyes wide. "I hope your day goes better than last night." He smiled. "Your husband's a lucky man."

After she smiled, Jason turned toward his office.

"Tech Sergeant Miller."

It was his turn to spin around and face her. His stomach tightened. He'd been out of line. Was she insulted that he mentioned her husband? Instead of scorn, her eyes glowed with mischief, her smile the brightest he'd ever seen it.

"No husband, sir. Just me and my boy."

Jason's mouth hung open as she jogged away.

"Might want to close your mouth, Sarge," his friend, Jackson, joked as he walked by. "Those nasty gotchya bugs are flying around."

Well, hot damn. No husband. The day started looking up.

* * * *

Kelly sat at her desk unable to make sense of the blurry numbers on her computer monitor. Fatigued, she rubbed her eyes, sighed and glanced at the clock. *Two-thirty. Half an hour to go. Ugh.*

After a long night of no sleep, tiredness had finally taken its toll. Home, bed...that's what she wanted. Unfortunately, with a two-year-old son waiting at home, that wasn't what she'd likely get. Oh, but he was worth it. Being a single mom was difficult at best, downright scary at its worst. Bottom line, though, she'd never change a thing. Cole was her life.

She thought about this morning, and her grin grew into a full-blown smile. Jason Miller. Now there was gorgeous hunk of a man. Not much taller than her five-foot-three inches, he still held a commanding presence. Lean muscle and sinew covered by naturally light brown skin from his Pilipino heritage.

For the two weeks he'd been running with her she'd been able to admire his strength and determination and his cute, tight butt whenever she pretended to fall behind. Today, though, he'd finally found a way to ask her something personal. *Your husband's a lucky man.*"

Had he been fishing for information? She didn't know much about him, only that he worked on the flight line, was divorced, and was five years older than her twenty-four years. Oh, yeah, she knew she'd been attracted to him from day one.

"I see you're working really hard."

Kelly recognized the husky voice. The man she'd just been daydreaming about caught her doing just that. Surprised, she spun the chair around, and her breath caught as her gaze hit him. Holy-handsome Batman, the guy was in his civvies: a well-worn pair of jeans and tight white tee. Heck, the shirt could've been second skin the way it showed off every well-defined muscle in his chest and broad shoulders.

Unable to clear her throat, Kelly spoke through a dry mouth. "Tech Sergeant Miller. This is a nice surprise. I gather from your lack of uniform you're not working too hard yourself."

He grinned from ear to ear. "No, ma'am. It was an early day. I was hoping I'd catch you before you left."

"Well, you caught me slacking alright."

"That's what I wanted to talk to you about."

Uh-oh, maybe this wasn't a social call. He wasn't in her division, wasn't in any of her chain of command, but that didn't mean he couldn't report her to her First Shirt. Wait just a minute. What would he have to report? Her staring at a computer monitor?

"My slacking?"

He shifted from foot to foot. "No. I wouldn't call you a slacker on your worst day. I was hoping to ask you to dinner tonight."

Her heart performed a little flutter. "Dinner? I'd love to, but as you know my son wasn't feeling well last night. The sitter said he's been better today, but I need to get home and be with him tonight, just to make sure. Besides, she's watched him all day. I couldn't ask her to watch him tonight too."

"Well, I wasn't actually suggesting we go out."

She raised an eyebrow.

"Just hold on before you get the wrong idea. If it wouldn't be too presumptuous, I thought I might bring dinner to you and your son. You've got to be tired, and it'd save you the trouble of having to cook. You could relax on the couch while I prepare the meal. What do you say?"

What did she say? Is this guy for real?

"Seriously?"

She smiled as his brows scrunched together and his beautifully kissable lips turned downward into a frown.

"Kelly, I'm sorry if I crossed a line. I didn't mean to insult you, but I thought you looked like you could use a break."

"Jason, wait. I'm not mad—quite the opposite. That's the best offer I've had in a long, long time. You don't mind putting up with a grumpy two year old?"

His smile broadened again, and he stood a little straighter, if that were possible. "Heck, no. I figure it can't be any worse than some of the guys I supervise."

They both laughed.

"I don't know about that," she replied. "Let me know if you still think so after tonight." Shutting down the computer, she wrote her address on a scrap of paper. "I live in Commando Village. It's still part of the base so don't forget your ID at the gate."

"Great, any requests?"

"Nope, Cole and I aren't picky. We'll be happy with anything."

He walked her to her car. "Is five okay?" he asked as he opened the door for her.

"Perfect. See ya then." Before he was out of sight, she hollered to him. "Jason?" He turned to her.

"Thanks."

He gave her a salute and left.

* * * *

Kelly's doorbell rang at five after five. Her heart stuttered, and her stomach started doing somersaults. *Good grief, calm down girl, it's just dinner.* She opened the door to Jason with his arms full of take-out from Bobby Jo's BBQ. Grabbing a bag from him, she laughed at all the food he'd brought and ushered him in.

"Really, Jason, do we look like we eat this much every night?"

He shrugged. "I couldn't decide on what to get so I think I ordered one of everything from the menu. Except their cornbread. I got about four of those."

Around the corner, the speeding blur of a two year old bounded into the kitchen dressed in Spiderman pajamas. "Mommy? Mommy, is the dinner man here?"

Jason raised his eyebrow and glanced at Kelly, who laughed. "I've been telling him every five minutes, for the past hour, that a man is bringing our

95

dinner. He wanted to know why I wasn't cooking, and an hour to a two year old is a lifetime. He hasn't learned patience yet."

Jason's dark eyes sparkled back at her. "I see. So being the dinner man is a good thing?"

She bent to pick up her son. "Oh yes, being the dinner man is a *very* good thing, isn't it, Cole?"

Cole started bouncing on her hip. "Dinner man, dinner man. Yay."

"As you can see, he's feeling much better."

Jason deposited the rest of the bags on the kitchen counter and began to pull everything out. "That's good to hear. Maybe tonight the both of you will get a good night's sleep."

Pulling the high chair up to the kitchen table, she settled Cole in it. "From your lips. He's just barely started sleeping through the night, but it didn't take me long to get used to it."

With a menagerie of food spread out on the table, Jason found the plates, silverware and cups and set the table. "I brought iced tea. Is that okay with you?"

"My gosh, yes. You've got enough here to feed an army. Stop waiting on us and start eating."

She dished out mashed potatoes and cut up BBQ chicken for Cole, and they dug in to the rest of the food. Half an hour later, they'd barely put a dent in the food, but she couldn't eat another bite.

"What in the heck are we going to do with all this food? Cole and I will never eat it all."

"I'll take care of everything. You just go sit with your boy and relax."

He really wasn't for real. She knew this now. He was a figment of her imagination. Maybe she was still dreaming from the night before and had yet to wake up. Still not convinced he wasn't too good to be true, she unbuckled Cole from his highchair.

"Okay, if you say so. We'll be back after we get cleaned up."

* * * *

An hour later, the washed dishes gleamed in the drainer, food rested in containers tucked into the fridge, and the kitchen had been wiped spotless. Kelly sat on the couch with Cole in awe of the man strolling into the living room. He actually looked happy after kitchen duty. Amazing.

Cole jumped off her lap and clung to Jason's leg. "Dinner man, dinner man, may I pwease wead me a stowy."

Jason laughed

"Do you mean, will you please read me a story?"

"Noooo, I can't wead. You wead me."

Kelly's thoughts bounced between amazement and laughter. She figured she'd better save Jason from having to read a bedtime story. "Honey, Mommy's gonna read Goodnight Moon. Climb on up here." She gave Jason an apologetic look.

Jason sat next to her on the couch and pulled Cole up on his lap. "I don't mind if you don't."

Another shock; there'd been too many to count tonight. "No, of course I don't mind," she replied.

By the end of the story, Cole slept soundly against Jason's chest. Kelly made a move to take him from his lap, but he shook his head and whispered, "Lead the way."

Kelly leaned against the doorway, staring at Jason tucking her little boy into bed and giving him a soft kiss on the forehead. A lump the size of a softball formed in her throat, and it was all she could do to keep from blubbering like an idiot. In one night this man formed a bond with her son; no one besides her parents had ever bothered to try.

Jason joined her at the door and placed his arm around her shoulder. "He's a beautiful little boy, Kelly. You've been blessed."

She nodded. "Yes, I have."

They returned to the couch and set the TV on low.

"So how do you like Florida and Hurlburt Field so far?" Jason asked.

She snorted. "I transferred from New Mexico. Being here, right on the Gulf, is like paradise."

"How long have you been in the Air Force?"

"Six years. I joined right out of high school. I actually had my physical and swearing-in on September 11th in Albany, New York. I was only a quarter through the physical when they stopped it. At the time, nobody knew what was happening or where the next attack would be so all federal and state buildings were shut down and they sent us home.

"The next week, my recruiter was pretty blunt. He told me we'd be going to war. I hadn't signed on the dotted line yet, and he said there was no shame in changing my mind if I wanted to. I told him to reschedule the physical. I was in Saudi when the president declared war. It was scary, but my parents have always been behind me, and I've never regretted joining."

"That's admirable. Where do you call home?"

"Vermont. What about you?" She drew one leg under her and shifted, facing him.

"All over. I was an Air Force brat. Both my parents were enlisted. We traveled all over the place. It was great. I've seen so much and have friends all around the world. That's why I joined; it's like one big family."

They talked about family and the places they'd been, the things they'd experienced, and the time flew by. Before she knew it, it was eleven p.m., and the yawn she held inside finally broke free. Until now, she hadn't noticed they had managed to gravitate toward each other and now sat thigh-to-thigh.

He took hold of her feet, pulled them up into his lap, and gently started massaging first one, then the other. A groan of delight escaped from her lips. His gaze caught hers and held. The time that had flown by now stood still as they looked intently at each other. His eyes held passion and heat, but she also saw the promise of a stable, reliable man. She knew from hard experience that this breed of man was few and far between. For the first time in years, she didn't fear the idea of a relationship.

She laid her head against the couch pillows. He did wondrous things to her feet and calves, and she began to imagine what other magical feats his hands might accomplish. All too soon, he stopped and slid out from beneath her legs.

Leaning over her, one arm on each side of her head, he bent and whispered in her ear, "I had a great time tonight, Kelly. You're a wonderful woman, and, if it's okay by you, I'd like to get to know you and Cole a whole lot better."

Her heart thudded so hard she was amazed it didn't burst right through her ribcage. His warm breath tickled her neck and sent shivers of awareness down her spine.

"I'd like that too—a lot."

Brushing a chaste kiss across her lips, he moved to straighten, but stopped and held her gaze once more, raw heat burning in his eyes. "Not enough for me. You?"

She barely shook her head, and he dropped to the floor on one knee, gathering her in his strong arms. He paused only one more moment for permission and crushed his mouth to hers in a kiss that promised so much more. His hand smoothed the hair away from her face and settled in the crook of her neck, his thumb caressing her jaw. Tongues tangled and sought knowledge of the other.

Pulling back at last, they gasped for well-needed air. Her body tingled all over, heat ran through her blood stream, and it was difficult getting her breathing back to a normal rate and rhythm. "Wow! You pack a punch, Tech Sergeant Miller."

He stood, notably uncomfortable, and laughed. "So do you, Senior

Airman Fuller. So do you."

Kelly started to sit up, but he stopped her. "Stay right where you are till I'm gone. If you walk me to the door, I'll need another goodbye kiss. If that happens, I can't guarantee I'll leave. Sleep well, Kelly. I'll see you at 0600."

"Goodnight, Jason. Thanks again for tonight. No one's ever been so thoughtful."

"Well, that's a damn shame, but I'll be sure to change that."

* * * *

Over the next several weeks, Jason visited frequently. He took Kelly and Cole for picnics on the beach and boat rides in the gulf. They'd taken a drive to New Orleans, had gone to the zoo, and had dinner on a paddleboat.

It was difficult at times to wrap her mind around the knowledge that men like Jason existed. She'd been dumped so many times. Cole's father had been the worst heartache she'd ever experienced. He'd just signed off his rights and walked away when he found out she was pregnant.

She'd never met a man like Jason. He was sweet, thoughtful, and appeared to genuinely care for Cole, and Cole just loved the man. *Oh, God, Cole.* What would happen when Jason left? It wasn't just her she had to think about anymore. Cole was an integral part of her life. They were a package deal. What had she been thinking?

The doorbell brought her out of her musings. Jason had mentioned he was coming over earlier.

"Hi." He brushed a kiss across her cheek as he breezed past her and into the hallway.

Warmth flushed through her face, and she shut the door behind her.

"Where's the little man?"

"Napping."

In two strides he stood directly in front of her. "Then how about a proper greeting." He framed her face with his hands and softly covered her mouth with his. By the time they came up for air, her breathing stuttered and her heart pounded.

"I love kissing you, Kelly. I could do it all day long."

"I'll bet you say that to all the girls."

The smile gone from his face, Jason met Kelly's gaze dead on. "I hope you didn't seriously mean that. You are the only one in my life. If I have my say, it will be that way forever."

"Jason."

"You don't need to say anything, Kelly. I know you don't trust what we have yet, but I do. Enough for both of us. I can wait until you catch up."

Kelly plodded into the living room and slumped on the couch. "It's not that I don't trust you, Jason. I do. But from what I've been through, I don't believe forever is anything I'll ever find."

Jason knelt on the floor in front of her. "You *will* find it. I promise. I'll be with you every step, showing you the way. I love you, Kelly. I won't give up on us." He stood and turned to leave but whipped around again. "Oh, by the way, you start Airman Leadership School tomorrow, don't you?"

Still dumbfounded by his declaration, she only nodded.

"It always runs late, and you'll have study groups and volunteer activities to do on the weekend. Don't worry about finding someone to take care of Cole. I have lots of plans for us men for the next six weeks while Mommy earns her sergeant stripes. And don't forget to give daycare a note so I can pick him up. See ya tomorrow night."

The door shut behind him.

The room swirled in front of her. Never mind that he just solved a major problem for her. She was still back at the I-love-you part. Could he possibly mean it? Suddenly giddy, Kelly jumped up and bound up the stairs to her room. Pulling her dress uniform out of the closet, she started to iron, starch, and arrange her medals. The next six weeks would be grueling—late nights studying, all the volunteer hours she'd have to put in.

She was now looking forward to all of it. If he meant what he said, he'd be the light at the end of the tunnel. *Oh, Lord, please let him mean it. Please let him be my forever.*

* * * *

Graduation night finally arrived. With the ceremony over, she strolled across to where Cole and Jason waited for her. This was one of her greatest accomplishments, and she was darn proud of herself. Though she couldn't have done it without Jason.

He'd come through more than she'd ever imagined he could. He'd taken complete charge of Cole, made sure he'd been fed, bathed, and read to before bedtime. On the weekends, the two had done "man things" together. Jason had spent many nights on the couch after helping her study. And now, here she was, headed toward the two most important men in her life.

Cole launched himself into her arms, draped himself around her neck, and slobbered her face with kisses. "Can we go now, Mommy?"

"You bet!"

Jason wrapped his arm around her waist as they walked to the car.

"There is somewhere special I'd like to take you before we go get that pizza we promised Cole."

Jason drove out to the beach and parked the car where they could look out at the water. Cole was half-asleep in the backseat watching a DVD, so they stepped out of the car and sat together on the hood. The moon sparkled across the water while a soft, warm breeze blew through her hair. It was beautiful here.

"So, have you found it?" Jason asked.

Confused, she looked at him and laughed, "Are you insinuating I've lost something? My mind, maybe? I know I've been a bear these past weeks. Thank you so much for putting up with me."

Jason smirked. "Well, that wasn't quite what I was talking about, but it was my pleasure, Staff Sergeant Fuller." He pulled a small box out of his jacket pocket. "I've been waiting six long weeks for this moment."

He knelt on one knee and held her hand in his. "But you are what I've been waiting for my whole life. I've known this since the day I laid eyes on you. You're a strong, caring, beautiful woman, Kelly Fuller. Will you marry me?"

Tears streamed down Kelly's face. "How can you be so sure so soon?"

"I know my heart. I know what it has told me for months now. Do you love me?"

Kelly pulled him up off his knee. "Oh, yes. Yes, I love you."

The stars sparkled in Jason's eyes, and he asked again, "Will you marry me? Will you and Cole become my family?"

Kelly threw herself in his arms and held tight. "Yes, yes, I will. We will."

He twirled her around in a circle and kissed her till her knees turned weak. "You asked earlier if I'd found it. Now I understand, and yes, I've found my forever."

Author Bio:

Debbie Gould has been writing for five years and has several novels published. She currently resides in Vermont with her husband and teenage son. An older daughter proudly serves in the Air Force and another son works for the family Well Drilling business. Debbie has also worked for eighteen years as a nurse.

Waking Up
by
Ava James

*In Iraq, Jaysen has treated many wounded men, but none touch her
heart like Sergeant Tiberius. Will she touch his heart too?*

Chapter One

Tanned and scarred, Sergeant Demetri Tiberius lay unconscious in
the fifth hospital bed, in the second row of the ward. Jaysen sponged his
wounded body. Water trickled down his chest, haphazardly following the
trail of hair and muscled grooves to pool in the soft spot of his sternum.

Day three of her bedside vigil of the Ukrainian Sergeant started the
same as prior days: vitals check, sponge bath, and a change of bandages.

With the back of her hand, she wiped the sweat from her brow and
dipped the sponge back into the cool water. She wrung it out and wished
someone would give her a bath for a change. Really, any kind of shower
would be nice. But she wasn't here in Iraq for her own comfort. She was here
for them, for all the people harmed by the destruction that war brought.

Thoughts of Alex crept into her mind, but she shoved them away to
focus her attention on Demetri. He was her one and only concern right
now. His recovery from the explosion that obliterated his truck and threw
shrapnel into his skull was her present goal.

On restless nights, when everything was quiet, sleep evaded her.
Thoughts of Alex would slip into her mind and keep her awake. Most nights
she would get up and walk down the hall to the patient wing to check on her
latest charge.

Last night was no different; she pulled up a chair beside Demetri's bed
and listened while he slept. His steady, even breathing gave her hope. He
was a fighter with a strong will to live. That much was obvious from his
body's resilience. The explosion should have killed him; instead, here he
lay comatose while his body grappled with his wounds. All she needed was
for him to wake up.

While he snored softly, Jaysen told him about her deceased brother.

She described Alex in physical detail and retold several of the happy
memories of their childhood. Summers in Wisconsin were a far cry from
the dry heat of Iraq, and in Wisconsin, there were lakes to jump into to cool
down.

Her attention veered back to the present. She folded the linen sheet down lower and exposed his genitals. With the curtains around his bed closed, no one saw the blush that heated her already warm cheeks. The feminine side of her could not help but acknowledge the appeal of his masculine body. But she was a nurse, so wasn't she supposed to be able to ignore such things? Wasn't it all part of the job?

She allowed her curious gaze to roam the muscled planes of his body. Her skin heated in reaction to the feast laid before her. She couldn't deny her admiration. Nurse or not, she enjoyed the sight of his naked body.

The strokes of the sponge across his midsection continued to loom dangerously low while she cleaned his pale bottom half. She found the contrast between his naturally fair skin and his tanned stomach, arms, and chest endearing. A moan escaped his parted lips as the back of her fingers accidentally brushed his bare belly.

Inwardly, she cursed her carelessness. Jaysen folded the sheet back up around his hips and returned the sponge to the basin. The heat of her blush started on her cheeks and radiated outward across the rest of her body. She grabbed the towel from the bedside table and started to dry Demetri. His hand in hers, she lifted his arm to remove the towel she had placed beneath him. His long, tapered fingers battered and callused. The knuckles of his left hand raw as she examined him. She pulled the towel out from beneath him, and his grip tightened on her hand. Jaysen's eyes shot to his face, her heart pounding in her chest, the towel forgotten as his startled gaze met hers.

Sapphire blue eyes opened wide, confusion clear on his features. He tried to sit up; his muscles contracted from the effort while pain from his injuries seized him. A tic started in his jaw. He winced, and his shoulders fell back, the breath leaving his lungs as his head hit the pillow. His eyes slid shut.

He'd passed out.

Jaysen stood beside him, his fingers still entwined with hers. She waited for him to wake once more, but he didn't.

His grip on her hand eased, and his breathing returned to normal. It was then that she released her withheld breath. Now that he had woken up, the chances of him making a full recovery tripled.

When Sergeant Tiberius was wheeled into the ward with shrapnel lodged in his skull, several nurses doubted he would last through surgery, let alone survive this long. Once the metal and debris were removed from his head, neck, and shoulders, Jaysen was charged with his care. She stitched and cleaned his minor injuries and monitored his head wound. There was no way of knowing the extent of his brain damage. As with all head-trauma cases, the early medical fears were of fluid build-up and swelling of the soft tissues.

But the Sergeant proved to be a resilient man. He experienced neither complication past the first night.

His body appealed to her, but it was his strength that caught her deep in the chest.

She changed the bandages on his shoulder and neck, and then attended the bandage about his head. He looked serene and almost fragile as he lay in his bed. She wanted nothing more than to protect him, to shield him from the pain and fear Alex must have felt.

Her thoughts had a bad habit of returning to her brother when she least expected it. Alex enlisted in the Army right out of high school. He said that it was his calling. How she wished he hadn't enlisted. She was a senior at the University of Indiana when she received that earth-shattering phone call: Alex was dead. Her father broke the news to her, but his voice stalled and fumbled with his words. She could recall the exact time and the outfit she wore right down to her underwear. Eleven-fifty-six, purple and pink polka dot bikini briefs.

That was when she decided to join the Red Cross. Two years later, here she was stationed in Iraq at a NATO Military Hospital. In a month, her assigned term would be over and she would need to make the decision to stay on or return home.

With each patient she helped, a small piece of her grief lifted. Now, she tried to focus on the good memories. Maybe that was why she felt the need to tell Demetri about him. It was all part of her healing.

* * * *

Demetri opened his heavy eyelids slowly. Light flooded the space above him and all around. He flexed his fingers and was rewarded with the sting of the IV needle in his right hand. He wanted to lift his head, but he remembered from his earlier attempt that it was a bad idea.

He wiggled his toes and thanked God he was in one piece. The last thing he remembered was Uri making a crude joke about a donkey, followed by a loud bang that rattled the truck they rode in. After that, everything was a murky blur.

There was one thing, though, that was clear...a voice. Soft, feminine, and soothing, it called to him in his hazy sleep. He couldn't actually remember a word of what the woman said, but he recalled her foreign accent. English... she spoke in English. That was all he could remember. He wondered if the petite brunette at his bedside was the same woman.

His head began to throb as he concentrated. Closing his eyes for what seemed like a second, he drifted back to sleep. When he awoke again, he opened his eyes to slits. It was dark now. Dim light originated from somewhere to his left; he couldn't see the source.

"I think you would have liked him," the familiar feminine voice said. "He was the class clown and a daredevil to the end."

He wondered whom she talked about. Thankfully, he knew English. His hooded gaze slid to the right to where the woman sat in a folding chair beside his bed. She was indeed the petite brunette from earlier. Her hair was no longer restrained in a ponytail. Instead, it lay braided over her shoulder, her fingers idly stroking the ends.

"You know, one summer, I think he was twelve or maybe ten, I challenged him to touch the bottom of the pond at Aunt Arleen's farm and bring back a handful of mud. I thought for sure that he wouldn't be able to do it. Well, he went down and was under the water so long that I started screaming his name and actually jumped in with all my clothes on, shoes too. When he popped up with a glob of slimy mud coating his hand, I could've killed him." She smiled as she stared off into the darkness at the foot of his bed. In the dim light, he couldn't see her clearly, but her voice trailed off into a tone of sadness. He wondered why such a memory would cause her to be sad.

He remembered her surprised features when he'd woken earlier, but that image was cloudy. Leaning back on two legs of her chair, she stretched her arms and yawned.

"I wish you could tell me about your family. About your childhood." Her head turned toward the bed, and Demetri hurriedly closed his eyes. He feigned sleep and listened. She leaned close to him. Her breath feathered across his right pectoral as she spoke. "Please wake up again, Demetri. Please do that for me," she whispered. Her breath retreated, and he heard her rise from the rickety chair.

With one eye open, he turned his head and watched her tired form walk down the hall.

Chapter Two

Pain was the first thing to greet Demetri when he awoke. Now that he was no longer in the murkiness of unconsciousness, noises interrupted his rest. Pain pounded in his skull as he tried to return to sleep. What he wouldn't do for a bottle of vodka right now!

At what he figured to be near five a.m., the drip-drop sounds of a leaky faucet and pans clattering broke the near silence. Women, nurses he assumed, meandered through the corridor and spoke in what he guessed to be Dutch. One nurse came to his bedside and checked his pulse. Within minutes, she moved on to the next bed.

A few coughs sounded from a bed across the room. Sporadic groans originated from all directions. At one point, a man toward the front end of the hall began speaking incoherently. His voice grew louder with each word. Demetri heard the footsteps of several people move across the room toward the frantic patient.

His legs felt restless beneath the linen sheets that covered him. To top it all off, he ached everywhere. His stomach rumbled, and he wondered how long it had been since he had eaten anything. Then nature called, he had to go—now.

Nice and easy, he rose to his elbows, slowly shifting to an upright position.

What the?

He reached down and felt a small plastic hose. He cringed at the realization of what the hose was: a catheter. It was going to be painful, but there was no way he would keep that thing in. He needed to pee and not into a tube.

He grabbed hold of the hose, took a fortifying breath, bit his tongue, and pulled. The tube stung like hell as it came free. He couldn't believe how long the hose to his bladder was.

He reached for the side of the mattress and leaned over. Dizziness assaulted him. He waited for it to subside before he tucked the catheter hose beneath the mattress to ensure no urine dripped onto the floor.

Fortunately, the upset man distracted the nurses. Demetri closed his eyes and took a deep breath. The pain didn't last thankfully, but it was by far the most embarrassing thing he'd ever done.

He searched about his bedside for a bedpan; it was on the floor, a good three feet down. He could sit up all right, but to bend over and reach the pan was going to be a challenge.

He placed a steadying hand on the bedside table, leaned down a few inches and stopped. A wave of nausea struck him. He brought his hand to his head. A thick bandage covered the right side of his skull.

What happened to me? A new fear accompanied his nausea as his hand rubbed over the bandage and down to his face. Gently, he tried to gauge the extent of the damage. His eyes worked, and he was almost certain his mouth was unharmed. His fingers caught on stitches; a gash ran horizontally across his cheek. The cloth bandage wrapped about his head covered the majority of his forehead and right temple. He applied pressure on the wounded area, and pain ensued, but his skull was solid beneath his hand.

Relief washed over him at the realization that he wasn't disfigured. The nausea passed, and he leaned the rest of the way over. It stung when he used the bedpan, but he was relieved to have the catheter out. Finished, he set the used bedpan on the bedside table.

With one ache relieved, he wondered when his petite nurse would return. He leaned back on his pillows and contemplated pretending to be asleep for another day. He liked having her around, and if he were awake, who's to say how much attention he would receive from her?

His decision made, he would play the invalid role. He lay back and rolled his eyes beneath closed lids. He flexed his fingers and toes. His knuckles cracked one by one. The urge to pop his neck and back was strong, but he wasn't going to push his luck.

With a head injury, who knew what could happen?

* * * *

Jaysen started everyday with a quick visit to each patient before she began work with one particular person. Since Demetri's arrival, she started her daily schedule at his bedside. She grabbed the chart from the foot of the sergeant's bed and read the notes the other nurse had jotted down. His catheter bag was empty, so she continued with her routine. She took his wrist into her hand and felt for his pulse.

122 beats per minute. She recorded the vital on his chart.

His pulse was elevated from the earlier vital stats. She set the clipboard on the bedside table and pulled her flashlight out of her pocket. She opened his eyes and waved the flashlight back and forth. Movement. That was a good sign. He had normal pupil dilation, and his eyelids tried to close reflexively.

She turned to pick up her chart and realized it was set on top of a bedpan. A full bedpan? Perplexed, she looked from the bedpan to Demetri.

"Nah," she answered her unspoken question. Another nurse left it here by accident, she mused. Chalking the incident up to mere coincidence, she hung the chart back on the bed rail and took the urine for disposal.

Then it hit her. Elevated heart rate, eye movement, urine in the bedpan. Sergeant Demetri Tiberius was awake!

And he's playing possum!

A smile curved her lips as she retrieved a sterile bedpan and bath supplies. There was one way to be certain, and so she intended to get an answer within the next twenty minutes.

Chapter Three

He listened while the petite nurse placed some items beside him. He heard the tug and scrape of metal rings on a rail from above. The air about him stirred, and he realized that pretending to be asleep was about to get much, much harder.

And hard was exactly what he didn't want to be. Just thoughts about what was going to happen began to bring his formerly limp member to attention.

Giant, hairy, brown moles. Cellulite, chucky cottage cheese thighs. Winter in the Ukraine! He tried frantically to distract himself.

Fingers brushed across his chest and rounded the edge of his sheet to fold it down his torso.

Maggot eaten sheep's intestines!

Her gentle hands grasped his arm, lifted it, and placed it back onto what he assumed was a towel. She walked around the bed and did the same to his other side. The next thing he heard was the splish-splash of water. She must have wrung out a sponge.

Breathe, he reminded himself as he waited for the wet sponge to make contact with his skin. His pulse surged out of control in anticipation. *Where would she start?* He wanted to open his eyes so badly. The apprehension and anxiety knotted his gut.

She began to hum. A warm, wet object that he identified as a sponge, slid smoothly across his collarbone. Left to right, lower and lower, a few inches lower with each pass until she pulled it away. The languid heat of the sponge fired his skin. With his eyes held firmly shut, all of his other senses heightened. He heard her every breath. The sterile smell of the hospital ward was methodically replaced with a lemon soap aroma that mingled with her minty breath. He felt each intake and release of air from her.

Returning the sponge to his skin, she started in tight circular strokes on his chest and upper abdomen. Warm tingles broke out over his body. Every nerve stood alert to her merciless ministrations. Her cool breath blew across his wet skin, and he nearly lost it. A shiver shot straight down his spine to curl his toes.

Rotten eggs! Uri's stinking boots!

He bit down on his tongue to try to lessen the impact of her attentions. The nurse thankfully removed her instrument of torture. She dipped the sponge into the water basin; the familiar splash-splosh noises filled the air. Demetri tried to calm his blood and breathing. He fought for four years in this bloody war to keep peace, so he could do this.

You can do this. He chanted in his mind while waiting for her next tactical maneuver.

Instead of feeling the wet sponge on his skin, the sheet lifted. Cool air met his heated skin as she folded the sheet lower. The linen settled just over his privates. He bit down on his tongue even harder.

Fat-gutted, smelly, toothless, hairy men!

The sponge dripped water onto his sternum, and warm droplets rolled down and down. Firm strokes caressed up along his stomach only to dip lower with each pass. No matter how many disgusting things he brought to mind, the sensations she created were winning. The pressure of the sponge increased, it lowered closer and closer to the center of his alarm.

"Ready to give up?" she asked, her voice amused.

Stunned, he lay confused for a moment. Was she talking to him? He narrowly opened his eyes and glimpsed her smiling face. *She knows!*

"No," he stated, unsure how to feel about what just happened. The woman had known exactly what she was doing all along. She pushed him to the boundaries of what any man could stand. From the look on her face she was thoroughly enjoying his torture too.

"Well, you know what needs to be cleaned next, and I really can't fondle a patient," she set the sponge down on his chest, "so there you go."

Shocked, Demetri watched her disappear behind the sea-foam green curtain that surrounded his bed.

"Wait," he called, half upright on his elbows.

"Yes?" she said, poking her head around the curtain's edge, a mischievous gleam in her alluring amber eyes.

He fumbled with the sheet and swung his feet over the side of the bed. The sponge dropped from his chest to bounce off his lap and land on the floor. He moved too quickly; dizziness hit him hard. Just when he thought he would fall to the floor, her arms wrapped about his midsection, her shoulder steadying him.

She leaned him back onto the bed and propped pillows behind his back so that he could sit upright.

"Sergeant Demetri Tiberius. It's nice to meet you, nurse...?" he said, curiosity in his voice. After all, he still didn't know his tormentor's name.

"Blake, Jaysen Blake," she replied.

Her smile dazzled him as he looked into her beautiful face. Jaysen's features were open and relaxed. In contrast, she'd pulled her hair back in a tight bun. He wanted to reach out and tug her hair free.

"Nurse Blake, is there a Mr. Blake?" he asked, using an American line he'd heard in one of the movies they had shown in the barracks.

"Of course." Her reply dashed his newfound hopes. She bent and retrieved the sponge from the floor. "Although my father likes to be called Jim."

Chapter Four

Four Months Later
Castle Rock Lake, Wisconsin

Jaysen rocked back and forth on the porch swing of her family's log cabin. Far from the desert sands and dry heat of Iraq, fall had changed the leaves on the trees surrounding the vast lake. The sun glowed pink and purple on the fluffy clouds high above, set against a deep blue early morning sky. The reflection glistened and rippled across the mirror-like surface of the water as the gentle wake lapped against the shore. The serene peace of it all warmed her more than the hot cocoa in the coffee mug she held. She inhaled the clean forest air tinted with a hint of chocolate thanks to her drink.

"Gorgeous."

She smiled at Demetri's comment, his voice a familiar rumbling purr. The fact that he was here was a miracle in itself. His recovery had moved at a break-neck pace, taking only two weeks after he woke up.

Demetri was relentless in his pursuit of her. He arranged for flowers to be sent to her room, a room she shared with ten other nurses about fifty feet from his wing in the hospital. The chocolates he managed to smuggle in from the market were the deal breaker. Chocolates were hard to come by for anyone; you could get all the dates you wanted, but good chocolates were rare.

She never intended to get involved with a patient; it was unethical. But Demetri possessed something that she couldn't deny. For the first time in recent years, she was able to laugh without guilt. And he made her feel wonderful. More than wonderful, he made her feel cherished.

Once the doctors ruled that he had no permanent brain damage, he was shipped back to his homeland in the Ukraine. After his departure, loneliness overwhelmed her, impeding her ability to help her patients. She couldn't stay at the hospital when her heart wasn't in her work. Jaysen finished her term and decided to return stateside.

Demetri wrote to her every day that they were apart. Likewise, she wrote to him just as much. Their letters ranged from the mundane day-to-day activities of their lives to their hopes and fears. It was painful to talk to him about Alex's death in combat, but it felt like the final healing of her wounded soul. Opening up to him, letting him into her heart, was the easiest thing she'd ever done.

Two weeks ago, when he received his discharge papers from the

Ukrainian Army, the first thing he did was book a flight to Wisconsin. Just where everyone always wants to go, right?

Before Demetri came into her life, she didn't believe in love at first sight. Now, however, she didn't think she could live without him. But she would have to. In four days, he would leave. Jaysen sighed and looked up at him. She stopped the swing with her foot.

His sandy blond hair brushed the tops of his ears. His cobalt gaze fixed on her face. The light sweater he wore concealed his broad shoulders and muscled body. A thin scar separated his right eyebrow and faded into his forehead, the larger gash that once marred his cheek all but vanished.

"What are you doing up?" she asked as she pulled her legs beneath her on the swing's seat.

He shrugged his shoulders and moved to stand in front of her. "I couldn't sleep."

She reached up and playfully tugged at his sweater. "Dad had you up way too early the past few days. I don't know why you indulge him and let him drag you out fishing at those ungodly hours."

"I like to fish. Besides, I like him, and we were able to talk. You know, when you grow up in an orphanage you miss out on simple things. You're lucky."

He was right. She couldn't imagine growing up in a cramped orphanage with no one to give him love. And no one for him to love in return. It must have been so hard for him as a child.

Jaysen took a sip of her cocoa. Demetri kneeled on the wooden floor planks and wrapped his arms about her sides. He rested his chin on her knees. "I want to talk to you about something."

She didn't like the sober turn of his features. Jaysen was painfully aware of his impending departure and she didn't feel like talking about it. She would rather enjoy their last blissful days together.

"Can't we—?"

"No, I want to talk about this now." When he used that stern voice, his accent thickened. It made her want to giggle despite his serious face. She straightened her shoulders, looked him in the eye, and waited for him to speak.

But he didn't speak. He turned his head on her knees and rested his cheek against them. He inhaled deeply.

"Jaysen, I don't want to leave you. Not Tuesday, not ever." He sat up and took a deep breath, his vulnerable gaze piercing. Even now, with his strong arms at her sides and all his wounds healed, she still wanted to shield him from all harm. The trepidation in his eyes tugged at her heart

113

and soul. "Will you marry me?"

Stunned didn't cover her emotions. Tears stung the backs of her eyes as realization dawned on her. She sat silent and stared back into his hesitant blue eyes. The fear she saw within them made her heart swell.

With shaking hands, she placed her cocoa on the seat beside her, leaned forward, and kissed him. With all the love in her heart, she pressed her lips to his and whispered, "Yes."

Author Bio:

Ava James is an avid writer and reader of everything romance. To learn more about Ava and her work please visit her at: www.avajames.weebly. com.

Under the Christmas Stars
by
Faith Bicknell-Brown

Do two wrong guys and a pair of pink mittens spell doom for Lana's love life, or will a kiss under the Christmas stars prove that love was right under her nose?

Snow fell in enormous cotton ball flakes. The thermometer hovered around the perfect temperature to dump several inches of snow; the evening weather report stated that six or more was possible. Lana tiptoed down the icy sidewalk with her mother, Ann. Her foot slid, and she grabbed her mom's arm. They both looked at each other in dismay. Struggling to maintain her footing, Lana tried to stay upright and hold her mother up as Christmas packages tumbled to the slippery cement.

"Hang on! I got you!"

Lana glanced up into a man's familiar face. Ron Richards grasped her and her mother by their elbows and steadied them. Fat snowflakes landed in his chocolate-brown hair, each one glimmering in the lamplights that had begun to pop on along the street.

"You two go ahead into the store," he said. "I'll pick these up for you." He grabbed hold of Ann, who had started to slide again. "I'll bring your packages and bags inside. Go on before the three of us land in a heap!"

Ann laughed. "Thanks, Ron. You're a dear."

As they practically ice-skated to the door of Tokens to Remember to finish their Christmas shopping, Ann whispered to her daughter, "I don't know why you don't marry him, Lana! Ron's grown into such a dreamy man! And so sweet too."

"Really, Mom," Lana grumbled. "You're worse than a teenage girl."

"He has it bad for you, honey. Why can't you see that?"

Lana opened the door, the bell over it tinkling. Hot air blasted her face. "Ron flirts too much," she said. She scanned the new items of jewelry displayed in the front glass cabinet for Christmas.

A disgruntled snort escaped Ann. "Ron is not a flirt—he's charming. There's a difference. The only time I've ever seen him flirt is when he sees you."

"Men who flirt too much are trouble, Mom." She pointed at a brooch in the case. It wasn't that long ago that someone else who liked to flirt had stomped all over her heart and followed it up by kicking it into the gutter.

115

"Anyway, I'm interested in someone else."

"Now, don't tell me you've already got a date for the company Christmas party this Saturday."

Lana whirled to see her heart's desire. "Derek! I thought you were leaving for Pittsburgh this afternoon?"

"The flight's cancelled due to snow." He grinned at her around the wrapped packages in his arms. "Finished your Christmas shopping, Mrs. Potterson?"

Ann shook her head and wrinkled her nose in distasted as she pushed the brooch across the counter to the clerk. Lana wasn't certain whether the nasty expression was for her taste in jewelry or men. The bell on the door jangled, and Ron entered, battling his way inside with their purchases.

"Will you accompany me to the company Christmas party, Lana?" Derek's grin widened, his eyes glittering mischievously. "Melody can ride over with us if she likes. I know her car is in the garage."

Ron reached them with the presents and rudely shoved by Derek. He handed the bags and boxes over to Ann. The bell over the door rang incessantly as customers filed in and out of the store. A large woman in a bright orange parka struggled past them, pressing everyone against the display cabinet.

Once the lady had gone, Lana said, "I'd love to go with you." She smiled so widely it hurt.

Ron shot her a wounded look; the disappointment in his dark eyes sliced through her happiness. She squelched an odd feeling of guilt.

"I'll let Melody know about your offer of a ride," she said and ignored her mother's disapproving glare.

"Great! I'll pick the two of you up at your apartment around six Friday night." Derek hefted the gifts tighter in his leather-clad arms. "I've got to run. Nice seeing you again, Mrs. Potterson."

Ann snorted derisively. "What kind of man asks two women out on the same date?"

"Mother!" Lana snapped. "He's just offering Melody a ride! After all, she is my roommate and works at the office too!"

Ann colored slightly at the surprised looks from other patrons due to their raised voices. "Why can't she borrow your car?" she asked, lowering her volume.

"See ya around, Lana," Ron said, his tone dull. "Merry Christmas, Ann."

"You too, Ron," Ann called after him as he moved toward the door. "Thanks for your help." She watched him shut the door and navigate the icy patches of sidewalk.

Lana glanced at her mother and followed her gaze. Ron crossed the street on his way to the coffee shop across from Tokens to Remember.

Spinning on her heel, Ann faced her daughter. "You hurt his feelings!"

Lana's mouth dropped open. "I hurt his feelings? Ron and I are co-workers, Mom, that's all."

Her mother replied softly, her I'm-the-mother-and-you're-the-daughter tone in full force. "Have you forgotten that the two of you are also friends and that you have been since you were both long-legged, freckle-faced brats?" She handed the sales clerk the items she'd been examining. "That man cares for you, Lana, and he knows bad news when he sees it—and Derek is bad news. Have you also forgotten that Ron supported and helped you get through the tough times after Nick walked out on you? I don't remember you squawking at him to leave you alone then." She glanced around, and so did Lana. A few patrons realized that their eavesdropping had been noticed; they colored and wandered away. "Let's go get something to eat," said Ann. "I'm shopped out for the day."

Outside, Lana waited for the streetlight to turn, her pride smarting. From the corner of her eye, she saw her mother look over at her.

"I'm sorry, honey. I should keep my big-mouthed opinions to myself more often. I just don't want to see you get hurt again."

Smiling, Lana hooked her arm through her mother's. "I know. Apology accepted. Now, where do you want to eat?"

* * * *

During the next two days, excitement kept Lana on pins and needles. She imagined what a good time she'd have as Derek's date. After the party ended, there would be ice-skating at the office manager's farm, so she borrowed a pair of skates from her neighbor across the hall and a fuzzy muff from Melody. After her fiancé, Nick, ditched her, taking all her savings in a joint account and nearly everything in her apartment, Lana stopped dating. So why was she going out with Derek? She couldn't resist his blond good looks and big muscles, that's why. Plus, he had a smile that could melt a gal's panties.

Regardless, it was mandatory that any employee who didn't show at the company party didn't receive their Christmas bonus. Lana needed her bonus to replace some of the things that Nick had stolen. What worried her most was another confrontation with Ron. For the past two days, he'd avoided her at work, which was quite a feat when their desks were only a couple of yards apart.

Her mother arrived about ten minutes before Derek did. "Here's my pair of Isotoner gloves, dear. I thought these would be more comfortable to wear than that muff you borrowed."

"That works out great," Melody said. Her pale blue gaze scanned the apartment. A frown marred the smooth skin between her strawberry blonde eyebrows. "I can't seem to find my pink mittens anywhere. I just wore them yesterday."

Lana tossed her friend the muff and accepted her mother's gloves.

"Where's my Chapstick?" Melody riffled through her coat pockets.

Rummaging in her purse, Lana held it out. "Here, you put it in my bag this morning." Looking at her friend, she experienced a wave of insecurity. What did Derek see in her when her roommate was a Tanya Roberts look-alike? Self-consciously, she brushed back her long hair and wondered if she had on enough eye shadow to bring out her plain green eyes. Oh, well, she was the one Derek had asked out so that counted for something, didn't it?

A horn blasted out on the street. Ann peeped out the window. "Goodness! A true gentleman would come to the door!"

Lana held the door open for Melody and hurried out into the hall behind her. "Lock the door when you leave, Mom!" Lana called.

* * * *

Midway through the party, Lana received her bonus and was extremely pleased with the amount. Alone, she stood in a corner, sipping spiked punch and nibbling a sugar-sprinkled cookie. What was keeping Derek? It was time to leave for the skating pond; several co-workers had already left the party. A few stragglers by the door debated about the stock market during Christmas, and clustered round the Christmas tree, the wallflowers discussed something about plans for New Year's. Worried and sensing the worst, Lana grabbed her things and hurried out to the smoker's area to see if Derek had left the building.

Cars pulled out of the icy parking lot. Down the street, the traffic light blinked from red to green and back again. Lana picked her way across the pavement toward Derek's Mustang. A filigree of frost had spread across the windshield and the passenger's side window. She checked the driver's door and found it unlocked. Maybe she'd get lucky and find the keys in it too. That way, she could listen to music with the heater on while she waited for Derek and Melody to come out. Surely they would realize she wasn't in the office and come looking for her.

Sliding behind the steering wheel, Lana shut the door. Damn. No keys.

Come to think of it, she recalled Derek slipping them into his coat pocket. Headlights swept the Mustang's interior. A disturbing thought flittered through her brain, and Lana twisted to look out the rearview window. Many of the employees had carpooled to the farm and would pick up their vehicles later. She hoped that Derek and Melody hadn't car pooled to the farm without her.

She started to get out of the car, but something in the backseat caught her attention.

Her mouth dropped open. Pain stabbed her gut.

A pair of fuzzy, pink mittens.

Oh, no. Not again.

"I can't seem to find my pink mittens anywhere. I just wore them yesterday."

Furious, she stepped out of the car and slammed the door—hard. How could she be so stupid *again*?

Determined to find Derek and confront him, Lana stormed across the parking lot. As she passed the side entrance to the building, a giggle erupted from the breezeway where the janitors had curtained it off to keep the snow from drifting there. She paused and backtracked. Dread pooled in her heart. She peeped around the edge of the tarpaulin, sensing the worst.

Derek stood with his arms around Melody, his mouth to hers, their bodies pressed so tightly together, the passion between them enough to melt the Polar Ice Caps. Her roommate whimpered with pleasure.

Humiliated, face burning, Lana retreated. She pulled her hat from her coat pocket and tugged it over her head. She didn't even bother to put on her Isotoner gloves, but jammed her hands into her pockets instead. Might as well go home. It was obvious her evening was a farce, and besides, everyone else had left, so she couldn't even catch a ride out to the farm.

She rummaged for her cell phone in her purse. A quick call to the two taxi companies only netted her more disappointment. All available taxis were busy at the business district where most of the Christmas parties were in progress. Her parents had gone to a friend's house, and Lana didn't know their name or number. What now? Dejected and fighting tears, she started walking home.

Two blocks later, she saw a little coffee-and-donut shop. Lana decided to stop in and drown her foul mood in a cup of joe. With a powdered donut and a cappuccino clasped tightly in cold, chapped hands, she sat down in a corner booth.

"Mind if I sit down?" Ron's voice rumbled behind her.

"Sure." Lana didn't turn around. She'd know that deep, voice anywhere.

"Someone told me they'd seen you walking and wondered if you were going out to the big blast the office manager is having." He signaled the waitress. "I thought I'd head this way and see if I could find you."

Lana shrugged.

"Where's Derek?"

"With a pair of pink mittens," she replied behind her steaming cup.

"Pink mittens?" He frowned.

"Melody."

Realization crossed his face. "Oh, jeez...I'm sorry, Lana."

She shrugged and bit her lip to keep it from trembling. Finally, she tried a bit of lightheartedness to change the subject. "Didn't you drive tonight? It's terribly cold to walk. That's why I stopped in here."

"No," he answered, "but you know the cold doesn't bother me. It's such a beautiful evening, I decided to walk. Plus, this coat is super warm." His gaze met hers. A strange flutter wound its way through her, as if a butterfly had lost its way. "If you don't mind some company, I'll walk you home."

The pleading, hopeful light in Ron's deep, dark eyes was too sweet for her to refuse. "I'd like that very much," she said.

They finished their drinks, bundled up, and left the café. Somewhere from an outside speaker Bing Crosby's *White Christmas* echoed across the frozen streets. Ron took her hand in his, something they had always done as kids, and together, they strolled toward her block. The clear night sky boasted a googolplex of stars, ones that glittered so brightly in the heavens that Lana paused to admire them.

"It almost looks like the stars could be hand-plucked from the sky, doesn't it?" Ron observed.

She smiled at him. Somehow, he always had a way of sensing her thoughts. She squeezed his hand, and they continued their stroll. The icy sidewalks shimmered in the streetlights; salt crunched beneath their boots.

A white cloud plumed around Ron's face as he spoke. "I'm sorry about what happened tonight." He didn't look at her.

"No, you're not." She smiled despite her smarting pride. "You don't like Derek, and now, neither do I."

Chuckling, Ron said, "No, I'm not sorry, but I am sorry you got hurt again."

"It's okay. I should've been aware of all the telltale signs. Derek was just using me to get to Melody, although I wish she'd been up front with me. I feel really stupid." She realized Ron's voice reminded her of velvet, and those brilliant dark eyes of his twinkled like polish onyx. "I'll share a secret with you."

He glanced at her, his smile tugging at her heart. "What secret?"

"I'm deliriously happy with my new escort." She relaxed, knowing she truly meant her words. "I'm sorry I've been so awful to you lately."

He paused and turned to look down into her face.

Taking a step closer, she reached out to him, but her feet shot out from under her. Ron tried to grab her, but his footing slid too, and he landed on top of her.

"You okay?" His worried gaze scanned her face.

Lana burst out laughing. "Good thing we have such heavy coats on! Any more winter insulation in this getup of mine and I would've bounced."

Their laughter filled the street, but just as quickly, Ron captured her lips with his.

The sensation of his mouth upon hers, his arms around her body, and the cold, winter breeze prompted a response from Lana that surprised her. She moaned and kissed him back.

Moments later, he raised his head, reluctantly breaking their kiss. "Are you okay with this?"

Lana nodded. Desire lit up his eyes, and a thrill spiraled through her body.

"Think maybe we should get up before we melt the ice with another kiss?" A huge grin spread over his face. "Might be pretty embarrassing if someone finds us frozen to the sidewalk like this in the morning."

With both of them laughing almost too hard to get up, Ron helped her to her feet. She shivered, and he pulled her closer. Lana willingly stepped into his embrace, his arms giving her comfort, as if she'd just come home.

They passed a Santa jingling a bell for the Salvation Army. Ron tossed a handful of coins into the kettle. Continuing around the corner, Lana snuggled back into his arms. Somewhere the street speakers' music switched to *Jingle Bells*.

"Do you want to start over or just make up?" Ron laughed, the sound warming her.

"I thought we just did." She shot him an impish glance.

They halted at the edge of the town park that had been over-decorated with festive lights. Every tree dripped with icicle lights, and each bush, park bench, trash can, and water fountain boasted twinkling colored bulbs. A glowing Santa with his sleigh and eight reindeer lit up the area in front of the wading pool.

Ron turned, facing her. "Those feelings I had as a kid have had a lot of time to grow."

Lana smiled. "That makes two of us. I just wish I hadn't denied it for so long."

"We forgot the mistletoe." A disappointed note crept into his voice.

"Do we need it?" She leaned against his body.

This time, Ron kissed her softly under the twinkling Christmas stars.

Author Bio:

Faith Bicknell-Brown also writes as Zinnia Hope and as J. Emberglass. She's represented by TriadaUS Literary Agency. You can learn more about Faith and her work at: www.faithbicknellbrown.com.

He's On The Menu
by
Savannah Chase

Waitress Jessie Patrick crashes her car into a tour bus that belongs to rock star Ian knight. Now Ian's ready to show her he's just the thing she needs on her menu.

Chapter One

The windshield wipers barely kept up with the pounding rain.

Jessie pushed the button for the emergency lights. The signals flashed as she drove below the speed limit. With minimal visibility in front of her, she gripped the steering wheel so tightly her knuckles turned white. Her eyes kept scanning the mirrors, and she did her best to see the road ahead of her.

Please let me get home in one piece.

The normally congested streets glimmered wetly. Crowds had taken refuge in the warm confines of cafés and bars; condensation shrouded the establishments' plate-glass windows.

Jessie shivered, and goose bumps covered her skin. She reached over and turned the heater's dial. She wished she was at home in dry clothes curled up with a soft blanket and a cup of hot tea in her hand.

She couldn't help but shiver from the water that continued to fall from her hair and down her neck. Droplets rolled down her waitress uniform now soaked through. At this rate, she'd end up with a nasty cold.

A sudden stop and the sound of crunching metal startled Jessie. She shrieked as her forehead cracked the steering wheel. Thank God she hadn't been driving any faster or the airbags might have deployed. Rain washed over the windshield, the wipers struggling to keep up, but she couldn't see anything beyond the car's grill ornament.

"Darn it! No! Please don't let me have hit someone." She shifted the car into park and turned the engine off. Jessie swallowed a lump in her throat. Frantically, she reached for her seatbelt with damp, shaking hands. Once the seatbelt clicked, her heart raced a mile a minute. Tears streamed down her face. She didn't know what she would do if she'd harmed anyone.

She opened the car door and got out. Dark clouds blanketed the sky, and the rain still fell fast, hard. Jessie inspected the damage and what she'd crashed her car into. Every possible thought ran through her head as she looked at the bus she'd just hit. It wasn't just any bus. Oh, no...this was a large, black-and-silver tour bus.

This couldn't be happening to her. How on earth would she explain this to her insurance company? How would she explain this to the owner of the bus?

Her shoes squeaked with every step she took. Water sloshed around her toes, and her running shoes were ready to fall off at any moment. She approached to knock on the bus's door, but it opened before she touched it.

"I'm sorry. I'm so sorry. I didn't see your bus parked here," she called out.

"My bus driver is going to kill you," a voice said.

Trembling, Jessie waited for someone to come out. She didn't mean to crash her car into anything, especially a bus. She only hoped that if anybody was inside that they weren't hurt.

"Achoo!"

"Bless you," said the voice. She looked toward the window and saw a shadow moving around.

Once the occupant finally appeared, she did a double take. At the top of the stairs, Ian Knight stood only a few meters away from her in nothing but a pair of dark jeans. He ran his fingers through his messy black hair in an attempt to tame it. Right away, the black-and-white dragon tattoos over his heart caught her attention. Each faced the other and breathed fire towards the middle. She'd seen the tat in photos, but it looked totally different in person.

I must have hit my head really hard to see Ian Knight. Maybe I'm not even here and this is all just a dream. With my luck, I'm probably passed out in my car drooling out the side of my mouth.

She closed her mouth.

The guy was a mega star. Ian Knight, the lead singer and guitarist of one of the biggest bands in the world—Full Service—had been topping the charts with their latest CD and cleaning up at award shows. Last she'd heard, their latest CD, *Take Me On,* had reached triple-platinum status and held onto number one on the Billboard charts since its release five months ago.

He walked down two steps and motioned her into the bus. "Don't just stand there, climb inside."

Jessie followed him up the steps, every part of her dripping water, and shivered harder. Her teeth chattered so loudly that Ian shot her a sympathetic glance.

Once she reached the top of the stairs, the door closed behind Jessie, and warmth surrounded her. The inside of the bus, complete with a mirrored ceiling, looked like an apartment furnished with black leather couches, a small kitchen that included a fridge, television, a booth to sit and eat, and so much more.

Ian disappeared for a moment, and she took that time to call the tow truck. He returned holding two large, white bath towels.

"By the way, you weren't hurt, were you?" he asked.

"No, I'm fine. But that's more than I can say about your bus and my car," she answered.

He opened one of the towels. "I'm glad you weren't injured. Now, dry yourself off. You don't want to catch a cold."

She reached for it, but he walked over and wrapped the towel around her.

"That's better," he said with a wink and a smile.

Jessie bit her lip. He didn't give her just any smile. He gave her one of his *sexy* smiles. The one that always made her insides melt. His signature smile for photos.

She needed to snap out of it. Ian Knight was a rock star with women all over the globe. He wasn't interested in her. Flirting was part of his nature.

Jessie had to admit that he worked fast, but she'd watched him closely the past couple of years. She'd read all about his sexcapades in the supermarket tabloids, always photographed with different women on his arm. She wasn't about to become another notch on his superstar belt. He could forget it. She wasn't a groupie, and although she might love his music and think he was totally hot, that was as far as it went.

Ian handed her the other towel and waited as she dried her hair.

"Thank you," she said and snuggled herself against the fabric. The bath sheet still contained the smell of fabric softener and a hint of men's cologne, probably Ian's.

"Why don't you have a seat and I'll make you something hot to drink."

"You don't have to go through all that trouble for me," she told him.

"Really, I don't mind."

"I'll have some tea, if you have any."

Jessie glanced around the bus as Ian prepared the drinks in the tiny kitchen area.

What on earth is he doing here all alone in the tour bus? Where's the rest of the band and the bus driver?

The whistling of the kettle jarred her attention back to Ian.

"So, I guess I should start by asking the beautiful woman who drove into my bus what her name is," he said.

Jessie's cheeks grew warm. "Again, I'm so very sorry for the damage I've caused. Is your bus driver really going to kill me?"

"No, Ben won't kill you. That's me just trying to be funny. He'll be angry, but accidents happen. It must be raining harder than I thought for you to drive off the side of the road into a parked tour bus. I'm just glad that you weren't hurt." Ian picked up both of the steaming mugs and moved toward her. A shiver crawled down her spine, and she crossed her arms to stop herself from trembling. He placed a mug down on the table in front of her. She caught the look he gave her. "Why don't I grab you a change of dry clothes? They'll be too big for you, but it's better than the ones you have on now. You really shouldn't sit there all wet," he said, his attention focused solely on her.

Oh, my goodness! He can probably see everything I've got on underneath. At least he didn't mention the stains all over my clothes.

"That's ok," she replied, embarrassment in her voice. "The tow truck should be here any time, and I'll be on my way. It's kind of you to offer. Thank you."

He smiled devilishly. "A beautiful woman like you is a pleasure to have around."

Jessie tore her gaze away from his and looked at the floor. She only hoped that the tow truck would arrive soon. With all his compliments and charm, Ian became more and more irresistible.

"Why the red cheeks?" he asked.

She needed to stop herself from turning any redder. *This is Ian, and this is all a part of his game.*

A period of awkwardness passed between them. The bus door opening interrupted the moment.

They both turned toward the stairs.

"Ian, what the heck happened to the bus?" a voice asked. "I leave for just–oh, Ian, I'm sorry, man. I didn't know you invited female company. What happened?"

"Ben, it's a minor accident," Ian answered firmly.

Jessie wrung her hands. *So that's the bus driver Ian mentioned.*

Jessie stood up. "I'm sorry. The accident is my fault. I crashed into the bus. The rain came down so hard...and I just didn't see the bus parked here."

"The bus isn't so bad, but your car is a different story. We need to have this rig looked at when we hit the next city. By the way, Miss, there's a tow truck parked outside."

The instant the words left Ben's mouth, the honk of a horn penetrated the bus.

Jessie reached inside her apron, produced a pen and paper, and wrote something down.

She handed Ben the paper. "Here's my insurance information, and my name is Jessie Patrick."

Ben walked to the front of the bus and returned with a business card. He handed it to her. "Here's our info," he said.

Jessie placed the towel on the couch and tucked the paper away in her apron pocket. "I better get going. The truck is waiting. Thank you for the tea, Mr. Knight," she said. She made her way to the front of the bus and down the steps.

Walking past the bus she heard the conversation between Ben and Ian through the open window. She glanced up and saw Ian looking out at her. Their gazes met. She sensed he wanted to say something but there was uncertainty in his eyes too.

Ben stood behind him. "Ian, we have to get going. We have to arrive in Toronto by five and we still have a long way to go. This fog is going to slow us down, so we need all the extra time we can get. The band is already there waiting for you."

Ian faced him. "I need five minutes, and after that, we're gone."

Jessie hurried to the tow truck and climbed in. She looked back, but the bus was no longer visible. Just like that, Ian was gone.

Chapter Two

Two weeks passed since Jessie's accidental encounter with Ian Knight. He left as if their paths had never crossed. She got her car fixed, her insurance increased, and life went on as if nothing had ever happened.

Ian was somewhere in Europe with his band, living the rock-star life, and she'd returned to working at Rock Around the Clock.

Friday's lunch shift was in full swing. Patrons packed the diner. Chatter came from every direction as orders were taken. Waitresses hustled between the tables carrying trays filled with plates and platters of food and drinks. The smell of just-off-the-grill hamburgers, golden toast, hot coffee and many other foods wafted through the air—all the aromas that made a person's stomach rumble the minute they walked in the place.

Jessie headed towards table eight, but one of the waitresses stopped her.

Mary balanced her tray of platters. "Jessie, the boss wants to talk to you about something important."

"Can you cover my tables while I'm gone?" Jessie asked.

"Sure, that's not a problem."

Frank probably wants me to pull an extra shift. He knew she would say yes. She always did.

Tucking her pen and note pad into her apron, she made her way behind the counter and to the back where Frank's office was located.

Although the door stood ajar, Jessie knocked on it. Through the small crack she heard the wheels of his chair slide across the floor towards the entrance. Moments later, the door swung open.

She pushed the door farther.

Frank covered the phone receiver. "Give me a second."

His office was small but always tidy. His supplies and folders lay neatly on his desk. "Uh-huh...uh-huh...okay. That can be arranged. Okay, we will see you tonight," Frank said. He hung up. "Sorry about that."

"Mary said you wanted to see me right away. What's up?"

"We have a customer who has booked the diner for a private event, and I could really use your help tonight. The diner will be closed to the public, and the company has booked the place until two in the morning. So, what do you say?"

Jessie shrugged. "That's fine. You know I'll be here. I don't have anything planned anyways. I can definitely use the extra cash."

"Oh, and the customer requested you as the waitress tonight. They said that you're one of their favorites," Frank added.

"That could be any one of my customers."

Frank smiled. "Okay, so I need you here at five."

"Do you know who booked the diner?" she asked.

"Nope, not a clue."

"Well I guess I'll find out tonight."

* * * *

After her shift ended, she only had enough time to go home, take a shower, and grab a fresh uniform. Her usual uniform needed washing badly. During the lunchtime rush, a little boy had decided to use her for target practice. Dark red ketchup stains covered her yellow-and-blue dress. There was no way she could wear the uniform tonight.

Later, Jessie pulled up to the diner's parking lot entrance, expecting to see the parking lot packed with cars and people arriving for tonight's party. To her surprise, not a single car sat in the lot except for Bobbie's, the evening cook.

The emptiness reminded her of how the place looked in the early mornings. She always arrived to an empty lot; birds chirped melodically and often brought a smile to her face. The fresh, crisp morning air signaled the start of each new day. Sometimes the fog would just be settling, and it made her think of something out of a scene from a scary movie. By this time, the aroma from the kitchen would be wafting around the lot. Steam bellowed from the vents, and the back door to the kitchen would be ajar to let in the fresh air. Driving towards the staff parking area, she glanced at the door. Both the entrance and vents were shut.

She figured the party would start later, but one thing still bothered her. Where was the other staff that would be helping out tonight? Five o'clock had already passed, and from the look of things, she was the only one who had arrived so far.

Jessie parked the car in the spot closest to the back door and went inside. Once she closed the door behind her, she noted the silence. No noises came from the front, no staff shuffled around getting things ready, no dishes clinked and no patrons chatted. A sudden unease slipped over her.

Slowly, Jessie made her way toward the front of the diner, and as she neared the entrance to the front counter, a dim light caught her eye.

"Hello, I'm here. Where is everybody? Bobbie, I know you're here. I saw your car parked outside," she called out, hoping someone would answer.

Soft music reached her.

When she finally stepped out onto the diner's black-and-white checkered floor, she gasped. A sea of small candles blanketed the diner. Shadows danced on the walls and over the booths' white seats. More tapers lined the counter and every table and booth in the place. The beauty of the room left Jessie in awe.

On the floor in front of her lay red and white rose petals arranged in the form of an arrow pointing to the last booth on the left.

Who could've gone through all this effort to set something like this up?

With her curiosity piqued, Jessie followed the arrow to the last booth. There, she found a white box in the middle of the table with one red rose on top of it. She picked it up with the attached card. The sweet smell of the rose wafted through the air.

The card read: Jessie open me.

This mystery person did all of this for me? I thought it was supposed to be a private party? She smelled the rose. Not wanting to waste another second, she placed the flower next to the box and opened the gift.

A gasp escaped her lips. She pulled out a beautiful red, strapless dress. She recognized the Jinjo original design logo. One of his items probably cost a month's salary or more. She could never afford something so fine on a waitress' paycheck. A pair of red high heels from the Jinjo collection accompanied the dress.

A black ribbon tied another card to one of the dress straps. This one read: Please put me on.

Jessie glanced around the diner. Was someone hiding? Watching her? She placed the dress down and walked towards the other end of the diner to be sure nobody hid in one of the other booths.

She returned to the table, picked up the box and all its contents, and headed for the ladies room. She opened the black wooden doors and searched around in the dark for the light switch. Upon finding it, she flipped it on and locked the door behind her.

Butterflies danced in her stomach. Curiosity assailed her. Jessie kept wondering who could have done all this. She obviously had a secret admirer. The only person who came to mind was John. As a regular customer at the diner, he always took the opportunity to flirt with her.

He's handsome, polite, and seems like a great guy. She'd found out from their numerous chats that he worked in the largest law firm downtown. She knew he could definitely afford to buy expensive clothes, especially the dress. He'd also asked her out before, but she'd turned him down; however, he didn't seem deterred by it. He'd said he'd find a way to get into her heart regardless.

Jessie changed into the dress. *It won't hurt to find out if it's John after all. Besides, whoever it is has gone through so much trouble for me.*

She did her best to get herself readied and touched up her makeup. Before she walked back out, she glanced in the mirror one last time.

In the dining room, she heard someone moving around in the kitchen. She neared the order window and peeked through it. The movement abruptly stopped.

"Hello, is anyone there? If you are, please come out. I want to know who did all of this for me."

Silence surrounded her. *What's the point of doing all of this if they aren't going to reveal themselves?*

Jessie noticed something different about the roses on the floor. This time, an arrow pointed to the other end of the diner.

This must all be a part of his plan; he wanted her to wait and wonder, to anticipate what's to come. Her heart beat frantically with every booth she passed. Slowly, she neared the last one. She'd checked it earlier, and it had been empty. He'd probably used the time she'd left to get ready to set the stage for the rest of his plan.

Jessie paused two steps away from the final booth. She inhaled deeply and tried to let go of some of her nervousness. It didn't help at all; her heart beat even faster.

She stepped up to the booth. Someone had rearranged the table for two people. Another red rose stood in the middle of the tabletop, and two white candles burned on each side of it.

"Hello, Jessie," said a voice behind her.

At that moment, she could have sworn her heart leaped out of her chest. His was a voice she knew all too well; a voice she'd heard numerous times before.

She turned to face her secret admirer.

"Ian," she said breathlessly.

He reached for her hand and lifted it to his lips. "You're surprised to see me?" he said.

Oh, his kiss was dangerous. Excitement rushed from her head right down to her toes.

Jessie pinched herself. She needed to make sure this wasn't a dream or even a hallucination. Maybe her crush on Ian was making her crazy. A part of her regretted leaving so fast the day of the accident. Although he was a famous rock star, she couldn't fight the fact that he affected her just like all the other women who adored him.

Nope, it's not a dream. It's really happening. There, inches away from her, stood Ian Knight dressed in a black suit, white shirt, and light blue tie.

No more tight black jeans, and his messy hair was gelled to perfection. *Oh, my gosh...and he smells divine!* This was the same man who rushed into her life like the storm had that day and he'd vanished just as quickly. The man that she couldn't get out of her head since.

"I-I am," she replied.

"So, I guess my plan worked?" he said, smiling devilishly.

"Your plan?"

"That day when you left, I went after you, but I was too late. You'd already left with the tow truck. I tried to track you down, but your number wasn't listed. I even tried to get it from the insurance company, but they wouldn't give me any info."

Surprise settled over Jessie. She couldn't hide her smile.

"I remembered your uniform, so I did some digging around and found out that the only place that used them was here at Rock Around the Clock."

Jessie smiled. "You did all that just to find me?"

"Yes. Why not? You're a beautiful woman who's hard to forget."

Speechless, Jessie gaped at him. She never would have imagined he'd remembered her for anything other than the woman who wrecked his tour bus.

"Now, Jessie, would you do me the honor of joining me for dinner tonight?" he asked.

A part of her was leery of his intentions. She'd read enough about him and all his women to know better. Maybe this was just another one of his ploys to get her into his bed. Still, no matter how much she tried to fool herself, she couldn't. Something about him made her heart race. She didn't know anything about Ian except the things that were written in magazines. Those types of facts she didn't want to know. She desired to know the *real* Ian. The type of man he was once the cameras weren't around, when people had stopped following him, and no screaming girls were throwing themselves at him as he walked by. So far, this side of him appealed to her, and she wanted to see more of it.

"I would probably hate myself if I turned down your request. So, yes, I'll join you," she replied.

Ian took her hand.

"You're such a gentleman." Her smile grew so wide her jaws ached.

He helped her sit down. Before he seated himself on the other side, he reached into his pocket and produced a phone. Shutting it off, he dropped it back into his jacket. She didn't know why, but his action impressed her. With his lifestyle, Ian was a busy guy, but he still made the effort to break away from his rock-star life so that he could spend the evening with her.

He's on the Menu

* * * *

The evening didn't come close to anything like she'd expected. The night turned out to be amazing and enjoyable. Ian thought of everything. They were served a tasty Fettuccine Alfredo with red wine. For dessert, he'd planned black-and-white chocolate mousse cake. Each meal Ian served himself. Bobbie stayed in the kitchen the whole time, only helping Ian when needed.

After they finished eating, Bobbie helped clear the table and returned to the kitchen, leaving them alone once more. Watching him go, Jessie smiled. Bobbie was not only a great co-worker, but a wonderful friend too. *I'll have to make a point of thanking him tomorrow for everything he's done—and Frank for letting Ian do this.*

Surprisingly, she found it easy to talk to Ian. He took the time to listen—really listen—to what she said. They sat and talked as if they had known one another for a long time. Ian showed her more and more that he was nothing close to what fame had made him out to be.

"I want you to know that tonight has been one of the best nights I've experienced in a long time," he said, placing his hand over hers.

Jessie smiled. "Me too."

Ian slid out of his seat and reached out his hand. "Dance with me," he said.

She placed her hand in his. Ian led her to the middle of the diner, and they danced the night away. Jessie knew she would never forget this one night, her very own fairytale.

Once the song ended, Jessie couldn't tear herself away from Ian's gaze. His warm blue eyes looked at her with passion. No man had ever gazed at her that way before. With him, she felt like the only woman in the world. His eyes spoke the words that he didn't. She wanted to stay this way forever.

He lowered his head toward hers. Jessie quickly moved a stray brown hair from her face. He smiled at her action and placed a gentle kiss on her lips. It took her breath away, and, as his lips left hers, she mourned the loss of the contact, a kiss that a woman could only dream of. One that she never thought would happen to her, and the perfect way to end a magical evening.

The following morning, Jessie awoke to the sound of the alarm clock. For a moment, she wondered if everything that had happened with Ian was only a dream. She shot up in bed.

The red dress lay on the back of the bedroom chair.

Her storybook evening hadn't been a dream after all. She squealed at the thought of everything that had happened. She'd spent an evening with Ian! Not Ian Knight the rock star but Ian Knight the guy who made her heart do summersaults. The man that made her melt whenever he looked at her.

Knocking startled her. Someone banged hard on the door—and at seven in the morning.

Jessie jumped out of bed and grabbed her robe. She looked through the peephole at a young woman with a large white box.

Jessie released the lock.

"You Jessie Patrick?" the young woman asked.

"Yes."

The delivery lady handed the box to her. She pointed to the clipboard. "Sign here, please."

Jessie held onto the box with one hand and signed with the other.

The second the woman left, Jessie locked the door and took her delivery to the table. She ripped into it like a kid at Christmas. Inside the box, she found two dozen red roses. A card attached to them read: Jessie, I want to thank you for last night. You truly are a beautiful woman, and you took my breath away. I had an amazing time. When can I see you again? Ian.

Jessie knew deep down in her heart that this was the beginning of something different, something special. She'd finally found the man she'd been searching for. The one man that wanted her just the way she was.

6 Months Later

Tuesday September 27, 2008
Rock on Weekly

Many of you know Ian Knight as the lead singer of Full Service. He's made women scream until there was nothing left for them to scream with. He's been living the highlife traveling around the globe and playing sold-out shows to crowds of thousands. He's the envy of many men. His face is plastered on thousands of walls, and women can't get enough of him and his music. However, he's single no more. Ian has met the woman of his dreams. She isn't an actress or famous musician. She's not anyone you might have heard about before now. The gal who has stolen this hunk's heart is Jessie Patrick, a waitress at Rock Around the Clock, and Ian's the only one on her menu. Their story began on a rainy day with a car accident, but their paths crossed once again, all thanks to Ian. He'd arranged a secret meeting, and the rest is now history.

As I write this, I can hear the hearts breaking all around the world. All the ladies who have always dreamt that maybe, just maybe, they would one day catch his eye will have to bow out now. Jessie's tale is one that only happens in fairytales. Now Ian will have his eye on only one woman, the one who has captured his heart.

Author Bio:
  Savannah writes erotica and romance. Whether you want sweaty sex or sweet romance, she's written just the thing for you. For more info check out: www.savannahchase.com.

The Unexpected Gift
by
Lisa Alexander-Griffin

This story is for my mother Fay Treakle, and an unforgettable, dear friend—who I'll one day meet again.

Elise and Cade both grieve extraordinary past losses. Will a Christmastime miracle allow them a second chance at love?

Prologue
December, 2004

Elise wrung her hands, stared at the phone, and willed it to ring. She'd gone to the doctor just that morning to find out why she felt so fatigued, so nauseous.

The mesmeric twinkle of lights drew her gaze to the window. *Christmas Eve.* She should be happy, but she wasn't. Her chest tightened into a painful knot. Her husband's face, his love of life, surfaced in her mind. James had been gone for only two weeks, but a long and bleak future stretched ahead of her. An eternity.

She coughed, fighting the urge to gag. Food made her queasy. Like clockwork, she'd vomited every morning. *What's wrong with me?*

The phone rang shrilly, shattering the silence. Her nerves already shot, she jerked. *I should have died with him.*

Elise took a deep breath and reached for the phone.

"Hello," she said, cringing at the quiver in her voice.

"Elise," Dr Mansfield said. "Is that you? You sound strange." His voice faltered, and a chuckle rumbled through the phone. "I have what I hope is wonderful news. It seems that James has left you a miraculous Christmas gift. You, Elise, are going to be a mother."

Elise stared at the receiver. Her eyes blurred. *Even in death, James knows what I need and takes care of me from beyond the grave.*

She smiled for the first time in weeks. Proof of their love would live on long after she was gone. Although she couldn't share that joy with her husband, this baby would give her strength to endure the holidays.

Elise released a thankful sigh. "Thank you, Dr. Mansfield. I'll get back with you—when I've had a chance to digest this unexpected, but wonderful news."

"You've been under a lot of stress lately. I'd like you to call for an appointment soon."

"I will." She hung up the phone. Her hand fell to her stomach.

The baby was an answered prayer, a gift from God. Somehow she'd manage. The will to live surged inside her. She glimpsed light at the end of a long, dark tunnel.

Bowing her head, she wept.

Chapter One

December 2006

Multi-colored lights beckoned Elise. Perched on her hip, her daughter, Jamie, gurgled with delight. Elise pushed through the doors of Willingham's Toy Store, and the toddler's eyes lit with excitement.

They cruised the overstuffed toy aisles. A huge Christmas tree twinkled in the store's center. Nearing the tree, Elise spotted Santa with a child on his lap. She looked down at her daughter, her heart swelling with emotion. *I can actually enjoy Christmas now.*

Two long years had passed. She hugged her daughter tightly. Thanks to her precious gift, life moved forward in its never-ending circle.

Elise stepped into the long line and waited. When it came their turn, she moved near Santa's chair. Her gaze locked with the bluest eyes she'd ever seen. He smiled and took Jamie onto his lap.

"What would you like from Santa this year, little lady?" he crooned.

Jamie grinned, jutted out her two tiny lower teeth, and gazed up at him through innocent brown eyes. Drool spiraled from her mouth, dampening his hands.

"Ba-be," she babbled.

Elise laughed, and her daughter joined in. Jamie's tiny arms crossed. She imitated a mother rocking her child.

"She wants a baby doll," Elise explained. "Also a couple puzzles and a few fairytales. Jamie loves it when I read to her."

Jamie clapped her hands, giggled, and tugged Santa's beard.

"Be nice, honey," Elise scolded. She laughed, reaching for her daughter. "Let's not disrobe Santa. We wouldn't want to traumatize the other children."

The toy store Santa smiled, and Elise's breath caught in her throat.

"You may think me forward," the Santa said, "but I'd love to have coffee with you on my next break."

Shock shuddered through Elise. She stepped back and scrutinized the Santa. His eyes held kindness; his smile seemed genuine. What could it hurt to meet with him? She needed to move on with her life and stop hiding. In the coffee shop, they would be safe. She looked down at Jamie.

"What time is your break?" she asked.

The Santa glanced at his watch, his smile barely visible behind the snow-white beard. "In ten minutes."

Elise nodded, mesmerized by his twinkling blue eyes. She hefted Jamie on her hip and eased away.

Ten minutes later, doubt heavy in her stomach, she sat in a coffee shop booth. Reinforcing her hold on a squirming Jamie, she chewed her lip. Never had she acted so rashly before. Why had she agreed to this?

Christmas made her crazy. Why did the lure of a Santa suit and the warm glimmer of his eyes make her feel she could trust this man? *Damn, I'm just lonely.*

Elise gathered her things, pushed up from the seat, and turned to leave. In her haste, she bumped into a hard chest and looked up. A face like none she'd ever imagined stared down at her. Hauntingly familiar blue eyes twinkled.

The man was no regular Santa; he was Santa extraordinaire. Heat fused throughout her body, tingled to the tips of her toes. She averted her gaze only to glimpse bronze skin and a light furring of hair through the vee of his blue shirt.

Lord above, it's been a long two years.

Chapter Two

"I hope you weren't leaving." He stepped closer, gently nudging Jamie under the chin.

Her daughter cackled.

Elise smiled. "I'll admit it crossed my mind."

"Good thing I got here when I did." He clapped, holding out his hands. Jamie leaned toward him, her chubby hands reaching. Tiny fingers curled around his, and she held on.

Elise settled into the booth and rolled her eyes. *My daughter's such a little traitor.* Jamie patted the man's cheek. Elise grinned behind her hand. *And a little flirt.*

The Santa sat down across from Elise. His gaze locked with hers. He released a nervous laugh. "Guess we should introduce ourselves."

Elise lost herself in the depths of his azure eyes. She ripped her gaze away and wiped Jamie's chin with a napkin. "You first."

"Cade McPherson." He held out his hand. She laid the napkin aside and placed her hand in his. His fingertips circled her palms, and heat raced to her cheeks.

His expression softened. "Now, beautiful lady, what's your name?"

"Eli—Elise, Elise Terry."

He rubbed her ring finger. "I don't see a wedding band, but that doesn't mean no husband."

Her heart seemed to plummet to her feet. "No, not married. Widowed, two years now," she replied in an even tone. "There was nothing the doctors could do to save him. I was told later that he suffered a massive coronary."

"I'm sorry." He furrowed his brow, his gaze sympathetic. "That's a hard one."

Jamie reached for a saltshaker. Cade pulled her back and moved the condiment a safe distance away. He blinked. The crease in his brow deepened. "How old is the little one?"

"Nineteen months. Why?"

"Just doing the math. Widowed and two months pregnant? You must be a strong woman."

She worried her lower lip. A deep pain radiated throughout her chest. "I had no choice. You'd be surprised what a person can handle when left with no options."

"I'm sure." His gaze softened. "It would be hard knowing I'd missed a child this precious growing up." He rubbed Jamie's downy, sorrel locks. "I love children. That's one reason I play Santa here every year."

Jamie pressed her damp little mouth to his cheek. "Da-da-da," she babbled.

Pain sliced through Elise. She gasped and glanced at Cade. He smiled, but his eyes held a wounded look that tore at her soul.

"I'm so sorry," she said. "Jamie's never spoken those words before. I don't know what's gotten into her. She's usually not quite so taken with men."

The sparkle returned to Cade's eyes. "Don't apologize. Like I said, I love children." He chuckled and bounced Jamie on his knee. "Seems I remember inviting two lovely ladies for coffee. Guess I better live up to that invitation."

He passed Jamie across the table and moved to the counter. Now void of the Santa suit, Elise contemplated the man while he placed the order. Cade glanced over his shoulder. Unusual warmth spread through her body.

It had been a long time since she'd noticed a man. For almost two years, she'd thrived on being Jamie's mother. Although she wouldn't change her life, she needed more. A part of her died with James, but she wasn't an empty shell either. She needed to be a woman again, experience the sensations only a man could give her. James would want her to be happy, but could she move forward without somehow feeling she betrayed the love they had shared?

Cade dropped change from the coffee purchase into his front pocket, lifted the tray, and eased back to the table. He slid into the booth.

Noticing the chocolate donut, Elise quirked a brow. "Who's that for?"

His cheeks dimpled. Pink tinged his neck, white teeth flashed, and he laughed. "Jamie looks like a chocolate girl. I couldn't resist. Hope you don't mind."

"Not at all. I appreciate the gesture." Elise fought the urge to fan her face. The man turned her insides to jelly.

Carefully wrapping the donut in a napkin, Cade placed it in her daughter's hand. The toddler held the treat high and scrunched her tiny nose. "Tay-oo."

Cade's eyes rounded; his mouth gaped. "Did she say what I think she said?"

"Yeah, she learned to talk early on and hasn't stopped." Elise giggled. "At least she's showing signs of having manners."

Chocolate smeared Jamie's cheeks. She took another bite of the donut, and he ruffled her downy locks. "Aren't you the cutest. Just like your mamma." He glanced up, an unfathomable expression on his face.

Her interest piqued, Elise sipped her coffee. *There's definitely more to the man than a red Santa suit and a love for children.*

Draining his cup, Cade glanced at his watch. "Wish I had more time, but duty calls. I need to get back." He patted Jamie's cheek and stood. "I'd like to see you again, Elise."

His gaze seemed to burn into her soul. She flushed hot. *I need time to think.* "I'm sure we'll be back before the Christmas season is over. Do you work here every day?"

"Yeah, a man needs to keep busy to stay sane." The look she'd seen earlier resurfaced again. He grasped her hand and squeezed. "I hope to see you soon. Take care of this little angel."

He brushed a finger under Jamie's chin.

A sense of melancholy descended on Elise as he walked away.

Chapter Three

Cade made his way to the dressing room and readied for his Santa role. He glanced in the mirror, positioning the snow-white beard. With a quick tug on the belt of his red-and-white costume, he exited into the crowd.

Shoppers milled left and right. His mind wandered as he strode toward the makeshift North Pole. Elise's auburn hair cascading down her back, the tenderness of her smile when she'd looked at Jamie, and the haunted look in her green eyes flashed in his mind.

Another mother and child surfaced—blonde, laughing, and precious. The image was quickly replaced by the screech of tires, metal grinding against metal, glass shattering, painful moans, and too much blood.

EMTs had pulled him from the wreckage. A brief glimpse of the unmoving forms of his wife and child ended his world when they carted him away.

Cade jerked. A low, involuntary moan escaped him. He ground his teeth and balled his hands. Although not in the same way, the results were the same. He'd lost his family just as Elise had lost her husband. Somehow, he'd recognized her emptiness, the need and loneliness in her eyes.

He took a deep breath. Anxious and happy faces stared up at him. Settling into the chair, he focused on the children. They were what kept him sane and helped him through the holidays.

A small girl, no more than five, settled on his lap. He filed past demons away and looked down into her sparkling green eyes.

"What do you want for Christmas?" he asked, jostling her on his knee.

She giggled and blushed. "I've been a good girl. Mommy says so." She looked at her mother, who nodded in affirmation. "I'd like a Barbie and Barbie clothes, maybe a *cavertable* for her to ride in."

"I think you mean a convertible." He chuckled. "Ole Saint Nick can manage that. Just keep being a good girl until then." The child looked at him with bright, expectant eyes. He ruffled her hair and set her off his lap. In her tiny outstretched palm, he placed a candy cane. Clutching her mother's hand, she scurried into the crowd.

The children formed what seemed like an endless line. Finally, eight-forty-five rolled around, and the sea of eager faces thinned to a trickle. By nine, he'd dressed in street clothes and unlocked his truck. He thought again of Elise and prayed she'd seek him out before the Christmas holidays were over. She'd sparked his interest like no one had since Nicole.

* * * *

Elise gathered Jamie into her arms. She drew the diaper bag over her shoulder and grabbed the shopping bag with the baby doll and book purchases. In the future, she'd need to figure a better way to buy Santa stuff. Jamie would catch on soon.

She wandered through the mall, buying a few gifts for friends. Inside Gunther's, she spotted a slinky red cocktail dress. As things stood, she had no holiday plans and hadn't an inkling when or where she'd wear something so beautiful. She took the dress off the rack. Caressing the silk between her fingers, she made a snap decision. This holiday season would be for new beginnings. She couldn't remember the last time she'd bought anything nice for herself. Not when all her funds went to taking care of their home and providing what Jamie needed or wanted.

Passing a full-length mirror, she held the dress under her chin and studied her reflection. A scruffy man paused behind her. His cold, blue gaze seared her from head to toe. She shivered, shifted Jamie on her hip, and hurried to the cash register. Elise made her purchase and, juggling Jamie and the shopping bags, exited the building.

She eased the bags onto the asphalt and fumbled for her keys. A quick glance at her watch confirmed they had shopped longer than she'd planned. It would be dark before they arrived home.

She strapped Jamie into the car seat and retrieved the shopping bags. Once on the road, she breathed a sigh of relief, the strange man's clear and lifeless gaze, the expression on his face, lingering in her mind.

Along Main Street, Christmas lights winked in garland-strung store windows. She turned left on Henderson, leaving the small town of Sheraton behind. About four miles out, her car sputtered, shimmied, and died. Elise frowned. The fuel light glowed red. *How is that possible? I filled the tank yesterday.*

"Oh, my god," she moaned, scattering the contents of her purse on the seat. In her mind, she clearly saw her cell phone on the kitchen counter. Her hands had been full. She hadn't taken time to grab it because she'd never actually needed the darn thing before.

She looked in the rearview mirror. An exhausted Jamie nodded sleepily in her seat. Elise pushed the driver's door open and glanced skyward. Daylight faded fast.

Headlights flashed. Elise stepped out and waved her arms. The car slowed, pulling to the edge of the roadway behind her. A door creaked open. Silhouetted in the car's low beams, a man materialized, gravel crunching beneath his boots. Tiny hairs on her arms prickled and stood on end. A chill settled in her veins at the sight of his face.

The same scraggly, gray-haired man who'd watched her in Gunther's smiled and spat tobacco, his teeth stained and twisted. "Having a bit of car trouble?" He chuckled.

Elise stepped back. "Yes, it seems I've run out of gas, but I don't understand how. The tank was filled yesterday."

"Are you sure it's not something else?" He swaggered to the front of the car and raised the hood.

Elise followed him, peeking in at the engine. "I'm almost positive. The fuel light came on before the car died."

"Don't have any extra gas on me. I'll need to take you back to town." His gaze slithered over her body.

Please God—let someone else come along. I don't want to be alone with this man.

"How about it? You gonna stand there all night and gawk, or what?"

"N-no," Elise said. "I'll get my daughter." She unbelted Jamie's car seat, tugged it free, grabbed her diaper bag and purse, and locked the doors.

The man stretched to his full height and shoved his hands in his pockets. "Ready?"

Elise glanced up and down the road. "I'm ready." She expelled a ragged breath and, with doom heavy on her shoulders, walked to his vehicle. With her fingers on the door handle, she glanced at the darkening sky. No way could she carry Jamie and make it home on foot and in the dark. She'd never hold up to the distance, or the weight of her daughter. What choice did she have?

A strange gleam surfaced in the man's eyes. Never once did he offer assistance. He smiled, and she shuddered inwardly. Leaning into his car, she secured Jamie into the back. Opening the passenger door, she slid in across from him.

He U-turned in the middle of the road and headed toward Sheraton. Elise rested her arm on the window's edge. A prick on her underarm drew her attention to the door panel. Her stomach rolled. A scream welled in her throat. The door lock had been removed.

Three miles out of town, the strange man maneuvered onto a dirt road not much more than a trail. Elise's heart palpitated. She glanced at her daughter asleep in the back seat and yanked the door handle. It didn't budge.

The man spat tobacco juice onto the floorboard and chuckled. He braked to a stop, stepped out, and locked the door. His gaze darted in all directions. He rounded the vehicle, grabbed her hair, and dragged her out.

"Oh my god, no!" she screamed. She kicked and flailed, her nails raking his face. He backhanded her. Pain thundered through her head. She bit her lip to keep from moaning and struggled harder. *I have to get away. What will he do with Jamie after he's done with me?*

He pinned her against the car and tried to kiss her. "Be still now. I deserve a little payment for picking you up. I could've left you stranded."

Tobacco smeared the side of her face. His lips missed her mouth, his breath a repulsive mixture of beer and tobacco. Elise frantically searched her coat pocket, her fingers curling around a metal hair comb. She worked it between her index and middle fingers, its tips extended outward, and plunged the comb into his neck. The man grunted. Reinforcing his hold on her arm, he slapped her again. Blood trickled down his throat and through the fingers of the hand he'd pressed to the wound.

"You little tease," he rasped and pulled her hard against his chest. "I'll teach you a thing or two."

Chapter Four

Cade maneuvered through the holiday traffic. On Henderson Road, he punched the gas. His leg throbbed from sitting in one position for so long, a grim reminder of the accident. His stomach rumbled. Home would be a welcome sight.

Ahead, he spotted a car, hood raised, sitting on the edge of the roadway, another car parked close behind. He passed, easing up on the gas. Dumbfounded, he watched Elise disappear inside a beat-up Delta eighty-eight Oldsmobile. The man, unkempt and dirty, gave him the creeps.

Cade made a quick decision, U-turned, and drove back. The Oldsmobile did the same and headed toward town. Strumming his fingers on the steering wheel, he followed at a distance. *I just need to know she's safe.*

The Oldsmobile suddenly veered onto an unmarked side road. A dark sense of foreboding enveloped Cade. How likely could it be that she lived down nothing more than a pig trail? He paused in the middle of the road, rapping his fingers on the steering wheel in indecision.

Damn, I've gotta know!

With the headlights on high beam, he turned down the rough dirt trail. The man had Elise pinned to the ragged-out Olds, her back bowed against the fender.

Cade blasted the horn. He locked the brakes, hurling himself out the driver's door. The man's eyes widened in surprise. He cursed and sprinted into the woods.

* * * *

Winded and shaken, her mind a mass of confusion, Elise staggered to the rear of the car. Gravel crunched. She stiffened and whirled, her breaths coming in short gasps. A man's shadow loomed above her. Terror rocketed through her. She balled her hand and swung.

Strong hands gripped her wrists. "It's me, Elise."

She looked up into azure eyes and melted against his hard frame. "Cade! Oh, God! I thought you were that vile, ugly man." Her gaze darted around. "How did you find me? How did you know?"

"I travel Henderson Road every day on my way to and from work. I noticed the vehicle on the roadway's edge. I passed, and you were getting into that car. Something about the man bothered me. I had to come back and make sure you were okay."

Cade's large hand cupped her head, and he held her tightly. A sense of security enveloped Elise. His lips brushed her cheek. She shivered and stepped back.

"I need to check on Jamie. She's in the back seat." Elise fumbled with the rear passenger door. Her hands shook, her grip slipping on the handle.

"Let me."

Cade's warm hand settled over hers, his gaze searching her face. She moved aside. He tugged the door handle, and on protesting hinges, the door opened.

Elise scampered inside, unbelted the car seat, and hauled Jamie out. Cade carried the sleeping toddler to his truck and deposited her gently inside.

"Stay here, Elise. Lock the doors. I'll be back."

"Where are you going?"

His expression hardened. "To find the scum who abducted you. God only knows what else he might have done." He strode toward the thick copse of trees.

"Don't go," she called. "Let the police handle him, Cade."

He either didn't hear, or chose not to. Elise slammed the door and locked it.

Damn! I'd give every dime I have right now for my cell phone. She twisted in the seat. Something hard nudged her thigh. She felt beneath her leg and pulled out Cade's phone.

Dear God, don't let it be dead. She punched in nine-one-one. The phone rang. She held her breath and waited.

"Nine-one-one. What's the emergency?" a female dispatcher's voice echoed.

"We need an officer four miles out and east, just off Henderson Road." Elise glanced around to gain her bearings and looked down at her daughter. "Some sort of pig trail to the right, about a mile this side of my disabled car. The road must lead to a field or something. My vehicle's in clear sight, hood raised, so you'll have no trouble spotting it." Elise gulped in air, panic surging anew. She fought to stay calm. "My daughter and I were abducted. Thank God a friend found us, but now he's gone after the guy. They're in the woods somewhere. Someone's likely to get hurt. Please hurry," she said, her voice cracking.

"Stay on the line. I'm dispatching a patrol car now."

"Hurry," Elise gasped.

"Okay, a cruiser's en route. Stay put and on the line until officers arrive."

"I will." Elise scanned the tree line but saw no sign of Cade. Where had he gone? What was happening? Jamie stirred, and she gently rocked the car seat. "Please stay asleep, sweetheart," she whispered. "Now isn't a good time to wake up with Mommy so distraught."

Sirens shrieked in the distance, passed by, and died. Moments later, one cruiser followed another, lights flashing, sirens screaming. The cars sped in behind Cade's truck. Police officers exited the vehicles, pistols drawn. She released the door latch, held her hands high, and stepped out.

"It was me who called. My daughter's asleep in the vehicle, and a friend's out there looking for the guy who abducted us. He needs help. You guys are wasting time."

One officer eased to the truck, looked inside, and saw Jamie. "She's telling the truth, guys. Let's move out."

The men advanced in pairs toward the copse of trees and entered the brush and bramble. Elise's legs trembled. She sat in the truck seat with the door open, her panic surging anew. Everything was so quiet.

She tapped her foot on the runner board. A man cursed, leaves rustled, and he cursed again.

"Over here, guys!" someone shouted.

She stiffened and held her breath.

An officer emerged from the woods, the scruffy, beady-eyed man in tow, hands cuffed behind his back. He glared at Elise through swollen and bruised eyelids; his bloodied lips curled in a sneer. She shivered and averted her gaze.

The three remaining officers stepped from the tree line, then Cade, his face battered and dirty. A cut above his left eye oozed blood.

Elise scurried from the vehicle. "Oh my!" She covered her mouth with her hand and bit back tears. "What did he do to you?"

Cade grinned and flexed his hand, the knuckles scraped and raw. "Not much. He fought a little, but I pinned him down. Maybe he'll think twice before forcing himself on another woman."

Elise barreled into his arms and clung to him. "I'm so glad you're okay. I've lost one good man. I couldn't stand to lose another," she mumbled against his neck.

Cade stepped back, his mouth curving into a painful smile. "Does this mean you'll see me again, go out with me?" He rubbed her arms. "I can only imagine what you've been through. I don't want to pressure you into something you're not ready for."

She gingerly touched her lips to his. "When James died, I learned never to take people for granted or the moments given with them. None of us is guaranteed tomorrow. No one knows how much time they have left." She smiled. "Guess we'd best find out where this bizarre acquaintance leads."

He touched the tip of her nose, wrapped his arm around her waist, and escorted her to the truck.

Jamie, now wide-eyed and alert, smiled at them and cooed, "Da-da-da."

Cade grinned. "Sit with Jamie. I'll talk to the police and see when they want to talk to you. I'll leave them information on how I can be reached and take you home. We'll worry about your car tomorrow." He squeezed her hand and moved away.

Powerful emotion gripped her heart. She released a ragged sigh. *Could I be in love with him? Nah!*

Chapter Five

A sense of protection engulfed Cade. He looked over his shoulder. Emotion welled, tightening his chest. *Deja vu* all over again. Another Nicole and Tess, just a different scenario. He'd almost been too late.

He expelled a ragged breath. If he'd been moments later, two more beautiful and special lives may have been snuffed out for no rhyme or reason. Rage surged, heating his face. His temples throbbed. He moved to the cruiser and stared into the back seat.

The man glared back at him, a smug smile on his face. With his hands clenched, Cade strode toward the officers clustered around the Olds.

"I'd like to take Elise home. She's pretty shaken. The baby needs fed too." He shoved his hands in his pockets and rocked back on his heels. "Thought I'd leave my contact information. We can come by the station tomorrow, sign whatever papers need signing."

"That'll be fine," the officer nearest him said. "I'm sure she's eager to get her daughter home. Just write down your name, number, and address. I'll need to see your ID."

Cade handed over his driver's license, and the officer entered the information in the cruiser's computer. He flipped a notepad open and handed it to Cade, who jotted down his address and phone number.

"See you in the morning." Cade ambled back to the truck and slid behind the wheel.

Uncertainty etched Elise's face. "Can we leave?"

He reached for the ignition key. "Yeah, but I promised we'd go in tomorrow to take care of things." His gaze locked with hers. He wanted to wrap her in his arms and never let her go. *Why do I care so much? I don't even know her. Why can't I just walk away from this...whatever this is?*

He shifted into drive and braked to a stop at the edge of Henderson Road. "Which way?"

"Left. We live about three miles out."

He cut the wheel and maneuvered onto the blacktop. "We're almost neighbors. My place is five miles from here."

Elise's lips trembled; tears welled in her eyes. She turned to stare out the window.

His smiled died. He pulled to the side of the road and reached to comfort her. A sleeping Jamie wrapped her tiny hands around his arm, snuggling.

Cade supported Jamie's head. His heart filled with instant affection. God, he loved her baby smell, so fresh and pure. Nicole and Tess flashed through his mind. Intense pain washed through him. He gritted his teeth to hold back a moan. *Damn, I miss my family. Maybe that's why I'm drawn to them?*

He tousled Jamie's hair. "Let's get you guys home."

Chapter Six

"Turn here."

Cade slowed to make the turn.

She looked at him. "Don't expect too much. I've kept a tight handle on expenses since James died."

"Your husband's name was James?"

Elise gave him a bittersweet smile. "Yeah. It's been two years, but sometimes I miss him so much."

Cade braked to a stop in front of a quaint cottage-style home, its walkway lined with alternating pots of red and white poinsettias. "Have you not dated in all that time?"

"No. No one has interested me until now." She collected her diaper bag and purse. "Won't you come in? The least I can do is make coffee." Her amber-eyed gaze pierced his. "How do I begin to repay someone for not only saving my life, but that of my child too?"

"I didn't do anything that anyone in my position wouldn't do." He tunneled a hand through his hair and smiled. "But I'd love coffee."

Elise unfastened Jamie's seat and tugged.

"Leave it. I'll bring her in." Cade eased out and rounded the truck. He gently lifted the car seat and moved up the walk behind her.

She unlocked the door. He followed her to a bedroom in the back. Pink and frilly ABC-blocked fabric draped the windows, and a matching coverlet neatly snuggled the baby bed's mattress. Stuffed animals and books of every sort lined a white corner bookshelf. A toy box shaped like a dollhouse, the lid raised, overflowed with toys.

He settled the car seat onto the floor, unlatched the baby harness, and eased it over Jamie's head. Elise lifted her daughter onto her shoulder and tucked her into bed. She gently patted her bottom, then tiptoed out the door.

Cade accompanied Elise down the hallway and into the kitchen, where she set coffee to brew. She slipped bagels into the toaster, and he walked up behind her. "Are you really okay, Elise? The man didn't harm you?"

She turned and gazed up at him. "I'm fine. Although my nerves are somewhat frazzled." He massaged the tightness in her shoulders, and she sighed. "It frightens me to think what could have happened." Her brow furrowed. "What's strange is that I caught him watching me at the mall. I just happened to run out of gas. Seems he took advantage of my predicament."

Cade clenched his hands. "Maybe he siphoned your tank? The incident is too convenient to be coincidence, if you ask me."

Elise's eyes glittered with emotion. She released a quivering breath. "I never thought of that. Maybe we should've gone to the police department tonight."

The coffeemaker hissed. Elise grabbed cups from the cupboard and reached for the coffee decanter. Her hand wavered. She missed the cup, and hot liquid spilled onto the countertop. Cade steadied her hand with his, then sopped up the mess with paper towels.

Things were moving fast, but he was sure she'd been shoved into his life for a reason. His bond with Jamie had been instant, and his attraction to Elise so strong it scared him. His heart thundered. He had to know what it meant. God couldn't be so cruel as to tease him with a glimpse of what he'd lost, only to snatch it away again.

He sipped from the steaming mug of coffee and sat down at the kitchen table. His gaze roved the room. Bright red gingham toppers accented dark wood-framed windows. The round oak tabletop, smelling of lemon, gleamed beneath his hands. Place mats that matched the curtains adorned the table, and a basket of ceramic apples decorated its center. The tantalizing aroma of cinnamon filled his nostrils.

Sensing Elise's gaze, he looked into eyes that mirrored his inner turmoil. When he smiled, the fear vanished, and her shoulders relaxed. The bagels popped up in the toaster. She slathered their tops with butter and brought them to the table, settling down across from him.

Elise peered out the bay window into the night and worried her lip. He wanted to reach out, grasp her hand, and reassure her that she was safe. Instead, he wrapped his hands around the mug and drank. "Will you be okay here, alone?"

"Sure." She turned her gaze on him. "Jamie and I have been alone for two years. What happened today changes nothing. We'll be fine. I'm used to it." Her eyes clouded, and she looked away.

Cade finished the bagel, drained the coffee cup, and stood. "Thanks for your hospitality." He glanced at his watch. "I guess I need to be going."

Elise followed him to the door. On impulse and feather light, he brushed his lips across hers. For an instant, she responded. "Stay safe and remember, *he's* tucked neatly away in a jail cell and can't cause you any more grief."

"That's what I keep telling myself." She laughed nervously. "What time should I expect you in the morning?"

"I'll be here around eight, if that's not too early?" He chuckled. "First, I need to call in the reserve Santa. Irate mothers and unhappy children, I don't need."

Unexpected Gift

"Looking at you now, it's hard to believe you're the Santa in Willingham's Toy Store. If not for those eyes...." She dropped her gaze.

"What about my eyes?" He smiled and moved closer, pleased that she'd noticed something about him.

Her skin flushed a rosy pink. "They're the bluest I've ever seen and the first thing I noticed about you."

"So you noticed me, eh?" He grasped her hands and pulled her near.

She looked up at him. "You could say that," she whispered.

He released her hands and brushed a finger down her nose. "Lock up when I leave." He stepped to the porch and closed the door behind him.

Chapter Seven

Elise pressed her palms flat against the door's cool surface. Longing swelled inside her. What she wouldn't give for the comfort, the security, of a man's arms right now. *Just for tonight.* She checked the lock and moved to the couch. Memories of James surfaced. It seemed like only yesterday that they had been happy and planning a future, talking of children.

She eased down the hall to check on her daughter. The spitting image of her father, Jamie slept peacefully. She'd burrowed her tiny form beneath the blanket, thumb in her mouth. Elise caressed Jamie's sorrel locks, kissed her cheek, and tiptoed out and over to her bedroom.

Slipping on her nightgown, she tossed back the duvet and plumped the pillows. She lay down but couldn't sleep. Her mind whirled, her thoughts and emotions a jumble. One moment she longed for James, the next Cade's face and eyes teased her mind.

Elise stumbled out of bed and checked the front door lock. She glanced out the side window. Disbelief surged through her. She rubbed her eyes and looked again. Cade's truck sat parked on the edge of her driveway. Elise swung the door wide and stepped onto the porch.

A door creaked open. She shaded her eyes against the blinding porch light. Cade emerged from his truck, a sheepish smile on his face. He sauntered up the walk, and she glared at him.

"What are you doing here?"

He hooked his thumbs through his belt loops and frowned. "Honestly...I don't know. I tried to leave but couldn't. Damn fingers wouldn't turn the key in the ignition switch, so I decided to stay."

Surprise rocketed through her. "You can't sleep in your truck all night. What did you intend to do? Camp out and pretend at eight o'clock that you'd just arrived?"

"Hadn't thought that far ahead, but your idea has appeal." He chuckled. "Elise, I was worried. Still am. I couldn't leave you and Jamie alone, defenseless." His blue eyes grew solemn. "I know this sounds crazy, and I've struggled with my emotions all evening trying to reason things out in my mind. The simple fact is...I care for you and Jamie."

He sat down on the steps. Elbows resting on his knees, he rubbed his face. "I lost my wife and daughter about the same time you lost James. The reason I play Santa is to fill a void in my life that can never be filled. Images of their lifeless bodies are burned in my brain. Although I was pulled from the wreckage, until now, my life was truly over. I've been a walking dead man."

A lump lodged in Elise's throat. Her eyes burned. She fought to speak, but no words came out. She sat down next to him and gathered him in her arms. Brushing her lips across his brow, she rocked him like she would her own child.

"I can't leave you here," he whispered. "I won't turn my back and allow you to be taken away like Tess and Nicole were. We've been thrown together for a reason. Give whatever this is a chance, Elise." He raised his head and kissed her. His misty blue eyes glimmered in the moonlight. "Don't be afraid."

Through the hurt, the loss and grief, her blood heated, and love bloomed. *I was right. From the start, I felt the magic, the attraction, but denied the possibility that I could love again.*

"Come inside, Cade. I'll make a bed for you on the couch."

He snuggled her against his chest. "Do you believe in love at first sight?" he whispered.

She attempted a nonchalant shrug. "Every day's a new day, miracles happen, and prayers are answered. God heard me—you came. I can't and won't turn my back on that."

Cade intertwined his fingers with hers. "Given this chance, and with Him on our side, how can we go wrong?"

She led him inside. Closing the door, she stepped into his waiting embrace. "I don't know how I know...but here is where I belong." She laid her head against his chest, near his heart, and breathed in his scent. "I'd say we've been blessed with a Christmastime miracle and given a second chance at love."

Author Bio:

Lisa resides in North Alabama with her husband and young daughter. A writer of contemporary romance, you can find her at: www.lisaalexandergriffin.com or www.myspace.com/destinyschoice8.

Whispers in the Wind
by
Kensana Darnell

Ali needs to grow up. Mitch wants to forget his past. Can they come together to give each other what they so desperately need?

"Today is the day!" Allison Braddock jumped out of bed with glee. She ran over and threw open the window. Leaning out, she let the warm North Carolina sun beam down upon her skin. A fresh morning breeze blew through her hair. Today was the day her new horse arrived. She dressed hurriedly and ran down the stairs.

"Ali," her mother called, "breakfast first."

"I'm not hungry," Ali yelled as she hurried down the hallway, past the kitchen and out the back door.

"That girl I swear—Allison Leigh Braddock!—you get back in this house this *instant*," Cora Leigh shouted out the back door.

"But, Mom, the truck—!"

"Don't 'But, Mom' me. The horse can wait."

Ali stomped her foot, turned around and rushed back inside. She passed her mother, mumbling, "You know I'm eighteen. I know when I'm hungry or not."

"And I'm your mother, so until you move into your own house, I'll tell you when you're hungry. Your breakfast is on the table, missy."

Cora Lee Braddock was a true Southern woman. Ali's mother married a rich man, but that never stopped her from taking care of her house and family as her mother before had taught her to do. Ali knew that *no* was not an option, but it was always fun to try. She sat down at the kitchen table and wolfed down the eggs and bacon Cora had prepared. She stood, her cheeks puffed out like a squirrel with its mouth full of nuts, grabbed the glass of juice on the table, and guzzled it down. Ali reveled in the level of shock and disappointment her hideous behavior could bring to her mother. Every day was a raging battle against becoming the proper Southern woman she was expected to be. Over the years, instead of being the beautiful daughter her mother wanted, she'd become the son her father never had, tomboy to the core. Today proved to be one more victory for Ali.

"Umkay done," Ali mumbled through the food. She took one big gulp and swallowed everything down with a defiant grin.

"Good Lord, just go, child."

"Thanks for breakfast, Mom."

She tore out the door and headed straight for the barn. The truck had arrived to deliver the new horses, and Ali's father had promised she could pick the horse she wanted. She ran into the barn, looking around for Tim, the caretaker of her parents' ranch. He'd been with the family since Ali was five; he was like an uncle to her. Ali made her way into the barn, a cloud of dust in tow.

"Well, good morning, Ali. You're up early. Can't imagine why." A mischievous twinkle appeared in his eyes.

"Are they here?"

"What? Is what here?" He grinned as she ran from stall to stall in search of the new horses.

"Aw, come on, Tim. Where are they?"

"They're out back in the stable. You can ask—"

Ali tore out of the barn and right into a hard, muscular chest. A pair of big, strong hands on her arms kept her from falling.

"Excuse me, ma'am. I didn't see you," the stranger said.

Ali raised her head. Her gaze swept over a massive chest and worked up to a face shadowed by a dark brown Stetson. The pair of hands released her, and she backed away. Squinting, she shielded her eyes from the sun's stinging rays, and the figure before her came into focus.

Droplets of moisture rolled down his forehead alongside his temples to a tightened jaw line. A wisp of sandy brown hair rested above a pair of hazel eyes. Her gaze fixated upon a hairless, chiseled chest revealed by his partially unbuttoned shirt.

"No, I, uh...should have been watching where I was going," Ali finally replied.

Timothy strolled out to them. "Ali, this is my nephew, Mitch Colbert. He's going to give me a hand with the stables for a while."

Ali extended her hand. "Pleased to meet you, Mitch."

The man touched the brim of his hat and nodded his head. "Likewise, ma'am."

"If you need anything," Timothy continued, "and I'm not around, Mitch can help you."

Oh, I'm sure he can. She smiled and looked down the private road to the ranch; her father's car headed their way. Ali sauntered backward towards the driveway. "Welcome to B-Ranch, Mitch." She rushed off to greet her father as he stepped out to encounter a crushing hug from his daughter.

"I guess you've already seen the horses," Nathaniel Braddock said to his daughter.

"Not yet. I was just on my way to the corral." She beamed with excitement.

"Well, why don't we head on over?" Nathaniel glanced at Timothy and Mitch standing outside the barn. He threw up his hand. "Morning, Tim. Mitch."

"Morning, Mr. Braddock," Tim called back.

"Ali hasn't been bugging you guys too much, has she?"

The men met Ali and Nathaniel at the corral gates.

"No, sir. She's no bother," Tim said. "Beautiful lot you have here, sir."

"Thanks. It was time to get some new stock, and someone wanted a horse of their own."

Ali looked up at her father. "And it's about time," she laughed.

"Well don't just stand there. Go pick out your horse," her father instructed.

Ali ducked under the corral fence and moved out to the horses. She scanned the herd of six. A beautiful cinnamon-brown Quarter Horse stood out from the rest. She sauntered over to him and stroked her hand down the bridge of his nose. Ali snuggled her face against its warm coat and closed her eyes, the sound of her father and Tim still yapping on about ranch business teasing in her ears. She opened her eyes to find Mitch watching her. He winked as her gaze caught his. A smile as intimate as a kiss shaped his lips. She took a deep breath, smiled and trotted back towards the men.

"Absolutely beautiful," he said, his attention still focused on Ali.

"I agree, he's a beauty," Nathaniel said.

"Yes...yes, he is, Mr. Braddock," Mitch responded.

Ali stepped up to the corral gate. "I've decided." She grinned from ear to ear.

"So does he have a name?" her father asked.

"Of course. I'm gonna call him Cinnamon."

"Great. Then let's go tell your mother the good news."

"Okay, let me grab my gloves." She looked around the ground where she and Cinnamon had stood. The gloves weren't there. "I must have left them in the barn. I'll run and get them and then meet you at the house."

Her father strolled towards the house, leaving Ali to the task of recovering her gloves. She tromped back inside the barn and checked every stall before she found them hanging from a post. She grabbed the gloves and turned around to continue out the barn, but Tim's voice stopped her in her tracks. She peeked around the doorway at Mitch and Tim.

"Beautiful, huh?" Tim asked.

Mitch removed his hat and wiped the sweat from his brow. He ran his hand through his hair and placed his hat back in place. "Yeah, it is a beautiful horse." A blush entered his tan cheeks.

"Yeah, right...the horse." Tim glanced at Mitch; his lips trembled to release a smile. Unable to hold back any longer they both burst into laughter. "Just be careful. *Horses,* no matter how beautiful, can be just as dangerous." He turned to face Mitch. The smile left his face, replaced by a grim frown. "And they come in different breeds and classes."

"I know, Unc."

"No, I don't think you do. Ali lives in a different world from where we come from. Don't go getting your head all turned around over a girl. You've suffered the consequences once—that gal, Stephanie—just left you high and dry. Her parents' money and power set her free and left you to rot for something that wasn't your doing."

"I was trying to protect her."

"Yeah, well, you did, and what did you get for it? I won't stand silent this time and have your life taken from you again. You hear me?"

"I hear ya."

"I ain't saying that Ali would...I mean, I've known her since she was a girl.... Just watch yourself, boy."

"I will, Unc, I will."

Ali slipped back against the wall and into the barn. *Who was this girl? What had she done to get Mitch into trouble? Had Mitch served time for her? Why? Was he in love with her?*

She had to find out more, but how? These were not questions for her mother, and surely not her father. There had to be a way to find out what had happened. Ali hurried out the back entrance of the barn unseen. Still pondering the questions, she approached the porch, and a resolution came to mind.

"Hmm...I'll just ask him myself." Struck by an epiphany that seemed to be the answer, she joined her father to share her news about Cinnamon.

* * * *

"Mom, I don't want to make this a big thing," Ali said.

"But it *is* a big thing: you're leaving for college. You should want to invite all of your friends to send you off. It's the proper thing to do."

"Yeah, if you're a Southern belle, which I'm not."

Cora moved closer to her daughter. She took Ali's braid in her hand and unraveled the tight twist of her daughter's hair. "I don't see why you're creating such a fuss. We'll go shopping for a new dress, shoes, and order some decorations. Oh, and Ali, we can rent out the country club. Wouldn't you like that?" She flared Ali's hair across her slim shoulders.

Ali hated parties, but even more, she hated the guilt trips her mother laid on her. But Ali would do what was asked of her; she always did. "Yes, it'll be lovely."

"Great. I'll start making the phone calls right away." She kissed Ali on the cheek. "It will be wonderful. Just you wait and see." And off her mom sprang into a Martha Stewart rampage.

Ali mumbled to herself, "Yeah, sure, it'll be a blast."

She got up from the chair and left the house, heading across the back fields toward the wooded area of the farm. Just beyond the trees lay her favorite place in the world: Braddock Creek. It was her haven, a quiet place to just think. She strolled down to the riverbank and climbed up on the big rock overlooking the water. The sun set on the horizon, leaving streaks of orange and purple in its path. A full moon had just begun to take possession of the sky.

"Beautiful night, isn't it?" a voice from behind her said.

"Oh my God!" Ali jumped up from the rock and lost her balance.

"Whoa, watch your—" Strong hands grabbed onto her, saving her from an unwanted night swim.

She regained her balance and tried to focus on her rescuer. "Mitch?"

"Yes, ma'am."

She could hardly make out his face in the fading light. "What are you doing out here?"

"Just taking a walk. Are you all right?"

"Sure, I'm fine, and dry, thanks to you." She giggled.

"Yeah, I guess you are."

"Wanna join me for a while?"

"I really should be getting back to—"

"Just for a little while." She looked up at him and smiled.

"Okay, for a bit." He removed his hat and sat down beside her on the rock. "I hear you're leaving for school in a few weeks."

"Yeah, that's right."

"Which school?"

"Duke University. I want to study medicine, and they're ranked in the top ten. I figure if I'm going to do this, I might as well learn from the best."

"Well, now, that's a fine school," he replied.

"Yeah, I guess. I didn't want to go too far from home but I wanted to get away. Does that make sense?"

"Sure. A bird's gotta learn to fly on its own; you have to leave the nest at some point."

"See? You get it, so why don't my parents?"

"They just want to protect you. Can't say that I blame them."

"I'm not a baby anymore. I just want to do something on my own without their help."

"I can respect that."

Ali lowered herself onto the rock and gazed into the heavens. "What a night sky. The stars are really bright tonight." A light southern breeze blew through the weeping willows along the banks. Ali cocked her head to the side. "You know, sometimes when the wind blows through the trees, I could swear I hear them whispering." She glanced up into Mitch's honey-brown eyes. Reluctantly, she turned away. The sound of the creek waters seeping slowly downstream provided a beautiful backdrop to the beauty of the twinkling lights.

Ali sneaked a peek at Mitch, hoping he wouldn't notice. She turned back to find his gaze locked on hers. He moved closer, the heat of his breath radiating to her lips. His face, beautifully lit in the moonlight, looked so handsome. Her heartbeat quickened. *God, please let him kiss me.*

"I've got to get going." He stood up and jumped off the rock before she could attempt to change his mind. He placed the Stetson back on his head, glanced at Ali one last time, and tipped his hat. "Goodnight, ma'am."

"*Ali,*" she said.

Mitch stopped short before he entered the wood line and looked back. "Pardon?"

"You can call me Ali."

"*Miss* Ali, I don't think that's appropriate."

"It is if I prefer it." Her lips curled in a grin.

"Okay, Ali it is then." He slipped into the trees and disappeared.

* * * *

"Congratulations, Allison." The loud cheer rose over the country club. Ali exchanged smiles and thank-yous here and there with person after person. She finally managed to escape, making her way onto the veranda. At last, she was able to breathe. She leaned against the rail and let out a long, exhausted sigh.

The emerald green gown she wore was beautiful. It brought out her eyes just as her mother had said it would, but Ali hated it. Almost as much as she hated how her auburn hair was swept up with sprigs of baby's breath— again, her mother's idea. She would have loved to wear a pair of blue jeans and her usual twisted braids. Ali stared off into the starry sky. Her thoughts wandered back to that night by the creek with Mitch. She had wanted him to kiss her. Wanted it so badly it hurt just thinking about it. *I wonder what his lips feel like. I wonder what his—?*

"Why, Allison Braddock," a whiny voice said behind her.

Ali looked over her shoulder. There, in the shadows, stood Bradley Templeton. Ali and Brad had dated during their first year of high school. Things hadn't worked out between them, but that hadn't stopped him from trying to get back together with her.

"Hey, Brad. How are you?" she asked.

"Great. You, uh, wanna take a walk?"

"I really don't—"

"C'mon, we won't go far." He offered his elbow. Reluctantly, Ali slipped her hand over his forearm, and they headed down the stairs. "My, you certainly do look lovely this evening."

"Thank you." Ali smiled. Brad was an ass but at least he was a polite ass.

"So, Duke, huh?"

"What? Oh, yeah. Duke."

"That's a good school."

Yes, it is." Ali noticed they had wandered back to the darker part of the grounds. "You know, I should be getting back to the party. I mean, it is in my honor." She turned and set out toward the country club.

"Hold on! You owe me a good-bye kiss." He grabbed Ali by her arm and drew her close.

"I don't owe you anything, Brad. Let go of me!" She struggled to jerk away, but he held on tightly.

"Not until you give me what *you owe me*." He slapped her across the face.

"I suggest you turn the lady loose." The voice was low, but sharp with authority. Ali breathed a sigh of relief as Mitch appeared from the shadows of the outlying pines.

"You're kidding me, right? The stable hand? Don't you have some horse droppings to shovel?" Brad sneered.

Unfazed by Brad's remark, Mitch replied, "I'm only gonna say it once more: turn her loose."

"You don't give me—"

Brad didn't finish his sentence. A crushing blow connected with his jaw. He landed on the ground at Mitch's feet. Mitch pushed Ali behind him. Brad wiped away the blood that drizzled down from his mouth. He looked up at Mitch, his eyes wide with disbelief.

"You struck me?" He got up, finally able to stand on his feet. "You'll pay for this, *stable boy*."

Ali stepped between them. "Before or after I tell my father what you tried to do?"

Mitch shoved her back behind him again. "Yeah, sure I'll pay. Now g'on—get!" He turned towards Ali and cupped her jaw. He looked over her face, checking for any injury. "Are you all right?"

"Yes, I'm fine. I don't know what I would've done if you hadn't shown up. Thank-you, Mitch."

"You don't ever have to thank me for helping you. Don't you worry your pretty little head about that. Nothing and no one will harm you as long as I'm around." A twinkle of moonlight showed in his eyes.

"So, does that mean you'll be around a lot more?" She stepped closer to Mitch. He took a quick step back; his reaction amused her.

"What are you doing, missy?"

"Something you won't." She rose up on her toes and put her arms around his neck, lingering only for a moment before her lips touched his.

The hunger of her kiss broke through his calm exterior; his body surrendered, pressing against her. The eagerness in his touch sent a heated rush through her body. His hands rested on the small of her back as he drew her closer to him. Suddenly Mitch withdrew from the kiss. She tried to hold on to him, refusing to let go of him or the moment.

"Ali we can't...," he whispered, his breath warm against her ear. Gently, he withdrew from her embrace.

His reaction took Ali by surprise, but she was more irritated than anything. "Why not? I like you, and apparently from the way you kissed me, you like me too. What's the problem?"

His expression grew still and serious. "Too many to count. C'mon, I'll walk you back."

"No, I won't accept that answer." Ali stood firm, her arms crossed against her chest. Mitch stopped in mid-stride and spun around. With a few quick strides across the grass, he stood in front of her. Tension straightened his body, frustration carving its way into his handsome face.

"You just don't get it, do you?" He turned his back to her. "I can't let this happen—"

"You can't let this happen *again*. Is that what you were going to say, Mitch? Let what happen?"

He looked back over his shoulder. "What?"

Ali reached out for him, but he pulled away. "Mitch, who is Stephanie? What did she do to you?"

"How do you know that name?"

"I...I was listening outside the barn the day I met you. You mentioned her when you were talking to Tim."

"*Tim* being the key word. Ali, you had no right."

"I'm sorry." She glanced at the ground. "I just wanted to know more about you."

He glared at her, the honey-brown color of his eyes darkening with anger. "Next time...just ask."

Ali watched him turn away and head back towards the country club. She'd pout if she thought it would do any good, but Mitch wouldn't break—it wasn't his way. They reached the lower staircase leading to the veranda.

"Here you go, safe and sound," Mitch said.

"Mitch, I'm really sorry. Please don't be angry with me."

He stepped over to her and cupped her face in his hands. "I'm could never be angry with you, little one. I'm angry with myself. My past is not your fault. I'm sorry if I upset you."

"You didn't, I'm fine. Hey, why don't you join me?" She knew it was a shot in the dark, but what did she have to lose?

"No, I don't think so, Ali. This isn't my place. These aren't my kind of people. I don't belong here. Go on, enjoy your night." He leaned over and kissed her on the top of her head. "I'll see you in the morning."

She ascended the stairway and stopped midway. She peered out across the grounds to the wood line where Mitch had emerged and looked back at him again. "What were you doing out there anyway?"

"I was just out for a walk. You take care now." He smiled, nodded his head and faded off into the night.

That man does more walking than anyone I know.

* * * *

Ali awoke early the next morning to take Cinnamon out on the trail. By the look of the clouds, it wouldn't be long before the rain started. She headed down the hallway, careful not to wake her parents; Saturdays were the only days they ever slept in. She closed the back door behind her. Early mornings were her favorite time on the ranch. The wisp of smoky mist from the early morning rain rose from mountain range. She gazed out admiring the view.

She made her way out to the barn where she found Mitch already at work. A smile on his lips was the only greeting she needed from him.

"Morning, Ali."

"Hey there."

"Listen, about last night—"

"Don't worry about it. It was nothing. I was gonna take Cinnamon out this morning. Is he ready?"

"Yeah, he's been watered and fed, so he's as ready as he'll ever be."

"Why don't you come with us?"

"Ali, I don't know...I've got work to do, and Uncle Tim won't like it if—"

"Take the two-way radio; if he needs you sooner, he can check in with you. It'll be a short ride, so we won't be gone long, I promise." She put on her best look of innocence, favored him with a smile laced with underlying intentions, and waited.

"All right. I guess a short ride won't hurt."

They mounted the horses and headed out on the trail. It was absolutely beautiful. Ali had always found a quiet peace when she rode. She glanced at Mitch. Riding seemed to have the same calming effect on him too. *Oh, God, what a smile. I could watch him forever.*

She hesitated for a moment before she yelled out, "C'mon, I'll race you to the top." She nodded her head towards the highest point in front of them.

"You're on—!"

She took off through the trees.

"Hey, that's cheating," he shouted after her.

Ali glanced back to find Mitch close on her tail. "Come on, Cinnamon, we can take 'em."

He caught up just as they broke through the tree line. The horses raced at top speed across the open field leading to the hilltop. The steeds ran abreast of one another. It amazed Ali how quickly Mitch had caught up with her. She peered over at him, and his eyes met hers. He winked slyly and took the lead.

"Hey!" She leaned forward, urging Cinnamon to pick up speed. Mitch reached the hilltop first; Ali followed a close second. "How did—?"

He dismounted and strolled toward her. "Five years on a rodeo circuit," he said, a trace of laughter in his voice.

"You are a man full of surprises, Mitch Colbert." Ali removed a blanket from her saddle and spread it out on the ground. "Come and sit with me."

Mitch hesitated for a moment, but finally joined her. They sat adoring the early morning sights and sounds of the Blue Ridge Mountains. Finally, Mitch broke the silence.

"She was a friend." His voice came out so gentle she barely heard him. His jaw clenched, and he removed the Stetson from his head.

Ali froze. *He must be talking about Stephanie. Give him time, don't push him.* She caught a glimpse of him from the corner of her eye; he stared straight ahead.

"Take your time and tell me what happened." She needed to have all the missing pieces of the story.

His expression grew hard and angry. "I met her at one of the rodeos. She and her friends liked to mingle with cowboys. She was a student in one of the elite schools in Asheville. We hung out a lot, got to know each other...I thought I knew her."

Ali sat quietly listening to the story unfold.

Mitch continued to speak. "She went out drinking one night with some friends. Driving home, she lost control of the car and ran it through some of the Biltmore shops."

"Oh my God. Was anyone hurt?"

"No. Luckily, it was about one in the morning, so no one was on the streets. She and her friends left the car, and she came running to me. If anyone found out she was responsible for the damage, she'd be kicked out of school."

"So, what did that have to do with you?"

"Steph wasn't innocent. It would be strike three for her, and she'd not only get kicked out of school, she'd do time. I couldn't let that happen. "

"You took the blame?"

"Yeah, she told me her parents would get a good lawyer to get me off. So I told everyone I had been driving. What I didn't know was there had been alcohol found inside the vehicle. Once I was arrested, she turned her back on me. The judge decided to make an example out of me. I was ordered to pay two hundred thousand dollars in restitution and serve three years in prison."

The shock of the events hit her full force. "She left you to do her time in prison? What a bitch! How did you make it in there?"

"One day at a time. Staying alert kept me alive. When I got out, I promised myself I'd never let another woman control me like that," he looked into her eyes, "and then I met you. My uncle warned me, but there's something about you, Ali. I've tried to fight it but I can't." He reached over and caressed her cheek. "Ali? Please say something."

Ali knew Mitch was a complex man and now she knew why too. It was plain as day. This girl had hurt him. She had made it so no other woman could ever get close to him again. His heart was damaged goods, but she was willing to help him heal. His eyes called out to her, and her heart answered with every beat. Ali's stomach fluttered.

"Ali?"

"Kiss me...?"

His lips touched hers, the kiss soft. His composure calmed the tingling in the pit of her stomach. Ali's thoughts spun out of control as he lowered her gently onto the blanket never releasing her lips.

"Mitch." The radio crackled. "Mitch, you out there?"

Mitch sat up and took the radio from his belt. "Yeah, Unc, I'm here."

"Where are you, boy? I need you down at the north side of the ranch. Looks like we've got a broken fence. Some of the steer have gotten loose."

"I'm on my way." He cupped Ali's face in his hands and kissed her. "I'm sorry, but I've got to go. See you later?"

"Of course." Ali watched him mount his horse and ride away. The clouds began to fade as the sun rose up over the mountains. The warmth of the sun touched her face. She sighed. "It's going to be a wonderful summer."

* * * *

Summer came to a close, and Ali had to make a decision. She had worked so hard for this opportunity. The career she had prepared for since she was a child awaited her. But the man who had become the most important part of her life over the summer months was here. It was a difficult decision, one she felt she shouldn't make alone. She had to talk to Mitch. Her feelings for him were strong, but Ali couldn't stake her entire career on a man she'd known for only a few months. She had to know exactly how he felt about her, about them.

She found Mitch in the corral training one of the new horses. *God, he's so sexy.* Ali loved watching the way he moved and worked. He handled the horses so easily. Memories of their days together and the nights they'd spent lying under the stars, while Mitch held her tightly, rose in her mind. She remembered the warmth of his touch against her skin, the way his lips felt when he kissed her.

Mitch looked back at her. He winked, and a smile curled his lips. She put her thoughts on hold for the moment and waved to him. He placed the bridle on the stallion and strode over to her.

"C'mon, want to help me with Jazz?"

"Sure."

She followed him to the barn and waited silently while Mitch put Jazz in the stall and placed some hay down for the animal.

He looked at Ali again. "You wanna grab that brush over there on the post for me?"

"Sure."

He took the brush from her hand and began to brush Jazz. "So...when are you gonna tell me what's wrong?"

She glanced up into his eyes; they beckoned her for the truth. "Mitch I...I'm leaving tomorrow."

He continued to brush Jazz. "Yeah, I know."

"I need to know...."

His back was facing her; he stopped brushing. "What do you need to know?"

She stumbled, searching for the right words. "I need to know what this...I mean...."

He put the brush down, extended his hands and beckoned her to come to him. She slid into his arms. He put his hand under her chin, drew her face towards him. "Go—do what you have to do. I can't be—no, I won't be the reason you stay or go. This is not my decision, little one, it's yours."

"I just want to make sure."

He held her close. "You just make sure you succeed, promise me that."

She put her arms around him and squeezed him tightly. "I will, I promise."

The next morning, Ali said her goodbyes and packed her things into her car. As she drove away, tears streamed from her eyes. She caught a glimpse of Mitch in her rearview mirror and missed him already.

* * * *

Ali had not been home in a long while. She and Mitch had decided to see each other only when she finished school. He didn't want anything to stand in the way of her success, not even him. Email and phone calls became her new form of communication with her family. Of course, the occasional holiday visit was always required in her mother's eyes, but other than that, she spent her free time on campus. For her birthday, she chose to stay on campus. Her mother decided being alone on campus was no way for Ali to celebrate her twenty-fifth birthday, so here Ali was, back on the ranch as requested. She pulled the car up the long paved driveway, which led to the house. As she parked, her thoughts drifted to Mitch. The anticipation of seeing him again brought goose bumps to her skin and that old familiar flutter in the core of her stomach began anew. She stepped from the car and looked up to see her mother at the front door.

"Mom!" Ali called out.

"Ali, baby, is that you?" Cora Lee dashed out to meet her.

Ali ran into her mother's arms. "It's so good to see you."

Cora Lee embraced her daughter at arm's length. "Oh my goodness, look at you. You've grown into a beautiful young woman while away."

"Oh, Mom, it's just that you haven't seen me for so long."

"And whose fault is that?" Nathaniel asked.

Ali looked up. Her father stepped towards them, and she scurried to him, her arms strangling his neck the way she had as a child. "Daddy, I had to concentrate on my work. I didn't want to break my momentum."

"I know, my baby girl...*a doctor*," he laughed.

"Not yet, I still have my internship and residency left to finish." She held on tightly to her father as they proceeded into the house.

A knock sounded on the back door. Tim stuck his head inside. "Welcome back, Miss Ali. We've all missed you around here. It's been way too quiet."

They all laughed.

"We're set for your birthday party." Cora Lee beamed at her daughter.

Ali glanced behind Tim. "That's um...great, Mom. Tim...where's Mitch?"

"Oh, Miss Ali, Mitch moved on a few weeks after you left," Tim said.

"Moved on? What do you mean? He wouldn't just leave, would he?" Ali asked. "What about the letters that I received from him? They were addressed from here."

Tim rubbed his hand across the back of his neck. "Well, uh, Mitch wrote those letters after you left. He left a box of them, told me to mail one out to you every week."

The room grew silent.

"What about the emails? I received messages from him almost every day. He never mentioned he'd left the ranch. Was it Mitch, or did you send those too?"

"Emails? No, Miss Ali, I don't know anything about any emails, only the letters."

"I'm not a little girl anymore. When was someone going to tell me?" Ali looked around the room as she waited for an answer.

"Sweetie, we didn't want to bother you at school," Cora Lee answered.

"It wouldn't have been a bother. Mitch...was never a bother *for me*." She frowned and turned to pick up her luggage. "I'm gonna go unpack."

She trudged upstairs to her bedroom. *I can't believe he's gone. He didn't even have the decency to tell me he was leaving.* She slung the empty suitcase to the floor and kicked it under her bed. A knock at her door broke into her silent monologue.

"Ali, may I come in?" her mother asked.

"Yeah, sure."

Cora Lee shut the door behind her. "You wanna talk about it?"

"No."

"Ali, *please*."

"Mother, there is nothing to talk about. Mitch is gone. I never should have made that deal with him. I wondered why he was never here when I came to visit. Why didn't he tell me? Why didn't someone tell me?

She sat down on the bed and motioned for Ali to join her. "Baby, that wouldn't have stopped him. Mitch didn't have anything tying him here once you were gone. We all knew he was hurting."

"What? How did you know there was something between us?" She took a seat next to her mother.

"Oh, honey, your father and I have known almost since the day the two of you met. At first, we weren't crazy about the idea with Mitch's history and all."

"Mother, Mitch didn't do anything wrong. He took the blame to help out a friend. Unfortunately, she was only using him. He was found guilty for a crime he didn't commit."

"Your father and I know that. Tim told us everything. He also told us about the incident with Brad and how he had come to your rescue. Mitch is a good man. He's such a good man that we had no choice but to accept him." She laughed softly.

"You know about that too?" Ali said.

"There's not too much that goes on around here that gets by us." She laughed harder.

Ali put her head on her mother's shoulder. "Mom, sometimes his letters or emails were the only things that got me through the day. All I could think about on my way here was how good it would be to see him again. How could he just leave?" Tears streamed down her face.

Cora Lee put her arm around her daughter. "I know, baby, I know, but you'll get through this. We'll get through this."

Thoughts of Mitch plagued her mind. She clutched her pillow tight and cried herself to sleep.

* * * *

God, I hate these damn parties. Ali stood in the barn doorway. The sloe lemonade she drank gave her a sense of calm that she needed right now. She watched the people arriving for her birthday party walk up the drive. She should have been excited; it was her twenty-fifth birthday, after all. No gift was equal to what it would mean if Mitch were by her side. She wanted to share this day with him. She leaned back against the doorway and closed her eyes.

"Miss Ali?" A voice interrupted her thoughts.

Startled, Ali popped open her eyes. "Oh, Tim, it's you." A relieved sigh escaped her.

"I didn't mean to frighten you."

"It's all right." She managed a wavering smile.

"How are you holding up?"

She searched the ground, as if looking for an answer. "I'm okay."

"I'm sorry you're so down on your birthday, Miss Ali."

"It's not your fault, Tim, but thank-you."

"All right, I was just checking. I'll leave you be." He patted her arm and strode over to her father.

"*Ali*," Cora Lee yelled. "Come on, sweetie, they're bringing out the cake."

Ali waved. "I'm coming." She took the last sip from her glass, placed it on a fence post, and hurried to join the guests. She stepped up to the table and said, "I'd like to thank everyone for coming out today to celebrate my birthday with me. It really means a lot to me. So, have some cake, eat a little barbeque, and have a good time."

She glanced out across the lawn. Everywhere she looked there seemed to be a happy couple cuddled together. *I'm glad someone's having fun.*

"Happy birthday, little one," someone whispered in Ali's ear. A soft kiss touched her cheek, and a shiver ran down her spine.

"*Mitch?*" She spun around so fast she almost knocked him down. She jumped into his arms and threw her arms around his neck. "Mitch, you came back!"

"I wouldn't miss this for the world." A smile lit up his face.

She couldn't take the chance of losing him again. The pit of her stomach knotted. Today she would finally tell him how she felt.

"Mitch?" Stroking her hand across his arm, she looked into his eyes. She could drown in those honey-brown pools of his.

"What's wrong, sweetie?" he asked.

"I need to talk to you...alone."

"All right."

She took him by the hand and led him away from the party. They headed down to the creek under the weeping willows. The branches seemed to dance in the warm summer breeze. Under the cover of the trees, and finally alone, Ali turned to face Mitch. A frown formed across his brow as he stepped towards her and looked into her eyes. Ali sensed a change in him—maturity? Yes, that was it. She glimpsed the man he was meant to be fully displayed in his expression. Her wide-eyed innocence was gone, too, and she saw him now not through the eyes of an infatuated teen but through the eyes of a sensual, grown woman.

"What's this all about, Ali?" he asked.

A surge of emotion pulsed through Ali. She knew if she did not speak now she would lose her nerve. Now was the time to take advantage of an opportunity she thought lost.

"Mitch, I...." She stumbled over her words.

"You what?"

"Will you shut up and let me finish?"

"Okay, okay, I'm sorry." He laughed. "Please continue."

She took a deep breath, threw her hands out to her sides. "I want *you*, that's what," she blurted. "I've wanted you since the first day I met you. I want to be with you. I want to feel your lips pressed against mine. I want to feel you against me. Is that too much to ask?"

Mitch stepped closer, put his arms around her waist, and she relaxed against him. She thought her heart might burst from the sheer excitement of his touch.

"Ali, I can't give you all the things you're used to having. My pockets aren't deep; hell, they're practically non-existent."

"I don't care that you're not rich. I never did."

"All I can offer you is my heart. I hope that's enough."

"That's more than I could ever ask for."

He embraced her and kissed her passionately. She returned his kiss, and Mitch tightened his grip. Secure in his arms, she wanted to melt into him. He drew back only to take a breath.

"*Whoa*...." His lips rested in the crease of her neck. "Kissing you again is just as I remembered and somehow so much more."

"You've thought about us while you were away?" Ali whispered.

"Did I think about us? Only every waking moment, Ali. A day didn't go by that I didn't think of you. I just...needed to get away for a while. Everything here reminded me of you. I couldn't take it anymore. I barely got through the emails." He laughed.

"Then why did you send them?"

"Because *I* needed it; I had to hear your voice, even if it was only written."

"I thought you had forgotten me."

Mitch cupped her face in his hands. "Little one, I could never forget you. I couldn't if I tried. I want to spend the rest of my life with you."

He held her so tightly she thought she might melt right into him. A breeze blew through the trees. Mitch and Ali looked up into the waving and bowing branches, holding one another beneath the willows.

He looked at her and smiled. "Well now, what do you think *they're* whispering about?"

Author bio:

Kensana Darnell is an author of sweet romance stories of old. She resides in Asheville, NC with her family. Check her out at: kensanadarnell@ gmail.com, http://kensanadarnell.hostrator.com/Index.htm, http://kensanadarnell.wordpress.com.

Little Cowgirl
by
Nicolette Zamora

Greg, a grieving widower, investigates a party and finds a sexy cowgirl named Nan. Can she lasso his broken heart?

Greg Louison grumbled to himself. Why couldn't he have forgotten his cell phone? Then he would never have picked up his mother's call, demanding that he instruct her neighbors to turn down their 'wretched music.' Instead, he would be on his way home, ready for a cold brew and watching ESPN highlights.

Although his shift had ended, Greg figured that his uniform would be more inspiring, more conducive toward getting the partiers to quiet down. However, it shocked him to realize that he wasn't the only police officer there. Well, not that he had ever seen a cop wear a uniform that tight and with so much skin and cleavage showing. A costume party. Great. He'd fit right in. So much for uniform encouragement.

Greg maneuvered through the throng. Loud music played, and everyone enjoyed plenty of food and beer. People mingled, danced, and kissed on the front lawn. As Greg tried to locate the host or hostess, he couldn't help but wonder when the last time he'd been to a party was. Years ago. With Helena.

He sighed and shook his head. He didn't want to think about Helena right now.

"You seem a little out of place," a gentle voice said.

At first, Greg thought he'd imagined it.

"Well, I...." He cleared his throat and turned around. With gleaming hazel eyes and a small, up-turned nose, the woman demanded his appreciation. Greg wondered if she had any flaws. She was a natural looker with no make-up, yet her slightly provocative cowgirl outfit, a tight fringe vest over a white t-shirt, and extremely short shorts didn't match her gentle voice.

Laughing, she raised a curved eyebrow. She didn't seem to mind his lingering glance, although she did self-consciously tug at the bottom of her shorts, drawing his gaze to her long legs. "You aren't on the guest list, are you?" she asked.

"Not exactly," Greg said. "You see, my mother lives next door." He pointed to the house on the left. It was nine P.M., so his mother should still be up watching the Game Show Network, but there wasn't a single light on in the house. Was his mother even home now? "She...ah, called me and wanted me to ask if someone would turn down the music. I don't really think it's that loud. Not too loud at least."

The striking woman laughed again, revealing strong, white teeth. Greg stared at her lips. They were a little too large, he decided, so her beauty wasn't flawless after all. It made her more approachable.

"I wouldn't mind the music being turned down a little either. Better do it while Meg's busy." She flipped her long, wavy hair over her shoulder and gestured toward another woman who wore a bar wench's outfit with a tiny, tight mesh shirt that barely covered her breasts, and a skirt so short she didn't dare bend over.

Her face reminded Greg of the cowgirl's, only more severe with firmer features and harsher lines. "Your sister?" he guessed, following the cowgirl.

"Yep." She reached the speakers and turned the music down. No one else noticed as the party seemed to grow even livelier. "Nan Windslow."

"Greg Louison." He held out his hand and hoped she wouldn't notice how callused it was from his part-time hobby of woodcarving. "Does she throw parties often?"

"No. But when she does, she really knows how to throw 'em." Nan smiled.

Greg found himself smiling back. Maybe he would just have his cold brew here.

* * * *

Nan headed over to the drink table. Pouring herself a gin and tonic, she fought her annoyance at herself. Here she was at yet another one of her sister's famous parties; Nan hated being dragged to them, sometimes even feigning illness to skip out. But Meg emphatically insisted this time around, claiming that Nan absolutely had to be there. So she'd thrown on some faded jeans, some old boots, a white shirt, and a fringed vest. A pink cowboy's hat finished the simple costume.

Nan showed up at the party ten minutes early, feeding into her sister's demands. Meg took one look at her costume, pursed her thin lips, and shook her head. "We have to do something about that. Way too tame."

"But it's fine!" Nan protested.

"Not for this party." Meg dragged Nan into her bedroom and practically stripped her. Meg stared at her sister, now clad in only her underclothing, and remarked, "The bra too." Her sister handed her the shortest pair of jean shorts that Nan had ever seen.

"No." Nan stomped her foot. "I'll wear the so-short-you-can-see-my-butt shorts but I'm leaving the top as is."

"But you could be so much sexier if you just...."

Nan ignored her sister and dressed again. Before Nan could examine her appearance in the mirror, Meg stepped forward and tied the two ties of the vest, forcing Nan's breasts together. Nan admired her updated outfit and admitted that she looked like a sexy cowgirl. Her large breasts were ready to explode from their constraints. Thankfully, the white t-shirt allowed for a slight amount of modesty, but she didn't feel natural. And she was certain she would be out of place.

It turned out that Nan's modified costume retained more modesty than the rest of the women's, who all tried to reveal the most skin. Women wore bikinis to mesh tops and virtually nonexistent bottoms. Nan gaped at the array and decided she needed a couple of drinks to get over her shock and embarrassment. Even her sister dressed as a sexy bar wench!

Nan finally began to unwind, but she spotted a tall, handsome cop. From the way he kept looking around, she wondered if he was searching for someone. She saw a glint from his left leg—a gun—a real one. *He must be an actual cop.* She waltzed up to him and said, "You seem a little out of place."

He was even more handsome up close. She noticed his eyes first; they were a deep azure, bright and beautiful. Under normal circumstances, his uniform and strong build would make him an intimidating figure, but at the costume party, he seemed to have lost some of his authority. It pleased Nan that she'd allowed her sister to coerce her into wearing the sexier cowgirl version.

While Greg left to get them fresh drinks, Nan glanced around. Making eye contact with her sister, she smiled and nodded, and Meg winked back.

And just what was she intending? Nan shook her head. She wasn't the type of girl to let just any guy take her home. She certainly didn't want to seem bold or forceful but there was something about this man, this Greg, that made her act differently. *Of course, that might be the alcohol working.*

"Here ya go, little cowgirl," he said, his deep voice sending tingles over her body.

Nan gratefully accepted her drink. "Why, thank ya," she said, a smile in her voice as she adopted a Southern accent. She giggled at her poor attempt, and he laughed too. She eyed his beer. "I certainly hope you're off duty."

"I am." He swallowed a long gulp. "But that doesn't mean I can't still arrest people." He rewarded her with a teasing grin.

Little Cowgirl

Nan smiled. "You could arrest me anytime."

* * * *

Her smile really lights up her face. Mesmerized, Greg couldn't take his gaze off her. "So tell me about yourself," he said. "Does the little cowgirl ride horses?" He had barely met the woman but already found himself drawn to her, wanting to know everything about her, her past, her present—so long as it didn't involve another man—and her future.

"No." She shook her head, causing her brown hair to swirl around her shoulders in waves. "But I always wanted to. What about you?"

"Just once." The memories of Helena were still raw, the nerve too tender.

"If it wasn't pleasant, then we'll just talk about something else."

But it had been pleasant. Too pleasant. Greg cursed himself for failing at his poker face and forced himself from the past. He focused on the woman in front of him. "I'm sorry. What where you saying?"

At that moment, Nan's sister wandered over. "Nan, I really need you. Some of the guys are getting out of hand." Her words tumbled from her mouth in a rush of panic.

"Anything I can help with?" Greg offered, not wanting his time with Nan to end.

"We're fine," Meg said without a glance, already dragging Nan away.

"It was nice meeting you," he called.

Nan offered him an apologetic wave.

Greg watched her retreating figure until the two women disappeared into the house. With his assistance not wanted, Greg had no choice but to leave. He sighed as he climbed into his car, a heavy cloud of disappointment hanging over him. Most likely, he would never see Nan again, and even if he did, he had certainly left with things on a sour note. Maybe he should reevaluate things concerning Helena first before trying to have another relationship. Yet the pain was still too deep, too sensitive.

* * * *

The next morning, Nan woke up in a foul mood. First, the emergency that Meg had needed her for so desperately was nothing; it was merely her sister's way of getting Greg to leave. The party queen had realized that he was, indeed, a police officer and not just dressed as one. Oh, no...Meg couldn't possibly have a *real* cop at her party, could she?

Secondly, she had been too tired and had had a little too much to drink to drive home, so she'd slept at Meg's place.

Thirdly, she couldn't take her mind off Greg's blue eyes. She hadn't realized eyes could be that shade of blue, so identical to the sky. She could just imagine being whisked into the heavens in his strong arms as she gazed into his eyes.

Fourthly, her sister had bounced into the room way too early. "Wake up, little sis! Come on, you promised that you'd go over for brunch today!"

"Brunch?" Nan mumbled, her face buried in a pillow. "Promise?"

"Yes. Just before you fell asleep last night, you promised to go over to Mrs. Louison's for brunch. And we don't have much time to get ready. The shower's all yours!" Meg hurried from the room, her voice chipper and bright.

Nan scowled as she entered the shower. The initial cold blast of water quickly revived her, but her annoyance remained. How dare Meg pry a promise out of her when she was in no condition to promise anything! Despite her displeasure, Nan dressed and readied herself in twenty minutes.

Later, at Mrs. Louison's, Meg rang the doorbell before opening the door. "Come on, she always lets me walk in."

Nan followed without a word, gawking at everything. Candles lit the hallway, and old, historical works dotted the walls. Obviously, someone was a history buff, or at least a collector of wonderful art. Nan lagged behind, taking in the scenery until Meg grabbed her arm and dragged her to the dining room.

"How are you on this fine morning, Mrs. Louison?" Meg said, easing herself into a Queen Anne chair.

"Doing just fine." Mrs. Louison's sharp emerald eyes seemed to miss nothing.

Nan smiled politely. *Greg must have his father's eyes.* She sat down next to her sister.

Mrs. Louison asked, "And this is...?"

"My younger sister, Nan. I hope you don't mind that she tagged along," Meg said smoothly.

"It's nice to meet you," Nan said with a smile.

Greg's mother just stared at Nan. Despite feeling uncomfortable, Nan refused to look away.

"The food is in the kitchen. Would you be a dear and bring it in, Meg? My arthritis is killing me today."

"Certainly." Meg jumped up and left the room.

"I'll go help," Nan offered, half out of her seat.

Little Cowgirl

"There's no need," Mrs. Louison barked. "Meg can get it."

An awkward silence fell over the room and hovered like a storm cloud. Nan heard Meg talking and laughing in the kitchen, but the words were barely audible and Nan couldn't distinguish between them. *Who else is in the house?*

Mrs. Louison leaned back with a happy sigh.

"I hope that the music wasn't too loud yesterday," Nan said, attempting to destroy the pervasive stillness.

"The music?"

"At Meg's party yesterday. You sent your son over to ask us to turn it down."

Mrs. Louison laughed, the sound a harsh crackle. "I sent my son over so that he might finally have a chance to get over Helena and meet a nice girl. Meg should do just fine."

With a sinking sensation, Nan guessed that Meg was flirting with Greg right this second. And between the two of them, what guy would pick the shorter one, the plainer one, the shy and quiet one when he could have a roaring-good time with the party queen?

Nan swallowed hard before venturing, "I met him yesterday; he seems nice enough."

"Nice isn't the word to describe my boy," Mrs. Louison said with pride.

Greg and Meg entered the room, both carrying trays loaded with food: pancakes, waffles, toppings, scrambled eggs, sausage, and bacon.

Nan stared at Greg. He smiled in a way that he hadn't the night before, and Nan felt a familiar wrenching pain in her gut. She should be used to it; after all, Meg had stolen two other guys from her before.

"Morning, Mom." Greg kissed his mother on the cheek and sat down at the table.

"How long have you been here? And you just now decided to join us?" his mother snapped.

He ignored her.

Nan watched as he loaded his plate with so much food it hung over the plate's side. She attempted to catch his eye, but he seemed to see through her. She sighed unhappily. *He hasn't even noticed me.*

"Aren't you hungry, Nan? I know I'm starved!" Meg said a little too brightly for Nan's taste.

"Yeah," Nan mumbled, taking a plate and putting the closest foods onto it.

Greg glanced up, surprise on his face. "Nan! I didn't know you were coming!"

So Greg knew all about the brunch and Meg coming over. Nan couldn't hide her disappointment and said nothing throughout the meal. She sneaked glances at him as she eyed his broad shoulders, comparable to most cops, but without the gut that some had from too many sweets on long stakeouts. If he always ate like this, he must work out often to be so fit.

The instant she finished eating, she wanted to bolt, but Meg, Greg, and his mother were talking. Nan didn't even know what the conversation was about; she just stared at her plate, feeling miserable, lost and alone.

Second place, second rate.

* * * *

Something was wrong. When Greg woke up the morning after the party, he knew it. Sure enough, his mother had left a message for him to come over for brunch—immediately—and he had better dress nice too. This meant she'd invited some girl over in an attempt to play matchmaker.

Greg sighed. For all he knew, that was exactly why she'd sent him over to the party in the first place. *She means well, but sometimes...she seems just...mean. She doesn't care that I'm still grieving.*

Helena. Greg glanced at the picture beside his bed. They were together, smiling, lovingly trapped in a frozen moment of perfection. She had captured his heart and soul, an all-American girl with perfect curly blonde hair and bright blue eyes. Although Helena had carried around an extra ten pounds, she'd been just as outdoorsy as he was and loved hiking, riding horses, and camping. One weekend, they had planned to go rock climbing, but at the last minute, Greg had been called into work.

"Go ahead. Don't change your plans on account of me," Greg had told her. And those had been the last words he'd ever said to his wife.

That had been three years ago. Longer than the two and a half years they had been married, more than enough time to have moved on. Yet, he couldn't help comparing each woman he met to Helena.

Until Nan. Greg couldn't stop thinking about her. Even when he'd left the party and his thoughts had been on Helena, Nan had been in the back of his mind too. But how could he see her again? He didn't know where she lived, and her sister had been rather abrupt last night, so he wasn't sure she would give him the information. Meg seemed to be a domineering woman, too similar to his mother. Good looking, yes, but something drew him to her sister.

When Greg arrived at his mother's, he'd immediately headed toward the kitchen. His mother had the food ready—more than enough for an army.

Three glasses were set aside, although the drinks were still refrigerated. *Three's a crowd.* Greg scowled.

Footsteps startled him, and he whirled around. As if he had conjured her from his thoughts, Meg stood in front of him. If only her sister had appeared instead.

Greg didn't know what to say, but Meg didn't give him the chance. "Hi. I don't think I've had the pleasure of meeting you. I'm Meg Windslow. I sometimes help your mother around the house and gardens."

"Greg." He nodded, trying to smile since hers seemed to cover her entire face; somehow, Greg couldn't help but feel repulsed. Did she honestly not recognize him from last night? Or did she not care that he had been spending time with her sister? Either way, Greg couldn't help but feel as though his initial impression was correct: she was much rougher and harsher than her seemingly gentle and caring sister. Plus, he vaguely remembered his mother mentioning a neighbor who sometimes helped with her garden. His mother had complained that the girl pulled out more flowers than weeds. If Meg was that girl, his mother must be desperate to find someone for him.

Unexpectedly, Meg laughed. "All this food! It looks so delicious!" She gave him a winning smile.

Grabbing a tray of food, Greg was struck by how different the two sisters were. Nan was more reserved and yet more open. Meg just looked for a good time, expecting men to fawn all over her.

"You know," she said, "on second thought, you do look a little familiar. Have we met?"

"Yesterday," Greg acknowledged. "Your sister...."

"Oh, that's right. The police officer! I must say that uniform looked so realistic!" She laughed again and leaned over to touch his arm.

Greg maneuvered the tray to avoid her. "Let's go."

Once he sat down, his stomach grumbled. He was famished and loaded his plate with breakfast treats, a forced smile on his face for Meg's benefit. When Meg mentioned her sister, Greg glanced up, surprised. He'd been so wrapped up in his thoughts he'd honestly missed that Nan was at the table! Looking cute in a black spaghetti-strapped tank top and jeans, she appeared uncomfortable and a bit pale. *She must have a hangover.*

Even though she kept to herself, Greg continued to stare. Some syrup dripped onto her lower lip, and Greg wanted to lick it up. Her lips were full, but perfectly kissable. He quickly looked away, embarrassed by the thought. He hadn't kissed a woman in years, hadn't even thought of it, and yet Nan was firing his imagination in ways that he'd long ago laid to rest.

The conversation flowed, but Greg only responded when his mother or

Meg expected him to. Only after everyone had their fill did Greg clear away the dirty dishes. Nan had been so overlooked by his mother and Meg that she'd eaten with no drink. He'd only brought in the three glasses his mother had set aside. Greg felt horrible but, by the time he returned to the dining room, the women had already left. He glanced out the window in time to see a blue mustang leave from Meg's driveway, presumably Nan's.

"Thank you for the food. It was delicious," Greg said woodenly, resuming his place at the table beside his mother.

"Oh, stop being such a poor sport. I brought over a gorgeous woman, and you hardly even looked at her, let alone talked to her!"

"In case you didn't notice, there were two women here," Greg said, his tone sharp.

His mother raised an eyebrow. "Yet you didn't talk to her either." Her voice contained a warning tone. "Seemed rather unpleasant, that one."

"And Meg is just so friendly," Greg snarked.

"Yes," his mother said too eagerly.

"You should have seen how many guys were hanging all over her yesterday. They were like dogs, ready to pounce."

Mrs. Louison narrowed her eyes. "Jealous?"

"Not in the slightest," he retorted.

"Well, the quiet one has nice enough eyes...I think. It was hard for me to see them, though; she was so engrossed in the food that her gaze hardly left her plate."

"Then she must have enjoyed your cooking. That can hardly be considered a slight," Greg said.

"Well?"

"Well." He sighed, annoyed with his mother's games. "I'll let you know."

* * * *

After leaving the Louison's, Nan immediately walked over to her car. "Thanks for letting me crash," she said as she unlocked the door.

"You don't have to jet right away. I mean, it's not as if you have a hot date or anything."

The slight was just too much for Nan. "And how many...?" The angry retort died on her lips. Nan could hardly blame Greg for preferring her sister, and her sister never cared about anyone other than herself. Was it worth getting into an argument over? One that Meg probably didn't even see coming, so blind was she to everyone else around her? "I need to get going. I'll see you." And Nan drove away before she could hear her sister's response.

For the next two days, Nan refused to think about Greg Louison. However, despite her best intentions, her mind wandered back to him. When she left for a walk to clear her mind, she ended up gazing at the sky, thinking of his dreamy eyes. When she washed her costume, she recalled his initial once over; it was the first time she'd felt desired by someone in a long time. And when she spotted a cop car driving behind her, her heart sped up. Could it be him? The lights flickered on, and Nan pulled over, completely at a loss.

"License and registration," the officer demanded, dipping his head to her open window. Nan complied, annoyed with herself for hoping the officer was Greg.

He held up her license and examined it. "Is something wrong?" Nan asked. "I swear I wasn't speeding."

The officer frowned at her. "The ever elusive Nan Windslow. You know, I've pulled over three other blue mustangs just to find you." He sighed. "And all because you're the reason why one of our officers has been so depressed lately. And it's killing morale. You see, Greg is usually the one to bring donuts into the office, but since he met you, he hasn't. Instead of talking about his wife like he always does, he'd rather talk about you and your gentle voice."

"Wife?" Nan mouthed. The word crashed into her like a thunderbolt. A cloud of misery loomed larger than her sister's betrayal. *He's married?*

"Can I get your phone number so the poor guy can ask you out already?"

Nan's shock was so great that she stammered her number. Finally, she yanked her papers and license back and drove away.

Married. The man who she couldn't stop thinking about, the man who she was nearly in love with, despite her sister trying to hone in on him, was permanently untouchable. She hadn't seen a ring on his finger, but that meant nothing. Many men didn't wear their bands, especially if they were trying to have a good time with unsuspecting women. And his mother thought nice wasn't good enough to describe him. *Lady, I have much more vulgar words for him now.*

Minutes later, Nan walked into her apartment with one thought creeping into her mind that refused to be banished. His mother had invited Meg over for brunch because of Greg. Could Mrs. Louison really be trying to help him cheat on his wife? Something just didn't add up, and Nan tried to focus on the suspicion, an anchor to a possibly safe harbor. It nearly prevented her from bursting into tears. Nearly.

* * * *

When Greg received the memo from Paul Runi, he immediately grabbed the phone and dialed. One ring, two, three. No answer. Deciding to call again, relief filled him as someone finally answered the phone.

"Hello?" a nasally voice said.

"Is this Nan? Nan Windslow?" Greg asked. The voice sounded so far from the gentle sweet one that haunted his thoughts he wasn't sure if it was from the same person.

"Yes. Who's this?"

"It's Greg."

"What do you want?" She sounded surprised and not exactly pleased, a combination of emotions that confused Greg. Hadn't Paul told her that he wanted to locate her?

"I was wondering if maybe we could get together sometime. Maybe have another meal together."

"And would you actually talk to me this time?"

Greg frowned. "I thought you were a little hung over that morning, so I didn't want to bother you."

"But you certainly had no problem talking with my sister. Are you sure you wouldn't rather go out to dinner with her?"

There was no mistaking the hostility in her tone, and Greg couldn't fathom why. "No."

"Or your wife?"

"Excuse me?" he said.

"Oh, wasn't your cop friend supposed to mention her to me?"

Greg closed his eyes and tried to inhale a calming deep breath. Instead, he swallowed the gulp of air in a rush and barked out, "Listen, you don't know anything about my wife and you really shouldn't be judging—"

"I don't think it's hard to judge a man who's sneaking around behind his wife's back, trying to make plans with another woman!"

Her harsh tone seemed mild compared to his coarse and aggressive one. "I would much rather have dinner with her than you anyway!"

"Then why don't you?"

"Because she's dead!" Greg yelled into the receiver and slammed it down. He covered his face with his hands and slowly rocked back and forth in his seat. Her accusing words continued to echo in his ears, and he stood up and stormed out of his cubicle and left the station. At home, he stomped into his bedroom and plopped on the bed, but he couldn't sleep, couldn't think, couldn't concentrate.

Opening his eyes, he grabbed the perfect picture of happiness and threw it.

The shatter of glass proved to be a comforting and welcome sound.

* * * *

"Greg?" Nan whispered into the phone, completely mortified. The harsh beep-beep-beep signaled a hang up. Nan slowly dropped the receiver in place. Again, her eyes welled up with tears. How could she have been so harsh with him? And those words that she'd said, the accusations! No wonder his mother had Meg over; she was trying to get her son to move on from his grief! *And I only added to it!*

How much more don't I know about him? Nan climbed into her car. She could only pray that he would give her the chance to find out.

During the drive, her thoughts ran wild. His extremely short blond hair intrigued her. Would it move if she ran her fingers through it? How soft or stiff was it compared to his hard, tight muscles? Now she might never know. The thought left her drained, depressed, and furious with herself. In such a short time, Greg had become so important to her.

At the local police station, Nan saw several bored officers behind the front desks. With mucus-colored walls and horrific green-tiled floors, Nan couldn't imagine a more dismal-looking place to work in.

She spied the officer who had pulled her over earlier that day and hurried to his desk. "Is Greg here? I really need to talk to him."

The cop stared at her for a long moment, sized up her swollen, puffy eyes and nodded. "He left. Went home, I think. Seemed a little upset."

"Oh," Nan whispered, a sigh escaping her lips.

"I can give you his address."

Nan shook her head. "I don't think he wants to see me right now."

The man laughed. "Of course he does. You're all he talks about!"

Nan bit her lip. "Maybe he did. But I...I made a mistake."

"Must have been a pretty big one if you think that he wants nothing to do with you."

"I didn't know that he was married until you said something about his wife. And I certainly didn't realize that she was...deceased," Nan said in such a hushed tone that the cop leaned down to hear her.

"Oh, well that certainly explains things," the cop said slowly, realization lighting his eyes. He now seemed much more approachable, less of a gruff papa bear and more of a teddy. "That's my fault."

"No."

"Yes, it is. Listen, I'll straighten things out with Greg for you. It's the least I can do."

"Thank you," Nan said with a wan smile. "I hope...." She sighed. "Thank you."

"Paul."

"Thank you, Paul."

"Just let me handle it." He winked.

* * * *

A half hour passed, and Greg hadn't left his bed. His gaze remained on the ceiling and he didn't bother to look away when he heard someone climb the stairs.

"Greg. Get up."

The voice belonged to Paul, a good friend; yet, Greg wasn't pleased to see him. He just wanted to be alone. He ignored Paul, who picked up the broken frame and placed the picture on the nightstand. Greg swatted at it but missed, his gaze still on the ceiling.

"What's so interesting?" Paul asked.

"Leave," Greg growled.

"No." Paul walked over to the computer desk and sat down on the chair. "A beautiful young lady came down to the station a little bit ago. Was rather distraught."

Greg didn't react.

"Seemed to be blaming herself for something that wasn't entirely her fault."

Greg blinked but refused to comment.

"You see, I happened to mention your wife to her in passing when I got Nan's number for you. I hadn't thought anything of it because you seemed so gone over her that I assumed you might've confided in her. I thought she knew. Seriously, Greg! How can you expect to move on when you can't even tell the prospective lady about your history? Helena is a part of you, yes, but she's a part of your past. Now there's a wonderful woman who is beating herself up because she made an assumption, a wrong one. And she hurt you, yes, but she didn't mean to. So maybe you should give her another chance."

"Why should I?" Greg asked hoarsely.

"Either give her another chance or live in the past. It's your choice, Greg, but I would much rather have a living, breathing woman with me than just a memory. It doesn't mean that you love Helena any less. But you can move on and live your life."

Greg watched Paul leave. He reached over to the photo and gently ran his fingers over Helena's face before placing the picture facedown on the table.

* * * *

Nan returned home. The instant she closed and locked the front door, her phone rang. She dashed across the room. "Hello?" she said breathlessly.

"Nan? Are you exercising? You sound out of breath."

"Meg." Nan sighed.

"Well, you hardly sound thrilled to hear from me."

"Can you blame me? You knew that I liked Greg. You knew he was the cop from the party, yet you did nothing but shamelessly flirt with him at the brunch. Do you have some kind of complex that makes you take away everything that means something to me?" Nan couldn't stop the rush of words and grimaced. After all, her sister couldn't come between her and Greg when she'd already seen to that herself.

"Excuse me?" Meg said, her voice icy. "You were hardly the life of the party at the brunch, not saying a word to anyone! I'm not surprised he didn't even glance at you!"

"Right, Meg. That's why he called you."

"N-no," Meg admitted. "But I'm sure he will!"

"So you admit it: you were trying to steal him."

"Well, it's just—"

"Just that you can't stand for me to be happy."

"Of course I want you to be happy!"

"Then why were you flirting with him?"

"Because I just wanted to make sure he was the right guy for you. If he took a liking to me, then he couldn't be good for you, right?"

"Meg, don't sugarcoat it."

"Okay, okay. I admit it; I was wrong. I shouldn't have done that. It's just...he seemed so nice and different."

"Different from the dirtbags you normally date?"

Meg paused. "Yeah. I guess you could say that."

"Well, maybe he has a brother."

"You think?" Meg asked eagerly. "Because...I'll be honest, he didn't seem interested in me."

"Well, I'm glad to hear it," Nan said with a laugh. She wondered a little at how open and genuine her sister sounded; it was completely different from her normally fake, cheery facade. "And I'll find out if he has a brother. Or cousin."

"Great!"

"So, why did you call?"

"Oh, I accidentally dialed your number. I meant to call Joe."

"Isn't he the guy you can't stand?"

"Well, he does have a cute butt and he's a good kisser," Meg said.

"And here I thought you wanted me to find you a good guy!"

"Hey, I can have fun while I wait, right?" She laughed. "I should get going. Talk to you later!"

"Bye." Nan hung up, feeling a little better since she'd finally stood up to her sister. Now, if only Paul would be able to get Greg to forgive her....

* * * *

Greg slowly sat up. He reached into his pocket for his cell phone. Instead, he pulled out a small piece of paper. The memo with Nan's number on it. He sighed.

Helena. Nan.

Although Nan had been furious with him, she'd also been protective of his wife. He could still hear the hurt in her voice, the betrayal that she'd felt. It warmed his heart to know how much she respected his marriage. Nan cared for Helena and had defended her without even knowing her. A thunderbolt of realization coursed through him. Nan was the kind of woman that Helena would have befriended. The thought seemed to ease the blow, and the knowledge made him willing to finally reach out to another woman.

He dialed the number before he lost his nerve.

"Hello?"

"It's me, Nan," Greg said.

"Hi, Nan," Nan quipped.

Greg laughed, surprised by how easy she was making this. "I think I owe you an apology."

"No! If anyone needs to apologize, it's me. When I think about all the things I said...."

"You didn't know the truth, and I really didn't get a chance to tell you."

"There's no reason why I should have known. It's none of my business."

"Yes, it is. Just because my wife is dead doesn't mean that I can't enjoy female companionship. And if that female company is a strikingly beautiful woman whom I can't stop thinking about and just may want to date, then she deserves to know about my past."

"Only if you really want to talk about it."

"Over dinner. Tomorrow?"

"Anytime," Nan said softly.

Greg hesitated. "Would you like to go horseback riding first?"

"Are you sure?" Nan asked, surprised. His reaction to horseback riding when they had first met sprang to mind. She could only assume he'd shared rides with his wife. Her heart rate accelerated. If he truly wanted her in his life, then horseback riding might be an excellent start.

"I'm sure. There's nothing wrong with making new, magical moments."

"No." Nan grinned. She longed to see him again. Now she would have her chance to run her fingers through his hair. She recalled her conversation with Meg and asked, "Do you have any brothers? Or cousins who are currently single?"

"Why?"

"I told my sister I would ask."

"I don't. And even if I did, I'm not sure Meg is ready for a real relationship."

"I know I am," Nan said, amazed by her confident tone.

"I am too," Greg replied. "But only with my little cowgirl."

After finalizing their plans for the next evening, Greg hung up. The smile on his face stretched so wide his jaws ached. He realized that his heart was big enough to love both Nan and Helena, and he couldn't wait to open up and confide in Nan, his little cowgirl, his newfound love.

Author Bio:

Nicolette Zamora loves romance from first kiss to I do, sweet or passionate. A new writer, she sheds fresh light on the wonders of love. For more information about Nicolette and her work, visit her website at: www. freewebs.com/nicolettezamora.

Forever Guy
by
Jambrea Jo Jones

Samantha has a crush on Jack. Now that he's back in town, she needs to convince him he's her forever guy.

Tired and dirty, Samantha Reynolds walked into her office. She grimaced as she wiped the mud off her cheek and sat down in her chair, blowing her hair out of her face with a sigh.

Will this day never end? What is it with those Thomas twins?

"Mac, I still need to go to the bank for my daily run through. Take care of the Thomas paper work for me, and then you can head home to Louise. I'm on call tonight so give her a kiss for me," Sam called out to her deputy.

Mac chuckled and replied, "Sure thing, boss, catch you tomorrow."

Mac's chuckles followed him until the door closed behind him, leaving silence in his wake.

Sure, he can laugh. He didn't have a farm animal run him over, causing them both to slosh through a mud hole. Oh no, that honor belonged solely to her.

Sam shook her head, still trying to wrap her mind around the fact that those boys thought it would be funny to let a pig loose in Widow Owens's house. Of course, she got the call from the hysterical woman, and now she had mud from head to toe with the bank walk-through looming ahead of her. She tried to fix her bun, but her hair had a mind of its own. She might as well just get the bank run over with so she could go home and take a nice long, hot bubble bath.

As the first female Sheriff of Port, she tried to always appear cool and collected.

I do have an image to uphold. With a town this small, I'll never live this down.

Sighing again, she pushed herself up from her chair and headed out the door, but not before running her fingers over the photo of her dad.

I will make you proud of me, Dad.

She still missed her parents and thought of them often. Mostly she thought of her dad anytime something wonky happened, like today. She didn't try to fill her daddy's shoes—really, she didn't—but she knew the town would always compare her to her father.

Sam smiled weakly.

They still call me Bobby's girl more than they do Sheriff.

With a lighter tread, she finally left her office, adjusting her gun on her hip. She whistled as she shut off the lights, her thoughts on the bank and the end of her long day.

On the way, Sam stopped to pick up a newspaper. Absorbed in a headline, she opened the bank's door and collided with someone.

"I am so sorry. I wasn't paying attent—" Sam looked up.

No, it can't be. Is it? What...?

"Samantha Reynolds! Is that you?" the young man asked.

Oh my goodness, it IS him. Stop thinking and say something before he thinks you've been struck dumb.

"Umm...I...." She struggled to hold back the flood of schoolgirl emotions his presence unlocked. With one look from him, she turned into a knobby-kneed girl who suffered the hots for her brother's friend.

Nice one, Sam. She mentally kicked herself and shook her head. She was the town sheriff, darn it, not some silly girl with a high school crush.

Get a hold of yourself.

Pulling herself together, she continued, "Jack, you're back in town? Are you visiting?"

There, much better. I don't sound desperate at all. Nope just a girl talking to a guy. Oh, he looks so good. Am I drooling? Shoot, I'm covered in mud. What must he be thinking? There is no way I look sexy caked in mud. Stop that. He's talking again. Pay attention to what he's saying, not how you look.

"I just got in today. Didn't Mitch tell you? I planned on calling him, but I wanted to get everything in order before the town closed down for the night. It will take a bit to get used to small-town living again."

"Mitch is buried in work right now, and I've been on call so he didn't have a chance to say anything. So...are you back for good? Are you finished with the military?"

His eyes darkened, and his face hardened. Sam wondered what thoughts ran through his mind.

"The teller is ready for you. Why don't you give me a call later, and we can catch up?" She directed him to the window. *Please say yes, please say yes.* She ripped off a piece of her notebook paper and wrote down her number for him. "I live with Mitch at our parents' old house, so I'm sure you have this number, but here you go, you know, just in case."

Great, now I'm rambling. Just turn, leave and hope he calls. Well, that is just stupid. Of course he'll call. Stupid, stupid, he's your brother's best friend.

Sam shoved the number at him, trying not to blush, and turned to finish her walk-through so she could leave before Jack had a chance to say anything. She had enough embarrassment for one day and she could just hope he called for her and not Mitch.

* * * *

Sam couldn't believe it. Jack called *her*. Not Mae or Jill, the two knockouts in town, but *her*: Samantha Reynolds, tomboy extraordinaire. Of course, she had given him her number and asked him to phone her, not to mention they knew each other from way back, but he had called, and that's all that mattered. He didn't even want to talk to her brother. It was just a quick talk asking her out to dinner. Her dreams of him might be within her reach after all.

In high school, she'd followed Jack and her brother, Mitch, around like a puppy. Even then she'd had a crush on Jack, and it looked like the crush still had her in its grips. Being just one of the guys and Mitch's little sister sucked. She wanted more and she planned on changing the rules tonight to get it.

Sam glanced into her closet and pulled out her new slinky, black dress. Shopping didn't thrill her, but this dress made up for any hassle it had caused. The hem fell just above the knees, and with a sweetheart neckline, the dress wrapped around her curves to give her an air of sophistication. The black of her dress stood out against her pale skin, offsetting her red hair, and black always made her green eyes sparkle like jewels. Jack would never know what hit him. Sam grew up right; she planned on showing him just how much of a woman she had become over the years.

Literally running into Jack yesterday at the bank had to be a sign of the fates shining on her. Her dreams of him still visited her on lonely nights; the fluttering started in her chest, and her heart jumped as his eyes flashed in recognition, a slow grin creeping across his face. To see and speak to him after so long brought back the memories of the last time he walked away from her. Jack had left her no air to breathe and had broken her heart, not once looking back to see the girl she had been crying for him to come back.

Picking up the pieces took time, but to his credit, she never told him how she felt before he joined the military. She needed to grow up, and as Jack left for the Marine Corps, she felt it too soon for her to express her feelings for him. She needed to make sure her emotions weren't mere puppy love. Sam had no intention of making the same mistake twice. This time, she wouldn't let him leave because they belonged together in the forever kind of way.

Sam shook off the memories and raced to get ready for her evening. Tonight, her dreams would come true.

* * * *

Sam arrived at the restaurant with seconds to spare, running late thanks to a question her deputy had about a break-in the night before. She had faith the officer could handle himself. She took a deep breath and opened the door. Butterflies danced in her stomach as her eyes caught sight of Jack sitting ramrod-straight. His military background showed in his posture, his back held away from the chair. A slight grin spread over her face as she walked slowly toward him. She hoped her nerves didn't show. The closer she got to Jack's table, the more the tiny flicks danced in her belly. Sam rested her hand over her stomach to calm herself. She almost floated to the table, and in no time, his chair loomed in front of her. He stood to greet her like a true gentleman, pulled her into a hug with a slight pat on the back; it was a sweet, friendly greeting between two old friends.

Sam held back a sigh and tried to calm herself by taking deep breaths, which proved a mistake. Jack's scent washed over her, powerful and musky, just as she remembered it. The sight of him made her ache, and his arms were so right wrapped around her. Sam held on tightly even as she felt him trying to back away; she knew she needed to release him before he thought her crazy. She wanted to take this slow and not scare him off too soon. Sam didn't want Jack second-guessing himself; they belonged together. Being his best friend's sister shouldn't even come into the equation. She walked a fine line in her quest of forever with this man. She knew they had both matured while away from each other and she couldn't wait to find out more about the man Jack had become.

More strength showed in his face after his time in the service. What struggles had he gone through to earn that vigor? The mystique spurred on Sam's curiosity and attraction. She lacked the presence of mind to really take a good look at Jack, to take in his raw power, but now her gaze drank in every bit of him.

She wanted to run her fingers through his black, closely cropped hair and mess it up a little. She figured the style had to do with his years in the military. It looked good on him. Better than the long hair of their high school years. Sam let out a small sigh as she sat down. Embarrassing herself by melting into a pool at his feet didn't seem like a good idea.

The waiter showed up soon after she'd taken her chair and asked if she and Jack needed a few more minutes. After the server left, the air turned heavy with the background noise of other patrons until they both spoke at once.

"What brings...?"

"How have you...?"

Sam laughed softly, lowered her hand, and said, "You first."

"I wanted to ask you how you've been. I've kept in touch with Mitch through the years, and he's very proud of you, but he never spoke of your life or why you stayed in Port. I thought for sure you would be out of here the first chance you had."

"He only says that so I won't arrest his sorry butt," Sam said with a chuckle. "No, really, I'm glad we're so close. With Mom and Dad both gone and—"

"I'm sorry, Sam," Jack said. "I wish I could have been here for the funeral, but...."

"No, Jack," she laid her hand over his on the table, "you were overseas. We knew you couldn't be here. Mitch and I both understood. I didn't bring it up to make you sad. Mitch said he talked to you about coming home, but he didn't say why. What brings you back to Port?"

Possibly me? She knew that wouldn't be his answer, but a girl could dream.

"After I got out of the military, I bummed around for a time unsure of what I wanted to do with my life. Mitch contacted me and offered me a job with his construction company. It's been awhile, but I like to work with my hands, so it's a good match. And here I am."

His soft lips caressing hers flashed through her mind, but she forced herself to focus on his last comment. Why didn't Mitch tell her about the job offer? Hmm...she needed to have a little talk with her big brother.

"Sam...Sam, are you okay?" he asked.

"What...? Oh, sorry, what did you say?"

"I asked how you got into law enforcement."

Heat climbed into Sam's face, but she soldiered on. "I followed in Dad's footsteps. I knew Mitch had no desire to get into law, but my fascination with Dad's work just made me want to be more like him. It helped that Dad was my hero and I would go to his office all the time and watch him work. It made sense for me to go to school to become an officer. I left for a while, but after Dad died, I came back and joined the sheriff's department here. Old Man Harris took over for a while until they found someone else to be sheriff, so I decided to run, and the rest, as they say, is history."

Sam glanced around the restaurant, seeing it with a fresh outlook. How could it be that she'd never noticed the romantic lighting or the elegant brocade tablecloth? She employed any tactic to avoid Jack's eyes as she talked, afraid of seeing only a friendly look glancing back at her. She wanted so much more from him, but what if he didn't want more from her? Sam peeked into his dark brown eyes. His gaze captured her, rendering her lost and unable to turn away. She thought she saw a flash of something, but almost as soon as the raw emotion appeared, the door slammed shut again. Did she really see an interested look in his eyes? Sam wanted forever with him, and, if she read his expression correctly, her dreams had a chance of becoming a reality.

Sam cleared her throat and looked back down at the table as their food arrived, but she sensed his gaze on her.

Jack reached across the table and grabbed her hand. She jumped slightly.

"Is everything all right?" he asked. "You seem a little distracted tonight. We can leave if you want. We can get our order to go."

Finally, she looked up at him.

"Oh, no, I'm fine. I'm sorry if I seem a little off tonight." Sam gave him a bright smile.

"Why don't we take a walk around town and maybe stop off for some ice cream before we head home?" he suggested.

"That sounds like a great idea."

Jack called the waiter over to settle the bill and requested their order to go. Once their food arrived, they left.

The night had chilled, and Sam shivered.

"Are you cold?" Jack asked. "Here, take this." He took his suit jacket off and helped Sam into it. The coat engulfed her, but it smelled of Jack, and she closed her eyes thinking this has to be the aroma of Heaven. She pushed up the sleeves a little and reached for Jack's hand. He let her lace her fingers through his, and they walked, content in each other's company; they needed no words.

Breaking the silence, Jack brought up old times.

"Do you remember that time Mitch put the frog in your room? I can still see the look of shock on his face as you calmly picked it up and handed it back to him. That moment was priceless. We had a lot of good times, didn't we?"

"We sure did. I've missed you, Jack. I really have."

Sam reveled in the fact that Jack continued to hold her hand as they spoke of the past. Jack guided them to one of the small benches that lined the street, helped her sit down, and pulled her toward him.

This must be a dream; I'm going to wake up any minute.

Sam snuggled closer to his warmth.

"I've wanted to do this all night." He sighed.

"What?" Sam responded.

"Be close to you, just hold you."

Yes, I'm convinced this is a dream.

Jack's lips descended to hers. Sam rose to meet him and slowly moved her lips against his, savoring a dream come true. She drew in a deep breath and sighed as his lips brushed hers again and again. She closed her eyes and raised her hands to his face. She wanted to hold him close, afraid he might tear away. Jack's arms captured her against him, pressing tightly for a moment before he leaned back. The distance between them became wider, no longer keeping her warm; empty and needy, she wanted his lips back. He rested his forehead against hers and held her hand to his chest.

"I'm sorry, Sam." He drew her in again and hugged her tightly to him. She rested her head against his chest and heard his heart pound against her ear, his breath uneven as his pulse raced.

"Jack, please don't be sorry. I've dreamed of this moment since high school."

Sam untangled her hands from between their bodies and put them on Jack's cheeks, tugging him down for another kiss; it was sweet, gentle and wrapped with all the emotion she could put into it. She knew she needed Jack for her own and Jack needed her. Like that old song said: it's in his kiss, and he was her forever guy.

Jack pulled away again and sighed.

"We can't do this, Sam, we just can't."

"Why not?"

He offered her no answer, but instead took her hand and led her back to the parking lot.

After helping her into her car, he said, "I'm sorry, Sam, I just...I can't."

Jack turned and walked away without a backward glance.

Sam didn't know what to make of his behavior. One minute he was kissing her, and the next, he was telling her he couldn't. She had to convince him that they belonged together, now and forever. She needed a plan and she hoped it worked.

* * * *

Sam walked into Mitch's building peering in the different offices looking for a sign of Jack. Mitch said he would be there today filling out paper work, but he'd failed to mention which office Jack occupied. She'd asked Mitch about not telling her Jack would be back in town, but he'd just shrugged and said he didn't want to make it a big deal. Sam shook her head. *Men!*

She stopped, finally seeing Jack in the last office, his head bowed over his work. Sam's breath hitched in her throat, and she had to remind herself to breathe. Looking at him warmed her from the inside out, and she wanted nothing more than to run her hands through his hair and draw him next to her. Forcing herself into action, she moved closer to the door.

"Knock-knock."

Jack's head jerked up; he looked shocked to see her.

"Are you here for Mitch? He just walked down the hall."

"No," she replied. "I thought we could go for a picnic. It's almost lunchtime, and I have the day off. Well, I'm on call, but things are usually quiet here." Sam drew Jack's attention to the basket she carried.

"Sam, I don't know...."

"Come on, Jack. It's just a picnic. I'm not asking for anything more than lunch. You have to eat, don't you?"

Jack's face changed from uncertain to accepting. She struggled to hold in her sigh of relief. It seemed she did that a lot around him.

"Okay, but I don't have much time. I need to get this paperwork done so I can get on site with Mitch."

"Did someone call me?"

"Hi, Mitch," said Sam. "I'm stealing Jack away for lunch. We'll be back in a bit."

"Lunch?" Mitch looked down at his watch. "I guess it is about that time. Have fun."

Sam smiled and reached for Jack's hand, guiding him from the building, but not before he took the basket from her. She smiled back at him. Very seldom did someone treat her like a lady. As the sheriff, most people acted as if she had no gender. Having Jack step up and respect her as a woman felt nice for a change.

"The place I have in mind isn't far. We can walk there."

"Listen, Sam, about last night."

"Jack, let's just enjoy the day. Ahhh, here we are. I told you, not far at all. Isn't it beautiful here?"

"Yes, yes, it is."

Sam looked back at Jack to find his gaze on her.

It's working. It has to be. I knew I didn't imagine things.

Jack glanced away.

Trying to bring his focus back to her, she pointed out where they would eat lunch.

"The perfect picnic spot is over by that tree. I have a blanket we can spread out and then we can enjoy lunch."

Sam busied herself with getting the picnic ready, trying not to grin like a fool. Once they both settled on the blanket, she started talking to Jack about old times in hopes of comforting him.

"Do you know what I remember most about growing up with you, Jack?"

"All the teasing?" he said with a slight grin.

Sam laughed. "No. That isn't it. But I do remember the teasing. I don't think I could forget it if I tried. I'm talking about how you seemed to always be there for me. I didn't have many heroes growing up, but you placed among the top of them. After you left, well, I had a big hole in my chest. A piece of me missed you in my life. Seeing you at the bank reminded me how much I really missed you."

Sam leaned closer and brushed her lips against his. He didn't pull back; she moved closer still, deepening the kiss.

Jack pulled back. "Sam...I told you. We can't."

"Why not? Give me one good reason why we can't."

"Mitch."

With that, Jack got up and left her alone in the park with her thoughts. *There has to be a way. This can't be it for us.*

Sam finished her lunch with a heavy heart.

* * * *

"That stupid jerk!" Sam screamed at her brother.

"What's wrong, sis?"

"Your dumb friend—that's what's wrong."

Mitch sighed and pinched the bridge of his nose. She didn't care if she caused him the headache. It had been two weeks since her lunch date with Jack, who now seemed to be ignoring her. He wouldn't even take her calls, and Mitch sat there taking the backlash like a good brother should.

"What did he do?" he asked.

"It's what he didn't do. He won't talk to me. Not one word." She sat down with a sigh. After her lunch disaster with Jack, she'd gone home and shared her plan with Mitch. At first, he didn't say anything and seemed a little upset, but she'd brought him around. Still, he'd warned her to be careful because Jack had been through a lot. Of course, Mitch wouldn't elaborate. Slowly, Sam's confidence that she belonged with Jack started to fade. Had she pushed teenage fantasy on the two of them by wishing for something not meant to be—or worse? Maybe it never existed at all.

Just one more chance; that is all I need. If I can't convince him we belong together I don't know what I'll do.

Sam tried not to cry as her eyes filled with tears. After this, if he still pulled away, she'd give up and just be his friend no matter how hard that would be.

"You have to help me," she said to her brother.

"Oh no you don't. I am not getting in the middle of this."

"But, Mitch...." She batted her green eyes at him. It usually worked.

"No, I'm not going to do it. You're on your own."

Sam frowned. "How can I convince him we're meant for one another if I can't talk to him? You have to do something. Invite him to dinner. Tell him I won't be here. That should work. Please...pretty please?"

"Enough with the begging. You're a grown woman. Go to work or something. I'll invite him over tonight."

Sam jumped up and rushed to Mitch, kissing him on the cheek. "You are the best! Thanks." She gave her brother another quick kiss and dashed out the door before he could change his mind. She had to get ready for work and she had plans to make.

* * * *

Sam shook her head, lamenting the fact that the Thomas boys were going to be the death of her with all their teenage pranks. It brought back memories of her brother's and Jack's escapades in high school. Miss Walker had called in to tell her that the Thomas brothers had been up to no good again. This time the boys targeted the school, and Sam really didn't want to know what mischief they had decided on for the evening too. She knew she might have to lock them up and throw away the key for their own good and the good of the community.

Pulling up in front of the school, Sam turned off her car as she spotted the boys off to the side of the building.

Please tell me they are not holding spray paint cans. They cannot be that stupid.

They were that stupid. Darn it!

"Boys, boys, boys. Why didn't you tell me you wanted a tour of the jail? I could have arranged it without the overnight stay."

The hissing of the spray cans stopped. The two dropped their arms and put them behind there backs.

"Sheriff, this isn't what it looks like."

She couldn't tell which boy spoke, so she addressed them both.

"You mean you aren't spray-painting 'school sucks' on the side of the building?"

"Okay, well maybe we are doing what you think we are, but we have a good reason."

"And that would be?"

"Oh...well...uhm. I guess I really don't have a good reason. I thought it would be okay just to say we had one," Matt Thomas explained.

Sam released a breath and blew aside the hair that had escaped her bun.

"Give me the cans."

They handed them over without a sound.

"Please tell me you aren't involved in the break-ins we've been having."

"No, ma'am," they both said a little too quickly.

"I'd better not find out differently. If you are involved, it needs to stop right here, right now. If not, I really will throw you both into a cell, and you don't want that. Now get out of here and behave. I don't want to be called out about you two again."

The two teens turned to go.

"And boys, you *will* be here bright and early tomorrow morning ready to scrub this off."

Sam grinned as their shoulders slumped.

Ah, to be that young again.

Sam got into her car and headed home. She only had a couple hours to get ready for the evening.

* * * *

The doorbell rang, and Sam raced down the stairs excited to talk to Jack. He had no choice but to speak to her. She didn't want to let him off the hook; she would not be ignored. Sam yanked open the door, and all the air left her lungs at the sight of Jack. She glanced up at him just as he licked his lips.

"Uhm...hi, what are you doing...? I mean, hi," Jack stuttered.

He looks so nervous. How cute. I could just kiss him.

"Mitch asked if I wanted to join in the game. I guess a couple guys couldn't make it, so he invited his girlfriend, Sarah, over too. It'll just be the four of us. Is that a problem?"

"No, not at all. Are you going to let me in?"

"Of course."

She stepped away from the door, allowing him to enter her home.

As the evening progressed, Jack left the table for the third time in the last half hour. She knew she made him uncomfortable and hoped he would rethink his position about their romance. She had to stop herself from doing more than running her bare foot up the leg of his blue jeans. This time, he left going into the kitchen to get a beer, and she had him right where she wanted him.

"I'll be right back," Sam said.

She stood and tried to act casual walking to the kitchen.

"Sis, we won't wait. I'm taking Sarah out. There is no way we are ever going to finish this game." Mitch winked at her and ushered Sarah out the front door.

Sam raced into the kitchen, no longer needing to act cool and collected. If she had her way, Jack would agree to see more of her, to become a couple and maybe establish a long-lasting relationship.

He turned as she opened the door, and she smiled as she slowly walked toward him.

"I just finished. Did you need—?"

She stopped him by holding her hand up.

"No, please. I think it's time you and I had a little talk. Mitch took Sarah out so it's just you and me."

Jack's gaze wandered all over the kitchen but wouldn't settle on her. She knew he wanted to find a way out, so she positioned herself in front of the door. He looked like he wanted to say something, but she stopped him again. This time, she moved close enough to put a finger against his lips and shook her head. Jack closed his eyes and inhaled. His breathing grew faster and warmed her finger.

"No, don't talk, just listen. I'm a big girl and I know what I want. Heck, I've known what I've wanted for years, but you ran off to join the Marine Corps, and I thought I'd have to give up my dream. But you came back, and I'm not letting you go again. You and me...we're a good thing, a forever kind of thing. That is, unless you don't want me. If you aren't interested tell me, say so, and I'll stop throwing myself at you."

This time *he* stopped *her* and took her hands into his.

"Sam, you're wrong."

Her expression fell. She just knew he would say he didn't find her attractive and wanted to be her friend and nothing more, that he had no romantic feelings for her.

"I'm not a forever kind of guy. There are things you don't know about me, things that might change your mind. I don't want to hurt you, and if we start something, you're going to get hurt."

Jambrea Jo Jones

Sam felt as if something heavy had been lifted from her heart and she smiled as tears filled her eyes. "No, you're wrong. Please let me show you how wrong you are. Give us a chance. Let me show you how good we can be together."

She took his hands, brought them to her face, and closed her eyes. She wanted to savor his touch, the feel of his palm against her cheek. Sam untangled herself to bring his face down for a kiss. He didn't resist. She wouldn't let him resist. Jack would be hers. Sam felt him relax against her and took advantage of his surrender. Finally, she pulled back, releasing him.

"Will you give us a chance?" she asked. "We could be so good together, so very good."

Jack tried to regain control. He relaxed his breathing and closed his eyes, resting his forehead on hers before he spoke.

"I'm willing to try, but there are things you have to know first. You might change your mind. No, don't talk, let me get this out. While in Iraq, I was hurt and in a coma for months. It took a while for me to get better. Luckily, I walked away with my leg intact, but it isn't pretty. I won't sugarcoat this for you, Sam. On bad days, I limp, and some days I don't even want to get out of bed. Sometimes I wake up screaming, thinking I'm still over there watching my men die."

She stopped him with another kiss.

"Don't you get it? I love you. None of that stuff matters as long as you love me too. I want to be there to soothe your bad dreams away, to make you forget. I want to be there helping you through the pain. I want it all, Jack. I want you, just as you are."

"But what about Mitch?" he asked.

"What about him? Mitch isn't involved in this; it's just you and me. It has always been just you and me," she replied.

"I still...."

She shook her head and watched his protective walls crumble.

Jack leaned closer, taking her lips with his, cupping the back of her head. Sam sank into his embrace to collapse into him, not knowing where his lips ended and hers began. They might have issues to deal with, but he belonged to her, and she never wanted to let him go.

Jack murmured against her lips, "I love you too, Sam. I guess I am your forever kind of guy."

204

Author Bio:

You can find Jambrea Jo Jones at: http://jambrea.wordpress.com or playgroundmystique.wordpress.com. You can also email her at: binojo2@yahoo.com.

When Time Stood Still
by
Kathleen MacIver

Matthew Garlinn never expected to find himself learning the ancient art of swordsmithing in the Scottish Highlands. And then there was her. The woman whose song haunted his dreams.

Chapter One

Matthew Garlinn sat on a stone wall under a sign that read *Alec MacCoinneach, Swordsmith*, and shook his head. Once upon a time, he would have laughed to think he'd one day find himself sitting in a place like this.

He was, of course, *outside* the shop because the door was locked and his key inside. But even that wouldn't have stopped him a few years ago. As it was, only his determination not to fall back into his old ways kept him from undoing the very easy-to-pick lock that guarded the back door.

No, what he found ironic was that he was not in the good old USA, not in a city, and not using either his wits or his tae kwon do skills to make a living. Instead, he was in the Scottish Highlands, staying in a village no bigger than one LA neighborhood, and learning the ancient art of swordsmithing. Definitely *not* where he thought he'd end up.

But what surprised him most was how he liked the life here. The mountains were harsh and unyielding, but beautiful. The people were friendly.

And there was *her*. The woman whose song haunted his dreams. Whose face had placed her in danger. Who had fled when he'd rescued her.

Maybe tonight, if he hung around the grocery store long enough, she'd come back and he'd see her again. *If* his boss would show up so they could get the day's work done.

He glanced at his watch and wondered what had happened. Alec was the kind of guy a person could depend on. *Not* the kind of boss to tell you to be at the shop at eleven to start work on a new sword, and then leave you sitting outside on a stone wall for an hour.

He hopped off the wall and walked half a mile down the road and back again. He made a list of all the repairs needed in the little old house he rented. He got out his knife and whittled on a scrap of wood.

Finally, he wiped his hands on his jeans and sauntered around back. There was no point in waiting any longer to open the old door. It wasn't like he was breaking in. He had been given a key, and Alec probably assumed he'd been smart enough to put it on his keychain.

The lock stared up at him stubbornly, and a closer look told him that it might not be quite as easy to spring as he'd thought. For one thing, it was rusted shut. For another thing, it was old...far older than any lock he'd ever picked before.

The rust slowly fell away, and he put his past experience to work until it finally gave way. He allowed himself a small smile and started to open the door, only to find an arm wound around his neck and his wrist pinned behind him.

"Thief!"

Matthew hesitated only a moment. That wasn't Alec's voice, and no one else had the right to tackle him here.

A shift in weight and a spin freed his arms, but his second spin failed to knock his assailant off his feet. Kicks that usually sent his opponents flying backwards met solid blocks. His fastest blows were returned, one by one.

Reluctant admiration filled him. Whoever this guy was, he knew tae kwon do as well. And was quite good at it.

But admiration wasn't going to make this guy leave him alone. Perhaps a few moves that were more of the street fighting variety might work. His determination rose, and with it, his speed...until he found a sword at his throat.

He froze.

Yes, this *was* a swordsmith shop, and there were dozens of swords inside. But that didn't explain why the guy holding the other end of this one looked so comfortable pointing it at people. No doubt he knew how to do other things with it as well. Things that he, Matthew, should obviously have learned before now.

"What are you doing?" the man demanded. "Trying to—?"

"Tristan!" The command exploded from around the corner of the building, and Matthew sighed in relief as Alec appeared. "That's Matthew, my apprentice!"

The sword dropped, and the guy named Tristan took a step backward.

"What's going on, Matthew?" Alec asked.

"I left my key inside."

Alec glanced at the open door, and his eyebrows rose.

"I've been waiting for almost two hours," Matthew added.

Alec remained silent for a moment, probably remembering things from that strange bout of soul-bearing he'd listened to a week ago. Matthew still didn't know what had come over him—he wasn't the confessing type—but he'd been sure that Alec would understand his more-than-checkered past.

He must have been right. Alec hadn't sent him packing that night, and he was nodding in acceptance now.

"Matthew, this is Tristan, my younger brother," Alec said.

Tristan held out a hand, evidently willing to let bygones be bygones. Matthew shook it as Alec continued.

"I'm sorry to be late. My cousin flew into Inverness this morning, and I had to go pick him up. We ran into traffic on the way back."

"Don't worry about it."

Alec shrugged. "It can't be helped, but we don't have time to forge that blade now. We'll have to leave it for tomorrow."

"So what should I do?"

"Do you want to come with us to Duncarragh?"

Duncarragh? *Really?* He'd wanted to see inside the castle since he'd learned that Alec had grown up there. "Sure," he said with a shrug. No need to look like he was *too* eager.

He waited while Alec went inside the shop to re-lock it, and soon, he found himself in Alec's crew cab pickup, sharing the backseat with two swords that were each nearly six feet long.

"So where'd you learn tae kwon do?" Tristan asked.

"I used to live above a studio," Matthew answered. "Why'd you learn swordplay?"

Tristan glanced at him over the seat back. "When you've got two older brothers who know how to wield a sword, you *have* to learn, just to survive."

Matthew chuckled.

"So the master of this studio taught you tae kwon do?" Tristan continued.

"Yeah. Why'd you learn it?"

Tristan grinned. "Being the youngest is also a good reason to make sure you know something your older brothers don't."

Matthew decided he liked Tristan.

Twenty minutes later, they came in sight of Duncarragh, standing guard on the shores of Loch Rhoswen. They drove inside the gates, and Matthew climbed out of the pickup as Alec and Tristan retrieved the swords.

They started toward what must have once been the great hall, just as twenty-some people poured out.

Matthew was given a flood of introductions, most of which didn't stick in his brain longer than a few seconds. The woman who kissed Alec was obviously his wife. An older man in surprisingly excellent shape turned out to be his father, Murray. Everyone else became a blur of faces.

Until he saw *her*.

She came from what looked like the stables, dressed in the same flowing skirt he'd first seen her wearing. Her black hair fell over her shoulders in the heavy braid that his fingers still itched to unravel. And her eyes were the same pale grey he remembered.

She smiled a greeting at Alec and Tristan, then her gaze met his, and she stopped.

Time stood still.

Her hand fluttered to her throat, and her eyes widened.

Please, don't run again, he begged. He'd probably make a fool of himself and chase her down if she did.

"Have you two met?"

Matthew swallowed as Alec's voice sounded in his ear, and time began again.

"Sort of," he managed. "She found herself in some trouble a few weeks back. I was fortunate enough to come to the rescue."

"Trouble?"

"A bunch of teenagers, behind that grocery store in town." His head was so muddled, he couldn't remember the name, not that it mattered.

"Thank you," Alec said. "I didn't realize we were in your debt."

Matthew looked at him. "I didn't realize you were either."

"Rhianna lost her family recently, so we consider her our responsibility. At least until we locate her cousins. Come, Rhianna," he said, turning to her. "Tell me why you said nothing of this."

They walked away, and Matthew followed her with his eyes. *Rhianna.* A beautiful name. A name that fit her. A name he'd never forget.

"I would forget about her, if I were you."

He turned to find Tristan standing at his elbow. "Why?" he asked as he eyed the sword Tristan still held. "You like her?"

Tristan shook his head.

"Then what?"

Tristan's lips tightened. "Just believe me when I say you're better of not thinking about her."

"It's too late for that."

Tristan sighed. "Don't say I didn't warn you. Come on."

"Where?"

"What you're about to see might interest you more than Rhianna."

Matthew glanced in her direction again. He wasn't at all sure that Tristan was right, but he followed anyway.

Chapter Two

Half an hour later, he realized that Tristan was closer to being right than he would have thought possible.

He watched in amazement as a sword-fighting tournament of sorts began. Every man there produced a broadsword like the one Tristan held and faced off against another, one by one. The men began commenting on the performances, while the woman cheered for their husbands and sons.

Except Rhianna.

She stood apart from the crowd, silently watching from the shadow of the castle walls.

He made his way toward her and waited until she glanced his way.

"Hello," he said.

"Hello."

She turned back to the action, action that no longer held his attention.

"Are you okay?" he asked.

"Okay?"

"After that night. They didn't hurt you, did they?"

She shook her head. "They thought I had coins."

"Coins?"

She hesitated. "Money," she clarified. "Thank you for your aid."

Her voice lilted against his ear with an Old-World flavor that enchanted him.

"Forgive me for running," she added.

"That's okay. Why did you?"

She shrugged. "I do not know many here. I did not know what to think of you."

"You haven't been in Scotland long?"

She didn't answer. She merely turned and continued watching the swordplay.

Matthew joined her, and they watched silently as several more matches were fought.

"Do you not have skill?" she asked.

He flushed. He had many skills, but he wasn't sure that tae kwon do, street fighting, lock-picking, or being a crack shot compared well against hefting a nearly-six-foot broadsword. "Not with a sword," he admitted.

"You are not from here?"

"I'm from the U.S."

"You Ess?"

She looked so genuinely puzzled, he didn't know what to think.

"America," he tried. "The States."

"Oh," she said. "Alec brought a cousin from there this day."

He nodded. Alec had mentioned it.

"That one," she said, pointing to one of the men getting ready to fight.

They lifted their swords and began the most impressive display yet. Their speed was dizzying, yet they fought far longer than anyone else.

"They are evenly matched!"

Matthew glanced at Rhianna. Why was she so surprised?

"Iain is easily the best here," she explained. "Or rather he was until this Jason arrived. See how Iain angles his sword and twists his wrists? See his speed? I have watched him disarm every man here with this, yet Jason returns his attack."

"Uh...." Matthew found his jaw dangerously close to falling open. It wasn't every woman that knew the intricacies of swordplay like this one evidently did. At least, he didn't think so.

She looked at him, wondering at his stupidity, no doubt.

"Which is which?" he asked.

A smile flashed across her face, further stunning his already muddled wits. "Forgive me. Iain is the younger. He is Murray's oldest son and Alec and Tristan's brother. Jason is their cousin."

He nodded and tried to decide which was more fascinating: the swordplay or the woman beside him.

"I do not think I have seen finer swordplay in all my life," she said.

He turned away from the display. "Have you seen a lot?" he asked.

She nodded but didn't offer any more information. Instead, she pointed behind him. "Tristan calls for you."

He reluctantly turned his attention elsewhere, and even more reluctantly left her to join Tristan.

"This is Kevin," Tristan said, planting his hand on the shoulder of the man next to him. "He wants to have a go at you."

"With swords?" he asked doubtfully. He wasn't one to shirk a challenge, but....

"Tae kwon do. Are you up for a match?"

"Oh!" That he could manage. He supposed he wouldn't mind the chance to prove that he had some skill in *something*.

The sword fighting seemed to be over for the moment, so he took up his stance opposite Kevin. Tristan threw down his hand, and they began.

It didn't take much effort to win the match.

"You're good," Kevin said as they finished and shook hands. "Can you take Tristan?"

Matthew glanced at Tristan. "I don't know."

"Come on, Tristan," Kevin cajoled. "I want to see if you can be beaten, for once."

Tristan flashed a grin. "Well, Matt?"

Matthew shrugged. "Sure. As long as your sword stays out of it."

Tristan laughed and took up his stance.

Kevin signaled the start, and again, Matthew decided that he and Tristan were evenly matched. He used every skill he'd ever learned and dug deeply for strength he hadn't used in a long while. In the end, he suspected that he only won the bout because Tristan had already spent a great deal of energy sword fighting.

"Thank you," Tristan said, holding out a hand.

"A pleasure."

"I'd be pleased to train with you any time you're willing."

Matthew considered only a moment. "How about a bargain?"

"Like what?"

"Teach me swordplay."

Tristan chuckled. "A fair trade," he agreed.

Everyone began turning away, and Matthew looked for Rhianna. He found her still in the shadow of the wall, quietly watching everyone and everything. What was she thinking? Had he redeemed himself and his lack of sword skill? And if he could learn, would she—?

"Matthew!"

He ground his teeth. Was *everyone* determined to keep him from talking to Rhianna?

"Come on, Matthew," Alec called. "I need to get home. I'll drop you off at the shop for your truck."

"Be right there," he answered. He turned back to Rhianna. "Will I see you again?"

She hesitated, then nodded.

"When?"

"When you visit Duncarragh."

"You live here?"

"At this time."

He nodded, and silence fell over them.

"Matthew!" Alec called again.

He sighed.

"Good day, Matthew," Rhianna said.

He forced himself to walk away, thinking that his name had never sounded so sweet.

Chapter Three

Rhianna permitted herself a smile of pleasure as she slipped outside. For the twentieth time in as many days, Matthew was here, preparing to drive himself to exhaustion in pursuit of sword skill.

She settled herself on a convenient rock and watched as he picked up the sword Murray had lent him.

He didn't do badly, she decided again, for someone who had not grown to manhood with a sword in his hands. At least, she supposed so. In truth, never had she seen a full-grown man learn swordplay.

She had watched her brother for years, though, and Matthew reminded her of him. They were of a height. They shared the same sandy brown hair and brown eyes. The same muscular shoulders and legs. And she fancied that when Matthew mastered his new skill, he would fight in much the same manner that Ranald did.

Or rather, he had.

The pain of losing her brother swept through her anew, and she swallowed the lump in her throat. He was gone, and she could not change that. Even Murray and Iain had been unable to do anything, though they had tried many times. And now....

She sighed.

Now she had the opportunity to watch a fascinating man whilst she rested in the safety of Duncarragh. It did her no good to worry about her future.

Matthew and Tristan put their swords away and turned to that other strange means of fighting they were so fond of. It never ceased to amaze her—the spinning and kicking and all else they inexplicably managed to do with naught but their hands and feet. It was fascinating—as was Matthew. Iain, Alec, and Tristan were not too unlike the men in her family. But Matthew was a mystery.

And a more appealing one than was good for her.

She didn't belong here. Murray would likely discover her kin in the next few weeks. Then she would be leaving Duncarragh, its warm welcome, and its fascinating visitors.

A pity she had come to like all three so much.

She watched until the shadows grew long and Matthew ceased his training. She kept her place as they spoke, and she tried to look as though his doings did not interest her.

Would he seek her out? She was a fool for wanting him to, yet....

"Rhianna."

She started. Truly, she *had* succeeded in distracting herself that time. "Off in dreamland?"

Dreamland. Yes, that described quite accurately where her thoughts had taken her. She searched for a distraction. "Your skill is increasing quickly," she said.

He smiled, and her heart picked up its pace. "Thank you," he said simply.

"You should ask Jason or Iain to train you. Either could teach you skills that would best Tristan."

He snorted. "They're so far out of my league, I'd look foolish even trying."

She did not know what he meant by his league, but she doubted he would look foolish. She shook her head. "You have the speed to manage the skills I am thinking of."

"And Tristan doesn't?"

"Tristan does, but his pride stands in his way. He wishes to learn all things himself. He will not ask."

Matthew grinned. "That sounds like Tristan. But he might manage it some day."

"Perhaps, but not as yet."

He cocked his head and studied her a moment. "How do you know so much about swordplay?"

Memories flooded her mind...Ranald working with a wooden sword as a boy...his pride when he got his first true sword...her pride when his skill was recognized. "I grew up watching my brother learn to fight," she answered. But those memories were followed by more that brought only pain.

She sought to change the subject. "Why do you seek this skill?"

He shrugged. "Why not?"

"Most men willing to pay so dearly for a skill have good reason."

"Isn't having the time and being interested enough?" he asked.

"You have nothing better to do with your time?"

He shrugged. "Nope. Unless it's talking with you."

"Why me?"

"Because you're beautiful, and I find you irresistibly fascinating."

He found her fascinating! She called herself a fool and studied her hands in an effort to stop the smile that spread across her face. "I am like every girl I knew," she said.

"Really?"

She nodded.

His finger nudged her chin until she had no choice but to meet his gaze. "You're not like any other woman I've ever met."

"How?"

He smiled gently...a smile that made her want to curl up in its warmth. "A million little reasons," he said.

She waited, but he didn't offer any of them. His gaze flicked down to her mouth for an instant, but he stepped away.

"Walk with me?" he asked.

She fell into step beside him.

"How long ago did you lose your family?" he asked.

She winced. "It has been five months."

"Oh. I'm sorry."

Relief coursed through her when he did not ask more. But the silence weighed heavily. She searched for something else to discuss. "Will you tell me why you came to Alba?"

He stopped. "Alba?"

"Forgive me. Scotland."

He smiled again. "Opportunity presented itself. Fortunately, I think. Does *Alba* mean Scotland?"

She nodded. "In the Gaelic. You do not have it?"

"No. How do you know it?"

"I was born with it."

Surprise covered his face. "Alec told me that almost no one grows up speaking Gaelic anymore."

She sighed. One more thing she did not know. One more thing to remind her that she did not belong here.

"So were you born with English as well?" Matthew asked.

She shrugged. "I have always known a very little. But there are many new words here."

"Here? Where did you grow up?"

She hesitated. It was a simple question, yet how could she answer without telling what she had sworn to keep secret? And why did so many conversations seem to end in her past?

"You don't have to answer."

She sighed. They had reached his truck, and he would be leaving in a moment. Perhaps a name would suffice. "Craeghall," she said.

"Craeghall?"

"'Tis where I was born."

A small smile flashed across his face. "I guess I need to study some maps. That means nothing to me."

"It is a very small town."

He nodded and glanced at his watch. "I guess I need to get going."

She nodded.

"I'll see you tomorrow?"

"I am here always."

He smiled and was gone.

Chapter Four

Matthew eyed his sword in satisfaction. He was finally starting to feel like he actually knew something about wielding it! And knowing that he had been the one to forge this blade made the skill he was learning even sweeter.

"Are we done?" Tristan asked.

Matthew nodded. "I'm done." He had other things to do.

He glanced at Rhianna, sitting on a boulder with her knees tucked under her chin.

"Then be about that other business," Tristan said. "I still advise you against it, by the way."

"Are you going to tell me why?"

"Nope."

Matthew studied Tristan for a moment. Did Tristan have a reason? Probably. But he seriously doubted it would be enough to keep him away from Rhianna. Heck, here he was, trying to figure out the best way to ask her out! He wanted *more* time with her, not less.

He stashed his sword in his truck and went to her. "Hi," he said for what seemed like the hundredth time.

"Hello."

He plunged in. "I want you to go out with me."

Her eyes widened. "Out? Where?"

"To a restaurant or pub, or something. Will you?"

She shook her head, but her smile encouraged him.

"Please?" he tried again.

Her smile grew, but she shook her head once more. "I cannot, Matthew."

He sighed. She could *not* expect him to give up when she said his name like that. "How about a walk?" he tried.

She cocked her head. "Why do you wish to do this?"

"Because I've seen you every day for five weeks, and I still don't know nearly enough about you."

Her gaze fell. "There is nothing of interest to know about me."

"That is where we disagree. *Everything* about you interests me."

She glanced up and began nibbling on her bottom lip, sending tantalizing thoughts through his mind. He turned away from them with an effort. "So, will you come? We can walk along the loch or go up the mountainside. Whatever you want."

His breath caught at the smile that bloomed on her face. If this is what he got for offering to take her on a walk, he'd do it every day!

She hopped off the boulder and headed toward the gates, and he fell into step beside her.

"Which way should we go?" he asked.

She glanced at him. "I choose?"

"Yep."

She pointed to the ridge above them. "Shall we climb to the top of this mountain?"

His eyebrows flew up. The top of the mountain? That had to be over 1,000 feet! Straight up! "This afternoon?" he asked. "Wouldn't that take awhile?"

She laughed merrily. "I love to stand on the mountains and see the glens and lochs below me. It does not take long to climb one as small as this. Come!" And she took off.

They reached the ridge a few hours later, and Matthew collapsed on the ground. His quads were screaming! Climbing uphill for so long evidently used muscles that tae kwon do didn't. He was breathing harder than he liked too.

He eyed Rhianna as she stood looking over the valley. She walked over to him easily, without the slightest trace of weariness.

"Shall we rest?" she asked with a twinkle in her eye.

He groaned. Difficult as it might be to admit, he'd just been outdone by a woman. "*Please*. This is something that you've obviously done more than I have." He stretched out on his back and tucked his hands under his head.

She settled herself beside him. "I have climbed the mountains many, many times. I love it."

"What else do you do like to do?"

She thought for a moment. "I like to sing."

He should have guessed that. He'd caught her at it more than once. "You have a beautiful voice," he told her.

She looked at him in surprise. "When did you hear me?"

"In the grocery store, the first time I saw you. I heard you from the other side of the shelves and went to see who was singing."

She chuckled. "I did not see you."

"I know. But I saw you. I got behind you in line, and I saw you disappear around the building. It didn't seem a safe place for a woman like you, so I followed."

"Like me?"

He sat up. "You're beautiful, Rhianna. Don't you know that?"

She shrugged. "Most say my eyes are a strange color."

He looked into those fathomless pools of grey and contemplated getting lost in them. But that might be dangerous. He turned his attention to the water below them.

"Have you seen the loch at dawn?" he asked, "When it's covered in fog, and the morning light makes everything seem magical?"

"Yes."

"That's what your eyes are like, only they're even more exquisite."

She smiled. "I am glad you like both my eyes and my song."

He liked a lot more than that, but perhaps now wasn't the time for it. "Will you sing for me now?" he asked instead.

"I do not know an English song."

He shrugged. "Then sing a Gaelic one."

She nodded, lifted her chin, and without the slightest bit of self-consciousness, began to sing.

He lay back on the ground again and let her weave the melody around him. He allowed his eyes to close. And he surrendered to the enchantment of her voice.

Chapter Five

"Matthew?"

He opened his eyes to find her leaning over him. Apparently she had finished her song.

"I thought you slept," she said.

"No." Although he *had* been dreaming. And having her so near and so relaxed tempted him to take those dreams a step further. He longed to bury his hands in her hair, trace the line of her jaw, taste the intoxicating sweetness of her mouth. All he had to do was draw her head down and—

"Matthew?"

He groaned and struggled to sit up. "That was a beautiful song." He searched for something safe to talk about. Something that wouldn't lead to thoughts of kissing her senseless.

"What else do you like to do?" he tried.

Her eyebrows furrowed in adorable contemplation, and she shrugged. "I find myself very often with nothing to do here."

"What do you *wish* you could do?"

She smiled wistfully. "I wish for a cottage to care for and a garden to tend."

He thought of the list of house repairs he had nailed to his door and chuckled. "If that's your idea of fun, you'd love my place."

"Your place?"

"Well, either Alec or his dad owns it—I'm not sure which. But the roof leaks, the windows don't open right, and the walls need work. My cleaning techniques don't seem to make a bit of difference in the place, either. And if that isn't bad enough, I've got nothing more than a bed, a table, and a broken chair to help me pretend someone actually lives there."

"That does not sound like a home."

A home. No, it wasn't, and it would take a lot more than soap, water, and repairs to change that.

He shrugged. "I've lived with less."

"Will you tell me of it?"

He looked at her, surprised. Tell her of his past? Perhaps he should. If she wanted nothing more to do with him, he'd have an easier time banishing the question that his lips kept wanting to blurt out. But if she still looked on him kindly....

He took a deep breath and began by telling her how he'd grown up fending for himself on the streets of Chicago, bringing home what food he could steal for his drunken father. He told her how he'd found his father dead one morning when he was eleven, how he'd felt when he'd been accepted into a local gang that had connections with a powerful crime ring, and how he'd worked his way up in the ranks of both, hating it all the while.

"Then I got caught."

She looked up.

"That could have been the end of me, but the cops offered me freedom if I turned state's evidence. I took it and left, determined to start my life again."

"Where did you go?"

"I ended up in Los Angeles, in a hole-in-the-wall apartment above a tae kwon do studio."

She smiled, and he nodded. "It didn't take me too long to discover that I liked the discipline of it. I learned everything Chung Wu could teach me and began saving every penny I could. My plan was to either buy the studio when Chung Wu was ready to retire, or start my own."

"Why did you not?"

"A sudden fire burned the studio and my apartment and killed Chung Wu."

"Oh!" she said in a strangled voice.

He shrugged. "It was a nasty blow, and I was sorry to lose my friend, but I'd started over once. I knew I could do it again. So the next day, I went to the library to search on the Internet for a job and a new place to live. Somehow I happened across Alec's advertisement." He paused. "That was two months ago."

He stopped and watched her, waiting to see what she would say.

"You have done well."

"Well?"

"To come from where you have."

He didn't quite see it that way. Sure, he was now on the right side of the law, but the memories.... "It's hard to leave it behind completely," he admitted.

"What do you mean?"

"The things I did."

"If you are not being sought for them, then surely they do not matter."

He hesitated as a particularly ugly scene sped through his mind. He met her eyes. "They matter to the mothers of the men I killed."

She didn't so much as blink. "Who were they?"

"Men who had sworn to kill me. Six of them found me alone one night."

"You killed all of them?"

"Four."

She hesitated, and her brows furrowed. "You regret this?"

"I have blood on my hands!"

"But they gave you no choice. There is no dishonor in that."

He was speechless.

"I wish my brother could have done as much."

He struggled to find his voice. "What happened?"

"Much the same thing. But after they killed my brother, they killed my aunt and tried to rape me."

His jaw clenched, and his hands curled into fists. If he'd been there—

"Iain found us and stopped them. But it was too late for Ranald."

"Your brother?"

She nodded.

"What about your parents?"

She began studying the twig she twisted in her hands. "They died when Ranald and I were eight years old."

"You were twins?"

She nodded again. "We cared for each other then, for there was no one else. He became as my father, and I, his mother. It is hard to believe that I have lost him."

Her voice caught, and Matthew wanted to reach for her. He wanted to pull her into his arms. Comfort her. Protect her. But she was lost in a world of her own.

He settled for giving her hand a brief squeeze. "I'm sorry."

She took a deep breath and rose. "We must return."

"I don't want to."

She glanced at him, and a smile flashed across her face. "It will be dark soon."

She had a point, so he got to his feet. "Can we come again?" he asked.

Her smile grew. "You see why I love it here?"

"Definitely."

"Then we will come again." She turned, and he followed her down the mountain.

Chapter Six

Rhianna watched happily as Matthew held Tristan at bay. Certainly, his skill with the sword was growing. It was evident that he had only been about this for a pair of months, but it was also quite evident that he would be formidable some day in the near future.

An hour passed, and with it came a subtle change. Matthew took the offensive. And Tristan was no longer defending himself as a teacher does his pupil. He was having to expend quite a bit of effort.

Three seconds later, Tristan's sword fell to the dirt. "Where'd you learn tha—?" He stopped. "Jason taught you that. Right?"

Matthew nodded. "Saturday. You were off with your girlfriend. Jason wasn't."

"Jason's wife is here. Alison isn't."

Matthew laughed. "The lesson was well worth it, to see the look on your face, if nothing else."

"I'm sure it was," Tristan answered. He picked up his sword again. "Come on. You won't manage that so easily again."

He raised his sword, and Rhianna permitted herself a small smile at his expense.

Matthew attacked again, and she sighed. She shouldn't be out here watching. She fell a little more in love with him every time they were together, and that was only asking for heartache.

They talked of everything now. Or tried to. But Matthew had ceased to talk of television when she told him that her family never owned one. He tried talking of government until her ignorance became apparent. Even family was difficult to discuss without revealing things she had sworn not to.

She simply did not belong in his world. And every conversation they had only served to make more obvious the fact that she never would. She did not even have time to try. Murray said he would find her kin in the next day or two, and then she would leave—

"Rhianna?"

Matthew's voice broke through her thoughts. She looked up and managed a smile.

"Are you okay?" he asked with concern in his voice.

She nodded brightly. "You're doing well."

"You tell me that every day."

"When you cease to do well, I will cease to tell you," she said. Although she was certain that would never happen.

He chuckled. "Come talk to me."

"Again?"

"Always."

She winced. How she wished that 'always' was possible.

They walked through the castle gates and skirted the walls until they reached the water's edge. She tried to put on a cheerful face and think of something new to discuss. Something safe.

"What's wrong, Rhianna?"

She sighed. "It does not matter." She could hardly tell him she was having difficulty not falling in love with him.

He stopped, and his touch was gentle on her face. He nudged her chin up and slowly caressed her jaw with his thumb. "It *does* matter. Won't you tell me?"

She tried to swallow the lump that was growing in her throat, but it would not leave. The tenderness in his eyes was too much—and too close to what she dared not hope for.

"Rhianna," he whispered.

Tears welled up before she could stop them. His hand moved to her shoulder, slid down her arm, and she was suddenly in his arms.

He drew her against him, and she surrendered. Perhaps this was all she would ever have of love. This month. This moment. Was that not reason enough to savor it? Because it could not last?

She nestled her head on his shoulder and relished his warmth and the feel of his breath on her hair. An osprey called overhead. The water rustled against the shore. The wind played with the hair she'd left unbraided for the first time, because Matthew had suggested it...more proof that she was a fool.

He pulled back slightly. She looked into his face, just as a gust of wind lashed his face with her hair.

"I should have braided it," she murmured as she tried to bring it under control.

"No, you shouldn't have," he said with a smile that made her feel that being a fool was well worth it, if it was for him.

He pulled her hands away and smoothed her hair back.

His gaze intensified, and the wind eased until it seemed as if the whole world held its breath. She lost herself in his eyes, in the feelings his hands gave her as they framed her face...tangled in her hair...touched her so gently.

"I've wanted to kiss you for weeks," he whispered.

She'd wanted that too, yet she'd convinced herself that there was no way she could have him. How could she?

His mouth touched hers, and she melted. His lips caressed her own... teasing, tasting, tenderly coaxing away her hesitation until nothing else mattered. Nothing besides Matthew. Being in his arms. Sharing her life with him, if that was possible—

But it wasn't. The difficulties were many. *Too* many. And though *she* knew that, he did not.

She drew back.

"Rhianna," he begged.

"Forgive me," she whispered.

"For what?"

"I should not have—" She couldn't finish. Should not have loved him? The idea was inconceivable. Tears blurred her vision, and she backed away. "I must leave."

"Where? *Why?*"

"To my family."

He reached for her. "You don't have to."

She shook her head in misery. Then she did what she had done in the beginning. What she should have done every day since.

She ran.

Chapter Seven

Matthew lay sleepless until the wee hours of the morning, and all he could think was that she was leaving.

The very thought was killing him.

He wanted to share his life with her, even though he had almost nothing to offer her. An old hut needing more repairs than he'd be able to afford in three years definitely wasn't what most women dreamed of. He had strength and determination, but those seemed next to worthless. Yet the thought of using them to make a life with her was tantalizingly sweet.

To think of having her always—believing in him, encouraging him, making him feel that his past meant nothing compared to the possibilities the future offered—the thought took his breath away.

He wanted her in his life. Her voice. Her beauty. Her understanding. The purpose that caring for her and protecting her would give him.

The first light of dawn began to reach through his uncovered window, and he still didn't have any answers. All he knew was that he had to see her.

He got up, made his way through the thick fog, and was soon pounding on Duncarragh's gates.

It felt like forever, but finally Tristan opened them.

"I want to see Rhianna," he said.

Tristan's eyebrows rose. "Aren't you supposed to be at Alec's shop?"

"Not for another hour," he shot back as he elbowed past.

He started toward Rhianna's door, just as she stepped through it. He stopped. "Please. We need to talk."

She hesitated for a moment before she nodded.

He turned to lead her through the gates again, only to find Tristan barring the way.

"Not this morning, Matt."

"Why?"

"It's not safe."

"You don't think I can protect her? Is that it?"

Tristan opened his mouth, hesitated, and shut it.

"I'd give *my life* for her," Matthew added.

Tristan sighed, and his look changed to pity. He stepped aside. "Don't go far."

Matthew ignored him. He hadn't been planning on going far anyway.

Rhianna followed, still not saying a word.

"We have to talk," he repeated.

"What of, Matthew?"

He turned to face her.

She stood there, her eyes calm pools that mirrored the water beside them. Had he only imagined those tears yesterday?

"We have to talk about us," he said.

Her eyes softened, but again, she shook her head. "There can be no *us*."

"There *can*," he insisted. "There already is...isn't there?"

She looked at the ground. "I must go to my kin," she said, her voice quiet and empty.

He lifted her chin. "Then I'll come to you."

Her calm deserted her, and the tears returned.

"I crossed an ocean to come here. I'll cross another for you if I must."

She shook her head again. "It is not the distance, Matthew."

"Then what?"

She didn't answer, and he could have sworn in frustration.

Instead, he took her face in his hands. "I love you, Rhianna. I know it's only been two months since we met, but...." He wanted to say that he'd dreamed of her all his life. That every minute they spent together was priceless...worth more than years with another woman could ever be.

Muffled hoof beats sounded through the mist, and Tristan's warning echoed through his mind, breaking into his thoughts of Rhianna. He dropped an arm around her waist, pulled her to his side...and his mouth fell open as a form took shape before them.

It was Murray, looking like something out of a movie. Dressed in the old Scottish clothing, he sat on his horse as if it were a throne. "I've found your kin, Rhianna," he said.

"Where, my laird?"

Murray named a place that Matthew didn't recognize, but that wasn't surprising. He had a hard time remembering any of the Gaelic names around here.

Rhianna nodded. "I have gathered my things."

The significance of her words tore at his heart. She was really going. For good.

She started to pull away, but he caught her hand.

"Rhianna," he begged.

"I must go," she whispered.

"I'll follow you. I swear I will."

Her eyes widened. "You must not!"

"Why? Where are you going?"

She blinked, and her brows furrowed as she looked at Murray.

Murray turned and began studying him with an intensity that put the worst

police interrogators to shame. "Can you be trusted with a secret?" he finally asked.

Matthew raised his chin. "I can."

"You will keep it as though your lady's life depends upon it?"

Matthew glanced at Rhianna in faint surprise. "I told Tristan I would give my life for her. It is all I have, but it is hers. You can trust me."

Murray was silent. Minutes ticked by. Finally, Murray heaved a sigh. "Rhianna's place of birth...is the Scotland of 1518."

Matthew was sure he'd heard that wrong. Fifteen eighteen? As in *the Middle Ages?*

He looked at Murray's clothing again. "And you, my laird?" he heard himself ask.

Murray nodded. "My mother bore me in the Year of our Lord 1455. I and my sons guard both the past and the future."

Matthew forced himself to swallow...to think rationally, even though the world seemed to swirl around him.

He focused on Rhianna's face and realized that, in some impossible way, it made perfect sense. Her ignorance of modern technology. Her story. Her response to his. Her knowledge of swordplay.

"And you have family there," he said slowly. "Family that loves you." And people that had a far greater claim on her than he did.

She looked at the hem of her skirt. "They do not love me, but they will accept me."

"Then stay with me! Stay where you're loved."

"How can I?"

"Marry me."

She looked up at him.

"I can do nothing for you in your world, and I know I don't have much to offer in mine. But I love you, and I can keep you safe. Is it enough?"

"But...." She took a step back and shook her head. "I don't belong to this world! I know nothing. I would shame you."

Shame him? He would have laughed, but he wouldn't hurt her for the world.

He reached for her shoulders. "I could never be ashamed of you," he whispered.

"But I do not think I can ever understand these microwaves, and televisions, and computers...."

He listened to her struggle with the words and thought of the mostly empty cottage he rented. "I don't have any of those, so why should that matter?"

Her eyes narrowed. "I've seen your cottage, and in my time, two families shared one smaller than it."

"Then why should I live there alone? Share it with me."

She sighed and dropped her gaze

He drew her against him, wrapped his arms around her, and silently breathed a prayer. If she left, he wasn't sure what he'd do. Following her was probably next to impossible. But so was living without her.

"*Please,* Rhianna," he whispered.

She lifted her head, but trouble still filled her eyes. "I do not think you understand how different this world is from mine."

"Perhaps I don't. But I wasn't born here either. I think the streets of Chicago might be closer to your world than you realize."

She looked puzzled.

"Never mind that," he said. "The world is what you make of it. As long as I have you in mine, I don't much care what else I have."

He watched as she slowly digested his words. She pulled out of his arms and turned to Murray.

"My laird?" she said.

Murray hesitated. "I can take you back to your time, lass. It can be as if time stood still. You can rejoin your kin a mere day after they left, and these months you have spent here would only exist in your memory and ours.

"But the choice is yours. Only you can know if you belong in that time or if you have found your future here."

He paused. "Matthew is a good man, and we would all welcome you both into our family, if that is what you wish. Choose wisely, lass."

And he rode away.

Rhianna watched him go, and Matthew waited. Eternity seemed to pass before she turned.

"Do you know what I thought when you fought off those men behind the store?"

He shook his head.

A smile gentled her face, sending a ray of hope through his heart.

"I thought I had never seen anyone like you. I wanted to know who you were and how you came to be there when I needed you."

"And now that you know?"

She hesitated only a moment. "Now I want you to always be there."

He reached for her again as relief and joy flooded his entire being. She wound her arms around his neck, and he kissed her again. And this time, he dared to believe that the future he'd hardly let himself hope for, was actually his.

Chapter Eight

Rhianna Garlinn smiled. Her new husband would come home soon, and she had managed to make quite a difference in the little cottage. Many repairs were still needed, but at least it was clean. And the thatched roof now kept the rain out, thanks to the mending skills Ranald had taught her.

She moved to the fire and checked the beef and potatoes in the pot. She supposed she'd have to learn how to use the cooking stove eventually, but Matthew didn't seem to mind her one-pot meals for now.

The door opened, and she turned. Matthew stood there, rain running down his face, and his shirt clinging to his shoulders. She thought she'd never seen a more beautiful sight.

"Welcome home," she said with a smile.

He looked around the cottage, noting the clean walls...the floors...the cloth on the table...the pot over the fire. His gaze returned to hers.

"Why do you say nothing?" she asked.

A tender smile lit his face. "You have given me what I never had."

"What is that?" she asked.

He stepped inside, and the door swung shut behind him.

"A home," he whispered and held open his arms.

Author Bio:

To learn more about Kathleen and her work, you can visit her at the following sites: www.KathleenMacIver.com or www.myspace.com/KathleenMacIver.

Wounded Hearts
by
Missy Lyons

After the devastating loss of Bella's husband, she never expected to find a love strong enough to heal her family's wounded hearts, or a man patient enough to try.

"Banzai!" Seven-year-old Bradley leaped into the pile of leaves his father had just finished raking. Colorful maple foliage flew in every direction as he splashed and kicked in the pile, his laughter broken only by the sound of the crunching. It had been a long time since Adam had seen his son this happy. When his mother left them, it had devastated the boy, and Bradley seemed to age ten years overnight.

Adam pretended to sound stern. "Now, Bradley, you did promise to help clean up this mess."

"Aw, Dad! But I wanna play!" Bradley sat with a bright orange leaf stuck in his hair. His boyish charm showed through the pouty expression on his face.

Adam chuckled, remembering his own childhood. Leaf jumping could have been a competitive sport for all the nice clean piles that he'd crashed into as a child. What kid couldn't resist a pile of neatly raked leaves just sitting there, begging to be demolished? It was like trying to find a substitute for a peanut-butter-and-jelly sandwich. Nothing else but the real thing would work.

"Me too." Without warning, Adam leapt into the pile, play-wrestling his son back into the leaves and tickling Bradley into fits of giddy laughter. Sammy, their black-and-white Border collie, jumped into the fray, frantically licking Bradley's face.

A noisy beeping sound interrupted their happy time together. A moving truck began backing up to the vacant house next door. Curious, Adam and Bradley stopped to stare at the new neighbors pulling into the driveway.

The old Victorian house had been vacant for three years, but despite its country charm, no one wanted to move into the old fixer-upper. It was beautiful with the hand-carved molding and the period architecture; however, that didn't make up for the fact that no renovations had ever been done to it. It was a money pit, and anyone who walked into the building and saw the gutted house knew it immediately. It would need a lot more than a little paint and love to make it livable.

A sporty, red convertible pulled up and parked behind the truck. The gravel driveway crunched loudly under its tires. Sammy let out a menacing growl, and Adam told him to hush, but the dog grew more and more agitated. The animal was off at a dead run before Adam saw what he intended to do. The black-and-white blur raced down the hill straight to the occupants just stepping out of the corvette.

"Sammy, get back here!"

"Sammy!" Bradley echoed his father's call, but the dog ignored them. He stayed on his bullet-like path toward the female driver who had her hands outstretched to ward him off.

Hopefully, she wasn't afraid of dogs. It definitely wasn't polite to have your pet meet the new neighbor before you did. Sammy would never hurt anyone, but some people were just fearful by nature. A burglar would be in more danger of being licked to death than bitten by Sammy.

"Come on, son. Let's go meet the folks moving in." Adam sighed in resignation. This wasn't the way he pictured meeting someone new to the community. Around these parts, a person didn't welcome people without a home-warming gift. It showed Southern hospitality to have a little something to hand them when you said hello, like an apple pie or fresh-baked cookies, a thoughtful present to say you cared. "We'd better get Sammy before he scares our new neighbors away."

The woman kneeled, greeting his dog with a brisk rubdown. Emergency averted, a sense of relief flooded Adam. Luckily for Sammy, the new neighbors were dog lovers. Sammy leaned against her long legs, his tongue lolling to one side. He was one fortunate dog, because if he had hold of him right now....

A little girl in pigtails squealed happily, wiggling from her passenger seat and running to greet Sammy. Adam jogged over to the driveway with his son following closely behind him. Within a few feet of the family, he called out, "Sorry about that. Sammy doesn't usually run off like that."

Adam firmly gripped Sammy's collar. "Sammy got away too fast for me to catch him. I hope he didn't scare you."

Her return smile captivated him. The breath caught in his throat as he perused her slim figure, her creamy skin, and intense eyes. She was just as polished and classy as her car. She straightened, dusted off her designer jeans, and straightened the low-cut aqua sweater to reveal a creamy shoulder. She scratched behind Sammy's ears, and Adam caught sight of the one thing that was enough to stop his body's reaction faster than the coldest shower.

A wedding ring.

"Easy boy," he said more to himself than to the dog. It wasn't like him to react to a woman on first sight, but it didn't matter. She was married. That meant she was strictly off limits to him, and it was one rule he never broke.

"It's okay," she replied, her warm blue eyes unafraid to meet his. "Madeline and I love animals, but we couldn't keep a dog in an apartment in the city. In fact, getting a dog is one of the things I was looking forward to when we moved out here."

The little girl stood quietly off to the side, too shy to come much closer than a few feet of Bradley or the dog. A sad, soulful look settled on her face, and Adam imagined she didn't smile much. "You can pet him, too, if you like," he tried to reassure her.

Slowly, she inched closer to the dog and petted him timidly on the back.

"Sammy won't bite you," Bradley said. "See? He really likes it if you scratch him on his nose too. Try it like this." He demonstrated by using two fingers to itch Sammy on the end of his nose. Immediately, the dog leaned up against his hand.

The little girl smiled and tried rubbing Sammy's nose. A wet, pink tongue licked her hand in appreciation.

"My name's Bradley. What's your name?" he asked.

The little girl refused to meet his gaze and stared intently at the grass.

"Her name is Madeline. She doesn't talk much," her mother intervened.

"It's okay. Sometimes I don't feel like talking either. Do you want to see some of his tricks?" Bradley asked. "Sammy loves to fetch sticks. He could run for hours and not get tired."

Hesitantly, the little girl looked up at her mother.

"It's okay, Maddy. You can go play. Just stay where I can see you, okay?" Her mother responded to the unasked question.

"Come on, let's go!" Bradley turned to run without looking back.

Madeline smiled broadly, immediately racing after Bradley. As soon as Adam let go of his collar, Sammy charged ahead of both children.

"Kids."

"Yeah, kids. I probably worry too much," she answered, turning her face away from him.

"As a parent, it's hard not to. They'll be fine," Adam reassured her.

"I know, and it's good for her. She needs to have some friends. Madeline's been so withdrawn this last year. She hasn't said a word since...."

A painful silence followed.

Adam's chest clenched. Something bad happened to this family, something so awful that she had a hard time even talking about it. "Since? Did she lose her hearing or something?"

"No. Nothing like that. She stopped talking right after Eric, her dad, passed away." Her free hand rubbed her wedding ring. "I've taken her to all kinds of different doctors and psychologists. They all say the same thing. There is nothing wrong with her physically. It's post traumatic stress, and she'll talk again when she wants to."

Surprise filled Adam. How could a little girl go an entire year without uttering a word? "She hasn't talked for a year?"

Her voice broke, her tone miserable. "Not a word. She hardly even plays with other kids. It's like she's in another world."

"I'm so sorry for your loss." She must have grieved terribly losing her husband, but this had to feel like she'd lost her little girl too. He couldn't imagine having his entire world altered like that.

"Thanks," she swallowed hard, her eyes brimming with unshed tears. "But a lot of people lost their loved ones that day. He was just another casualty. Another number on September 11th."

Adam didn't want to bring up such an obviously painful subject, but he needed to know about her and what she'd gone through.

"Hey lady! Where do you want us to unload this stuff?" one of the moving men yelled out.

"Most of the boxes are marked according to the room they belong in. Just take it in the house, please." She walked towards the truck to give better instructions.

Adam realized he didn't even know her name. He hadn't bothered to introduce himself either. Inwardly, he groaned at his rudeness. She'd just opened up, sharing a part of her life with him, and he forgot common courtesy in her presence.

The moving man nodded toward the house, holding the box tightly to his chest. "We need the house unlocked if you want them in there."

"Oh, I guess I forgot to do that." Her cheeks tinged the loveliest shade of pink. "Excuse me. I'll be right back."

"No problem," replied Adam.

He stood there awkwardly for a moment, debating whether to wait for her outside. She probably wanted him to wait for her on the grass, but he wasn't the type of person to stand around with his hands in his pockets. With his mind made up, he picked up a box and followed her in the house. The old, wooden stairs creaked under his footsteps; some of the boards were dry-rotted and would need replacing. The termites were fat and happy living here.

"Thank you. You didn't have to do that." She fingered a stray curl along her face as she held the door open for Adam and the moving men.

"It's my pleasure," he said, giving the house a once-over through the entryway. A thick layer of dust covered the windows, preventing anyone from seeing in. Wood paneling lined the walls, and a grand staircase led up to the second story. He crinkled his nose at the dusty-old-house smell. It was no place for a lady or a small child. "Where do you want this?"

"In the basement." She pointed to one door in the corner that stood open to a dark set of stairs leading down. "Most everything is going to be stored down there until I can get some of the renovations finished. We're planning on living in the basement for a while until the upstairs is done."

"Really?" Adam tried to bite his tongue. His heart clenched at the very idea of them living here. Maybe the basement was already cleaned up. "Okay. I'll just put this down there, then."

Flicking on the light switch, he made his way downstairs. The blue halogen light flickered for a moment before it finally stayed on. The mildew smell overpowered the house's other aromas. An unidentifiable black mold grew up the walls. An old, outdated kitchen took up one corner, complete with green appliances from the fifties. There was no way anyone could be happy living like this.

If she belonged to him, he never would have allowed her and her child to live like this.

The protective thought scared him. Why had his mind gone there? The idea wasn't unwelcome, but he'd never thought about marrying a second time. His first wife, Angela, was too self-absorbed and busy with her own life to be a mother, but if he she had been the right woman, he wouldn't have let her go so easily either.

Adam set the box down in a corner determined that his new neighbor was not going to move in anytime soon if he had anything to say about it.

* * * *

"All finished?" Bella felt her flesh grow warm at the reappearance of her handsome neighbor. She wasn't used to being thrown off balance by anyone let alone another man. It had been a year since her husband had died, and yet, she still felt like it would betray him to begin dating again. It had never been an issue before. It was easy to resist other men. She still loved Eric and she would always love him. When he'd died, she thought her heart did too, but her body was telling her that she was most definitely alive.

"Yep. Sure am. By the way, my name's Adam Jennings." He stuck out his hand. She grasped it firmly. The warmth from his skin encased her hand and spread up her arm. The gold in his eyes flashed with interest, letting her know she wasn't the only one experiencing the attraction between them.

Bella laughed. How could she not have realized that they hadn't introduced themselves? "I guess we did skip that part. I'm Bella Thompson."

He released her hand, leaving her cold. She didn't want to stop, but it would seem even more awkward to say, *I just want to hang onto your hand for a minute longer*. Her body must have gone into overdrive. Stupid hormones had her acting like a teenager all over again.

"My mama raised me to have good manners and she would never let me live it down if I blamed it on her." His voice, deep and sensual, sent a ripple of awareness through Bella. "So I'll blame it on being in the company of such a beautiful woman."

She managed to shrug and say offhandedly, "Ah, you're just saying that, Adam."

"No, I mean every word. My mama would have my hide if I didn't treat you like the lady you are, and Bella fits just perfectly, since it means beautiful and," he gave her a knowing wink combined with one of his devastating smiles that she imagined he saved for special occasions, "you are exceptionally beautiful. It's enough of a distraction to make any man forget his own name."

Any more compliments like that would go straight to her head. She tried to pretend his nearness didn't affect her, but it did. His nearness made her aware that she was very much a woman, and it might to be a bad idea to let him know it.

"Well, I guess I'm just as bad, because I should have told you my name a long time ago."

"So, what brought you to a little town like Ashville, Bella?"

"It's not that small."

"Yes it is. With a population of two thousand, it doesn't even get many tourists; farmers fill the town more than anything else. Most of the locals grew up here and never moved away."

She could understand his curiosity. People didn't just up and move here from the big city. Except people like her who wanted to start a new life and forget the old one. Every day, friends questioned how she was doing or feeling and it never let her heal. There were too many memories that haunted her.

"It looked like a great place to forget," she said with a sigh, motioning for him to follow her back outside where they could watch the children again.

"Forget? What do you mean?"

"It's tough when you lose someone you love, you know?" Eric had been so young. It didn't seem fair that she should be allowed to go on every day without her husband, or that her daughter should grow up without a dad. No one really understood the pain she had to relive on a daily basis. "More than anything, we moved out here to forget and to move on with our lives. Maddy needs a fresh start, and so do I."

Adam walked with her out of the house and back into the yard; he paused and looked intensely into her eyes. She felt as if he could see all the pain of her past through that small connection.

"I understand. I haven't had to live with that kind of pain, but we did lose Bradley's mother a few years ago. She walked out on us and never came back. It wasn't easy for either of us. It broke my heart to see my boy in that much pain. I hated it whenever he blamed himself for it."

"Did you love her?" She wasn't sure why she wanted to know, but she couldn't stop herself from asking.

"I thought I did." He nodded. "But we grew apart over the years, and she had a hard time living such a simple life out in the country. I loved her for giving me Bradley, but honestly, I'm not sure I was in love anymore by the time she left. We argued a lot that last year, and she thought she sacrificed too much of her life for us."

How could a woman feel like that? She felt like she was *sacrificing* by raising her family? Bella just couldn't understand his ex's reasoning. Being a mother and a wife had been the most fulfilling part of her life. Ashville seemed like an idyllic place to raise a family. Close to nature. Away from the crime and all the noise and pollution of the city. Kids could play outside, and parents didn't have to worry about their safety. Maybe it was too much for a woman who wanted to be entertained all the time or needed to be the center of attention. However, what kind of mother would abandon her child?

"So she hasn't once visited or called to see how you are?"

"Not once, but I hear she's doing fine. I had a private investigator help me track her down to sign the divorce papers. Angela's living in Atlanta now with a new boyfriend and going back to college. She's got the life she's always wanted and is working as a model."

It must have been devastating for a child to lose his mother so young. No wonder Bradley had a hard time "I just can't believe she did that," Bella said.

"Me either, but I'm glad that I got to keep Bradley. I couldn't imagine life without him."

Bella nodded. She understood completely. Life without her little girl would be intolerable. She could never go through that kind of loss and lose the love of her life in that manner. She didn't think she was that strong, and without her daughter, there wouldn't be a need to go on. Without love or family, what was there left to live for?

Nothing.

"So you said something about remodeling the house?" he asked.

"Yeah," she chuckled, "the plan is to turn the house into a bed-and-breakfast. This is the second time I have seen the house and I still love it, but I kind of wonder if I got in over my head."

His soft voice echoed, "Me too."

"Excuse me?"

"It's none of my business, but the house is a mess, Bella." Concern edged his smooth voice, but it still bugged her to have her neighbor nosing into her business. Who was he to question whether she could handle this remodeling project?

The house was beautiful; its period architecture, copper ceilings, marble fireplaces, and intricate woodwork couldn't be built new. The house deserved someone who would take care of it and fix it up, a family that would appreciate living here—like her and Maddy. "It's got good bones, and I know it will be a gem after the remodeling is done," she said defensively.

"The house has been on the market for years because it's so rundown. I'm not even sure it's safe to live in it the way it is."

"Well, we don't have a choice." Hands on her hips, she didn't like where he was going with this, but he was right that it was none of his business. "There aren't any hotels in Ashville, and we have to be close by to supervise the construction."

"I can help you with the hotel part if you want." His voice was calming, his tone patient. "Do you already have contractors picked out to help with the remodeling?"

"Yes. Jennings and Sons said they would be able to help. They hope to be done with the construction in a less than a year, and that's a total overhaul." She frowned. "What do you mean you can help with the hotel part? We can't exactly stay with you. The neighbors would be talking about me before I even met them."

"You sure? I would promise to stay on my side of the bed, and the spare bedroom isn't getting much use," he joked.

Warmth surged into her cheeks. "Adam. We just met. You can't be serious."

"I wasn't. I was only teasing, but my Dad does have a hunting cabin just a few miles from here that doesn't get much use at this time of year. It's got everything you need, and it's a heck of a lot cleaner than this house is right now. I'm sure I could talk my folks into letting you stay there until you get this place a little more move-in ready."

"Oh, Adam. That's so sweet, but I'm not sure I would feel right about staying there."

"It would only be temporary. I'm sure it wouldn't be any hassle. It would probably make my folks feel better knowing it wasn't empty and they wouldn't have to drive out to check on it every weekend."

"All right. I'll take a look at it." This sounded like a great opportunity. It was close by and would give her and Maddy the privacy and freedom to look after the construction of this house. The settlement from her husband's insurance would more than cover her living expenses and construction costs until she could begin work at the hospital again. "I hear it's not fun to live through renovations," she said. "I wasn't looking forward to it, but I've never lived in a town that didn't have even a little roach motel."

"The cabin is a lot cleaner than any roach motel. It's small but cozy. I go up there once in a while for weekends just to get away from the stress of it all."

"Away from it all? You call this stressful?" She laughed. He had to be joking.

"It's nice and relaxing. I promise you'll love it. The log cabin is surrounded by a forest, and a creek runs through the property. Deer will walk right up to your front door in the morning. We can go see it tonight, if you like."

Bella was too surprised by his offer to object. "Okay. I may just take you up on that offer, but that doesn't mean that I am moving in, Adam." To be honest, she wasn't looking forward to moving into that dark, musty basement, and it was nice to have an excuse to stay in the company of her new neighbor for a few more hours. She felt more alive today than she had in the last year.

"Okay. No pressure, but you know a tent would be better than this, Bella." Adam's mouth twitched with amusement.

There was no arguing with him there.

* * * *

Everything was news in a small town. Adam did nothing to stop the rumors that he and Bella were a couple. People were quick to draw that conclusion not long after Bella moved into his family's cabin. They spent enough time together that anyone would draw that kind of assumption. He kind of liked the idea of being a couple, but Bella was still a little too emotionally raw from the loss of her husband, and, despite the attraction, she said she wanted to give it some time before she began dating again.

He would give her the time she needed, but eventually, he wanted to explore what was between them. It was more than sexual. Bella was smart, compassionate, and giving. She was a wonderful mother too. It broke his heart that she had to sit back and watch her daughter's withdrawal from the world.

He often sat and watched the little girl play by herself. Surrounded by her silent world, Madeline ignored the people around her, watched quietly as life went by, and on more than one occasion, he saw her wipe away tears.

She would never get over the loss of her father, but she was just a child. She couldn't sit by and watch the world go by without her. Somebody had to do something to bring her back into the world, do something to help her care about life again. Madeline was acting far too grown up for her age.

She needed to learn to play again.

That was how he found himself on their doorstep, knocking on the front door with the girl's wrapped present in his hands. It was silly, he knew, but it was a simple thing he could do for her.

Bella opened the door, surprise evident on her face. "Hello!"

"Hey." Adam always loved to see Bella. Just being in her presence made him feel warm from the inside out.

"Hey, yourself. Why don't you come inside?" she asked.

"Sure." He stepped inside, brushing against her body. As always, a frisson of electricity passed between them. He didn't mean to stay and only wanted to drop off the present and go off to work, but it was hard to resist spending just a few minutes with Bella.

God, if she ever found out what she did to him, it would be hopeless. He would be totally lost. Tied around her little finger. He already was, but it was probably better if she never knew it.

"So, what are you doing here so early, Adam?"

"Oh, just thought I'd drop off a little something for Maddy. I heard it was her birthday." He held the small package out in front of him.

"Adam, you didn't have to go to any trouble. You've already helped us so much, but I'm sure Madeline will love whatever you got her." Bella closed the front door and yelled to the back of the cabin. "Maddy! Come here, sweetie. Adam brought you a surprise!"

Madeline slowly walked out of the bedroom. She always looked so sad. No smile lit up her face. No joy in her little life. He hoped he could change that just a little.

Motioning for her to come to him, he knelt down, holding the present out for her to see. Madeline took the gift, skittish as a woodland creature, as if he would take it back if she made a sudden movement.

"Go ahead and open it." It would take time to earn the trust of Maddie and her mother, but that was fine with him. He was a patient man, and it would be well worth it in the end.

Madeline opened the small box, allowing the colorful wrapping paper to fall on the floor. To her delight, she found a bug-hunting kit. Her face lit up with fascination and wonder. Her curious expression silently asked him why he would give her such a gift.

"Do you know what it is?"

Maddy nodded.

"When I first met you, I knew you would make a great butterfly hunter. You just needed to learn how and to have a few tools of the trade."

Her eyelashes fluttered against her creamy white skin, her little nose crinkling with laughter. Even her mother smiled. He couldn't be happier. If he could just help her be a kid for day, it would be a gift to remember. She spent so much time focusing on therapy. Once a week, she traveled an hour to see a psychiatrist.

"You already have everything else you need, courage, determination, and just enough of that adventurous spirit to find some of the most beautiful butterflies around these parts. Now you have the tools to go with it."

Opening the box, he removed the butterfly net and handed it to Maddy. Her tiny hands held it carefully.

Her soft voice was so quiet that he thought he almost missed it...her first words in over a year. "Thank you." Maddy looked up and asked her mother, "Mama, can I go play now?"

Bella's complexion paled, but despite the shock, she reacted calmly. Her heart just needed time to heal. Just like her mother's.

"Of course," Bella stuttered the words, but her face glowed with happiness. With unspoken emotion she added, "Just stay near the house where I can see you, Maddy."

"Yes, Mama," Madeline yelled as she ran outside, taking her net with her.

Bella's bright blue eyes welled with tears. She looked at Adam. They had witnessed a miracle. Something most people took for granted.

"How can I ever thank you?"

"No thanks needed. I didn't do anything special, really," Adam replied. He didn't expect Madeline to begin speaking. He just wanted to see her act like a kid again.

"You're amazing. We tried everything for an entire year. Then you come into our lives for just a few weeks, and Madeline begins to speak like she'd never stopped talking. I can't thank you enough for what you did today. With the construction. The house. With everything. If there is anything you ever need, just ask and it's yours."

"There's only one thing I want right now, but I would never ask you before you're ready." He needed her to know that he was interested, but he didn't want to pressure her. A broken heart required time to heal. She needed time to trust again.

"Whatever it is, I won't say no. You have been so good to me. To us. You deserve that."

His hands covered hers as he stared intently into her eyes. She needed to understand this was important to him. "I'm hoping that you'll give me a chance."

"You mean...like date you?" She sounded incredulous.

Ouch. Rejection hurt.

Adam nodded, swallowing his pride. He was putting his heart on the line, but he didn't expect bringing it up to be this hard. The breath caught in his throat; he awaited her response.

"I—I didn't want to date again after losing my husband." She avoided his gaze but didn't pull away from his touch. "It felt like I would be cheating on him if I did. I know it's not logical, but it was so hard to lose him. I wasn't even sure I could love again."

"I understand. That's why I want to give you time to think about it. When you feel comfortable with it, I'd like you to consider me. To consider us."

"Thank you." Her voice came out soft, low.

"I want to give you as much time as you need and I don't want to force you into anything. So no pressure, but when you are ready, will you tell me?"

"Yeah."

"Promise?" he asked again.

"I promise."

Bella ran her hands up his chest to lock them behind his neck, hugging their bodies close. He liked it, too much, but he really didn't want to push her into anything physical. It had to be her idea. She had to be ready for this and not just trying to please him. "What are you doing, Bella?"

"Showing you that I'm ready."

Happiness swelled in his heart as her head tilted up toward his, awaiting his kiss. Wrapping his arms around her, he took her into his arms. Elation rushed through him. Bella's blue eyes fluttered shut, and his lips touched upon her soft, pink lips in the gentlest of kisses. A butterfly kiss that promised hope and love for a future together.

Author Bio:

Missy Lyons loves to spend her free time spinning romantic tales of fantasy for her stories, which you can find out more at: www.missylyons. com.

CPSIA information can be obtained at www.ICGtesting.com
Printed in the USA
LVOW13s2344220414

382840LV00001B/218/P